Praise for The Goddess of Fried Okra

"Inspiring and touching."—*RT Book Reviews*

"With characters full of heart…and vinegar, Jean Brashear takes us on a road trip through the back doors of modern life. And we get to read every hilarious marker on the way."
—Pam Morsi, *USA Today* bestselling author

"Jean Brashear has that "it" factor. She is an incredibly talented writer who can hit every note with enough clarity to bring the reader tears, laughter, or just, "Oh, my, this is an amazing story." THE GODDESS OF FRIED OKRA is stunning, powerful and raw. Pea is on journey to heal herself, and find herself—and you will want to go with her to find her dear, dead sister—I do."
—*New York Times* bestselling author Stella Cameron

"A wonderfully engaging story of one woman's search for self. Jean Brashear tugs on your heartstrings and won't let go."
—Julia London, *New York Times* bestselling author of *A Courtesan's Scandal*

"THE GODDESS OF FRIED OKRA is a fabulous read. Riveting. Original. Those characters grabbed my imagination and didn't let go."
—Cathy Maxwell, *New York Times* bestselling author

a novel

Jean Brashear

Bell Bridge Books
Memphis, Tennessee

This is a work of fiction. Names, characters, places and incidents are either the products of the author's imagination or are used fictitiously. Any resemblance to actual persons (living or dead,) events or locations is entirely coincidental.

Bell Bridge Books
PO BOX 30921
Memphis, TN 38130
ISBN: 978-0-9841258-9-0

Bell Bridge Books is an Imprint of BelleBooks, Inc.

Printed and bound in the United States of America.

We at BelleBooks enjoy hearing from readers. You can contact us at the address above or at BelleBooks@BelleBooks.com

Visit our websites – www.BelleBooks.com and www.BellBridgeBooks.com.

10 9 8 7 6 5 4 3 2

Cover design: Debra Dixon
Interior design: Hank Smith
Photo credits: scene -© Orientaly | Dreamstime.com
sword/alphabet © Jaguarwoman Designs

:Lu:01:

Dedication

For my mother, Diane Roberson, who daily teaches me about being a strong and admirable woman (and one who was determined to have Pea for her own book clubs to read);

For Kathy Sobey, who has walked a few thousand miles with me over nearly twenty years of mornings (and some nights) being both laughing playmate and unpaid shrink;

For my cherished brother Buddy, who ignored most of my big sister bossing but somehow turned out pretty great anyway ;

For my beloved children, Jonathan and Seneca, and my adored grandgirlies Emma and Kate, who give my life meaning and my every day joy beyond measure;

And, as always, for Ercel, the love of my life, my rock and my greatest inspiration.

The Goddess of Fried Okra

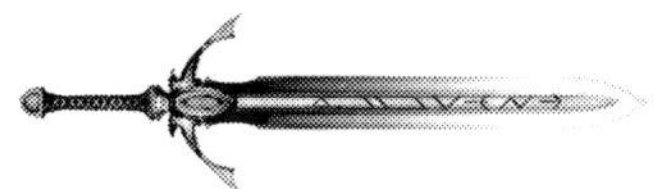

Jean Brashear

Bell Bridge Books

Mount Bonnell

Mount Bonnell was site of picnics and outings in 1850s and 1860s, as it is today. Legend has it that an excursion to the place in the 1850s inspired the popular song "Wait for the Wagon and We'll All Take a Ride." As a stunt in 1898, Miss Hazel Keyes slid down a cable stretched from the top of Mount Bonnell to the south bank of (then) Lake McDonald below.

Austin, Texas

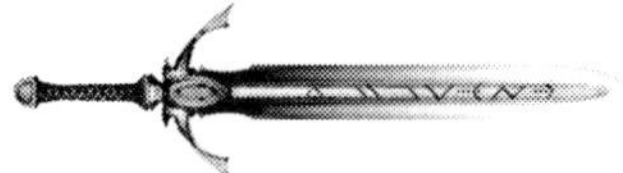

MADAME EVA SAYS

Nothing else could have put me on the road again, not after eighteen years of being dragged all over creation. The road was Mama's perpetual escape clause for boyfriends, bill collectors or just boredom.

Sister, she used the road to save me.

All those years, I swore up and down that once I was old enough, I would find a spot and no force on earth would budge me.

But I didn't count on Sister.

Sister gave up everything for me, see, and I owed her. She was only sixteen when Mama died; I was eight. Life could have been so much easier on her if she'd let the social services people have me like they wanted. Instead, she even chased off her no-good daddy Alvin when he showed up saying he would take care of us. She understood lighting-quick that what he really meant to do was lay on his sorry behind. Only get up long enough to take the child welfare money and buy lottery tickets. Sure as shooting, he would have let Sister do all the work.

But Sister turned those spooky eyes on him—I can still see him shrinking from them.

Sister, she had mojo. In spades.

Once she was gone, just shy of my twenty-ninth birthday, I lost everything I knew of home. Ten months went by, endless hours and weeks when no matter what I tried, I could not get comfortable in my skin. The hole in my heart was just too big to paste any more patches over. *If only I could see her, talk to her,* I thought, maybe the world would make sense again.

Especially if she would forgive me.

Yes, of course she was dead, but Sister believed in reincarnation, see, and she took great comfort from the notion of a do-over. Me, I couldn't quite say I shared her faith, but I was desperate. Sister had it in her mind that the first year was critical for finding a person's new body, and no matter how much I read on the topic—which I assure you I did, since a person cannot have too much information and anyway, I'd sooner read than breathe—I could not find one surefire source to say she was wrong. I couldn't even locate any proof that souls always took up residence in babies. Some people thought a person could have a near-death experience and awaken as someone else.

Others believed the soul could be an animal next time, or even a plant. I could find arguments about almost every dadgum thing, while details on the actual process were pretty much non-existent. That was too many unknowns for a person like me, but if there was a chance in this world that she'd been right, I had to try to find her. I was whole when Sister lived; what I knew of family came from her. I needed that again. Needed her.

And I was getting scared, real scared, that if I didn't hurry, I would be too late.

That was when I turned to Madame Eva, Sister's favorite psychic. I wasn't sure what to expect on my way over, but I kinda liked that little stucco house with its turquoise door and purple shutters, the riot of zinnias and marigolds tumbling along the cracked sidewalk. I was nervous, though, about going inside, wondering what all she might be able to see in my head.

She was nice to me, I have to admit. Took my hand real gentle, and if she spotted all the mistakes I'd made and the misery, she was too kind to say so. Instead, she told me if I opened my heart, I would find my family, but when I asked where, she only smiled and said the journey was up to me. That wasn't one bit what I wanted to hear from her, and I got too caught up in my disappointment and missed some things.

But you can bet that when she told me New Mexico might be in my future, my ears perked right up. Sister always swore she was descended from Pueblo Indians. *Someday, Pea*, she would tell me, *I'm going there to meet my people.*

Note she said *her* people, not ours, 'cause we had different daddies—well, at least she had one. My daddy I called Casper, like the Friendly Ghost, since he never came to visit. I don't think it was very friendly, though, not to show up even once.

Sister was short with brown eyes, like Mama and Alvin. My eyes were blue like Casper's. Sister said he was even taller than my six feet, but without all this mess of red hair. I read somewhere that my coloring meant I had Viking blood, and that was a comfort. Vikings were strong and fierce, and I cottoned to the notion that I had warrior maiden written all over me.

Well, except for the maiden part.

And also the muscles.

I probably could have used some warrior skills when I set off that July day that turned out to be only the beginning of my life's strangest chapter. All I owned in this world, once I'd gone a little crazy with grief and sold most everything we had, filled up the trunk and spilled into the back seat of the beat-up sedan she and I had shared. What I had left of Sister was a photograph and a tarnished Indian bracelet of Mama's that Sister treasured.

With my last paycheck from the store, my grubstake was six-hundred seven dollars and eighty-three cents, which the hospital collection agency would have dearly loved to snatch from me. But I had a mission, and I could not worry about the place that spit Sister out on the sidewalk and left her in the hands of the wrong person.

Namely, me.

The road, like a tongue-flicking serpent sidling up to Eve, called to me. Madame Eva said the stars were aligned, that Fate would lead me home.

Home could only mean Sister. All I could hope was that my hearing was good enough, even after all the loud rock and roll she and I used to dance to. I was desperate to hear when Fate would whisper to me *There she is, there's her new body.*

When I found her, as I hoped so hard I could, would she remember me, I wondered, or would I need to introduce myself?

Would she give me a chance to talk or just turn tail and run from me? Or what if she was a man this time? Boy, that would be rich, given that the women of my family had, at best, an uneasy relationship with the male of the species.

Stop it now, Pea, she would say if she were here right now. My real name is Eudora O'Brien, but Pea is for Sweetpea, the name she gave me when I was a baby. *You are frettin' again.*

Like one of us didn't need to. I was good at it, and I never liked to get out of practice.

The steering wheel about fried my hands when I grabbed it, but I held on. Started the engine and backed out of the stained driveway. I was a little scared to leave, but I had to.

I propped Sister's picture—one where she looked young and carefree in a way I'd never seen her—in the ashtray, and I pointed the car northwest. I decided I had best be alert; no telling where I might find Sister along the way. There were a lot of unanswered questions, I admit. Still, despite the heat of the day and the ache in my heart, I felt hopeful, for a change.

Hold on, Sister, I thought as I steered away. *I'm gonna find you, and when I do, I pinky-promise I will not let you down, not ever again.*

C.S.A. Salt Works

Located between Tow Valley and Old Bluffton, 15 miles NE. Since 1935 under Lake Buchanan. During Civil War made salt for table, curing meat and hides, feeding cavalry horses. A day's boiling in 100 iron, 250-gallon kettles produced 20 to 30 bushels of salt. Cooled, sacked and hauled out, this met Texas' wartime shortages.
First Llano County district court was held at salt works. Stagecoach stop was nearby. Brine here was from Cambrian sea waters trapped 500 million years ago in sand and strata. Indians led first settler here.

THE LATE SHIFT

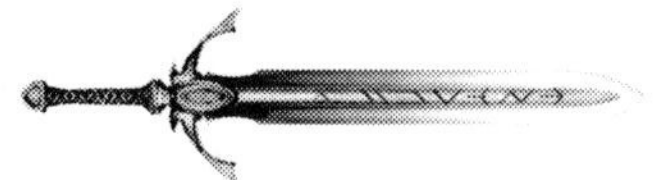

Texas has something like 220,000 miles of roads, not counting city streets, I read once. A ways down the road, the weight of them was pressing on me. Central Texas is a long haul from New Mexico, a direction I'd never traveled, and I had barely started. Plus, the car's radio wasn't all that reliable, and I was already a little tired of my own singing.

Then I remembered *Tell Me*, Mama's favorite road game. We would see something like, say, that fireplace and chimney standing alone in a field I had just passed, and we would fill in the story.

Mama would start with how the woman who lived there had had seven children and three miscarriages, then she would go on about how the woman would drag out the kettle and boil the wash water, then hang the laundry on bushes and trees until her man came back from selling the cattle. He would give her his hand-me-down rope for a clothesline, strung up between the big live oak around the side and that skinny one in back. Ropes, she told us, were valuable tools when you worked with cattle, and a fifteen-hundred pound bull required more strength to hold onto than a bed sheet.

We never knew where her stories would meander, but they could last for miles, and that old fallen homestead would linger in our memories forever.

Tell Me didn't have to be history, though. Take that cell tower ahead, loaded down with vultures. Mama would have gone crazy over that. I didn't have her storytelling gift, but I'd give it a try.

There was a pecking order, I decided. Not a one of them was perched closer to its neighbor than about three feet, and only one bird rested on the top rung. Below it were his lieutenants, swooping down to settle a fracas here and there or to spot the juiciest morsel that had slammed into the grill of an eighteen-wheeler.

Just then I spied a marker. Another of Mama's favorite travel pastimes was reading roadside historical markers, which are thick on the ground in Texas. Out of habit, I swerved to the shoulder and stopped. Mama wasn't much on reading in general, but the markers made perfect little snacks of information. Something to think about as you drove down the road. I myself was partial to the ones about women.

Leanderthal Lady

On Dec. 29, 1982, Texas Highway Department archeologists uncovered the skeleton of a prehistoric human female at the Wilson-Leonard Brushy Creek site (approx. 6 mi. SE). Because of the proximity of the grave site to the town of Leander, the skeleton became known as the Leanderthal Lady. Carbon testing indicates the woman lived 10-13,000 years ago. She was about 30 years old at the time of death and measured 5'3" in height. As one of the earliest intact burials uncovered in the United States, the site is a valuable source of information on the nation's pre-historic past.

Afterward, my brain's hunger was eased by the tidbit, but my stomach was a whole different story. I got back in my car and hoped I would find a convenience store soon. Just the thought of food, water and facilities—not to mention functioning air conditioning—had me focusing only on the road and no more sightseeing.

My car's A/C was always cranky, to say the least. Some days it was pure Arctic Circle, other days, *Cat on a Hot Tin Roof.* That day it was definitely Maggie, down to her slip and snarling at Brick. Mama was a big fan of old movies, and that was one I remembered vividly. Not that I was supposed to be watching, but I snuck a peek from behind the couch more than one night when Mama thought I was sleeping.

So when I got to Lampasas, I pulled into the first convenience store I saw, a hallelujah in my heart as I entered. The guy behind the counter looked up and nodded.

"Hey," I said and glanced around. With the shoulder move only the crème de la crème of us store clerks knows, he indicated the location of the bathroom. Singular. This wasn't your top-of-the-line Skymart of the future. No cappuccino. No twelve-flavor coffee bar.

This was the real deal, a convenience store the way God made them before Starbucks and yuppies messed up everything. I looked around on my way to the john and couldn't help feeling homesick. Cracked linoleum, Cashier-Has-No-Large-Bills signs and all, I had found a world where I belonged and there I had stayed, except for the times I had to work two jobs to keep Sister and me going once she got sick.

The last extra job had been at Fat Elvis, the bar where I met Jelly, my former boyfriend and good riddance. Fat Elvis was a miserable place to work, but you could rake in good tips if you played your cards right, and I needed money, even if it meant wearing those ice-pick heels. Like anyone could have missed me if they needed a fresh drink.

Mostly, except during the Fat Elvis period when I had to switch to days as a clerk, I had worked nights. People think that's really dangerous, but it's all in the eye, in how you smile and carry yourself. I was only robbed once, and the kid apologized before he left in handcuffs. What can I say? I'm a professional.

Rust-stained porcelain and walls that could use a good scrub, handles that were crying for a toothbrush to root out the gunk—this bathroom needed a firm hand. Not everyone takes pride in professionalism, but they ought to. Especially when women have to share a facility with a gender that never seems to think it needs to wash its hands.

So I used a towel to turn the handles, washed up and sprinkled water over my face and chest. Not that more humidity was exactly desirable in Central Texas, but in those precious seconds, the water cooled me as the air slid over my skin. I whirled like some ballerina, lifting my arms, letting my head fall back, my hair swirl behind. When I was little, I imagined myself a dancer of heartbreaking grace. I still could, if I didn't look in the mirror. Imagination can be your best friend, you know.

If I hadn't stayed to dance, I might've never heard the mewing. I stopped spinning and concentrated. The sound was coming from behind the back wall, some very young kitten, from the sound of things.

I always wanted a cat, but Sister had insisted I was allergic. Nonetheless, I couldn't just leave that little creature in distress. Walking out the door, I headed for my colleague. "Storage behind the bathroom, right?"

He was making change for a big black dude and only shrugged. "It is, indeed," he said, his accent the rich, thick melody of Egypt.

Another shiver of homesickness rippled up my spine. I didn't wait for his nod but headed that way.

Professional courtesy only extends so far. "You may not go there," he said. In his voice was his dilemma. Other people were in the store; he couldn't leave his register. Like postal workers or Guardians of the Pearly Gates, my colleagues and I do our job with rain-nor-sleet-nor-snow, 24/7/365, never-leave-your-post kind of fidelity.

"Don't hit the button. It's only a kitten." I tried the handle and found it unlocked. Opening the door, familiar scents assaulted me—pine cleaner, Windex out the wazoo. Flipping on the light, I waded through mops and buckets and extra shelving.

And there it was, tiny and trembling and weak. Not to pick it up would have taken a harder heart than mine. The kitten was a puffball, a faint and furry tickle against my skin. "Oh." My eyes began to water, but I couldn't put it back. That little creature was as alone as I was. I could have been quaking just like that if I let myself.

"You come out of there. It is not allowed," my colleague shouted. "My finger is on the button. Do not make me use it."

His threat snapped off my shiver at the stem. The Skymart stores are flush with automatic systems to monitor everything imaginable, but our Old Faithful kind of real-people stores relies on a video camera at the register and one button under the counter that will summon the cops.

"Oh, baby, it's okay," I crooned to the shivering black-with-orange-spots creature in my hand. "All right, all right, I'm coming," I hollered.

The kitten blinked and quivered until I thought its little body was going to shake apart. "Where's your mama?" I asked softly. I took one last look around but saw no other living being. With a hesitant finger, I stroked the tiny, spindly back. The cat arched under my hand, and I fell instantly in love.

But I couldn't have it. I walked out, cradling precious cargo. "Here, see? It's just a little bitty thing."

"You must take it away from here," he insisted. "No pets allowed inside."

Well, of course I knew that. Any idiot would, much less a professional of my stature. "I can't have a cat, and it needs a home."

"Put it in the alley. It must not stay here."

My clutch was instant and too tight. The kitten yelped. "Don't you have a friend who could take it?"

The black dude was still at the door and laughed, robust and deep. "Anwar? A friend? Get out." The skin around his eyes crinkled in that way I like so much.

"How about you? Look—" I extended my arms. The kitten, who had just begun to purr, screeched. "Did you ever see such a love?"

"Looks to me like it's already got a home."

"I don't even have a home myself." Both of them frowned. Anwar glanced out toward my car. "I mean, I'm not homeless—well, not exactly. It's just that I don't have a place to live right now or a job—"

Anwar's eyes lit. "We need someone to work the late shift here. You, I believe, know something of this work."

Late shift. My favorite. The time of night when the odd, sad and fascinating come out to play. Besides, I got lots of time to read on the late shift, and I could read my way into a coma and die happy.

Oh my . . . it was tempting. I didn't exactly have a bundle of cash, after all. Six hundred seven and change plus smoking-hot plastic were all I had in the world, and I was on a mission.

I glanced at Black Dude, who urged me with a nod. I shifted to Anwar, whose eyes gleamed.

But Sister was waiting, and I was pretty sure she wasn't inside either of these guys, or they wouldn't have been telling me to keep a cat who'd make me sneeze. "No." I shook my head with true regret.

"I'm sorry. I wish I could."

Black Dude shrugged. "It was worth a shot. You woulda jazzed up the joint." He looked me over once, long and down and up, with a slow smile and a wink. Of course I knew that he might just be really hard up, but still . . . a good, long, slow down-and-up can cure a multitude of ills.

"Then you must remove that animal from my store," Anwar said, yanking me out of slow-melt mode.

"I can't have a cat. I'm allergic."

Black Dude smiled. "Then why ain't you sneezin'?"

Frowning, I looked down at the dandelion puff in my hand. "I don't know."

"I heard about some kind of cats allergic people can tolerate, I think." He wrinkled his brow. "Don't know where I heard it, though."

"Really?" I always, always wanted a cat. But how fair would it be to take that baby and then find out Black Dude was wrong and have to leave it somewhere else? At least there, it would be close to home.

"Really. Besides, she looks pretty happy to me."

"How do you know it's a she?"

"Calico coloring—see those orange spots and that little white patch beneath her chin? Black, white and orange makes a calico, which only happens to girls. My Granny told me that once, and she's the only woman never lied to me."

A girl. Not having a boatload of good experiences with the male gender, it seemed fated.

Which is how I came to be on the road again, but not alone. With cat food for her, peanuts and a Dr. Pepper for me. As it turned out, I didn't sneeze once that first day, so I took another big step and named her.

Isis, the Egyptian goddess of rebirth. A very clever high priestess, she tricked her brother—the sun god Ra, who cared nothing about his people—into revealing his secret name and thereby captured his powers over life and death, becoming the most powerful of all the gods and goddesses. She used those powers to help out the common people, among whom she liked to walk. I learned about her in a book I read to Sister when she could no longer leave the house.

A woman with power was something I could sure stand to be, and cleverness was always an asset. Plus in the event that Sister's soul turned out to be wily, I figured the ability to find out secret names just might come in handy.

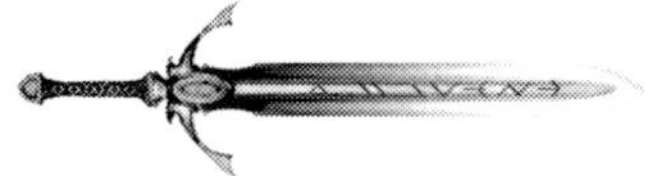

As the miles rolled by, I wished for a friend to touch base with, someone who'd care if I was safe or happy, but I had lost the knack of making friends long ago. When you moved all the time, you went one of two ways: you never made real friends because it hurt too much to leave them, or you made them and never let go, no matter how unlikely it was that you'd ever see them again.

After I had to move away from Becky Marie when I was nine, books became my friends. You could keep them or, if you didn't have room to pack all of them or money to buy replacements, you could go to the library—even if you didn't dare get a card—and visit. And some of them could be with you forever. Some of my dearest friends were in the trunk of the car at that very moment: *A Wrinkle in Time, Where the Redfern Grows. A Prayer for Owen Meany. The Secret Life of Bees* and the poetry of Mary Oliver.

Sometimes I imagined a bookshelf filled with my friends, sitting in the same spot for two—heck, let's be ambitious—five Christmases in a row. A luxury I could barely imagine.

Every new town, each new school, I would be up sick all night before the first day, worrying over not knowing what clothes would look right or if anybody would talk to me, never mind the incomprehensible mystery of how to be popular. That was beyond my wildest dream.

Sweetpea, Sister used to counsel me on those long nights, *You have got to stop caring so much about what other people think. If people love you, they love you. If they don't, you can't make them. It's their loss.*

I wanted to care as little as Sister did, but I couldn't. Maybe it was being an afterthought with no daddy. Maybe it was being five foot nine in sixth grade. Whatever it was, as I drove down the highway that July afternoon, I just knew that I desperately wanted to belong again the way I had with Sister.

But at least now I had Isis curled up on my lap, purring like an outboard motor. For a little speck of a thing, she could purr like there was no tomorrow. Even though the A/C still wasn't working, I didn't mind the extra heat. She needed someone. I wanted it to be me.

I even skipped a marker just to let her sleep. *You'll be sorry five minutes from now and have to turn around*, Mama would have chided, but I would just have to live with it. Isis felt perfect, snuggled in that way, like she belonged with me.

Then I remembered what I'd read about souls being reincarnated in animals. Cats are pretty mysterious, after all, and more than a little spacey. Maybe they'd make the perfect home for a soul. Whoever it was wouldn't have to think all that much, simply relax that go-round. Eat and sleep in the closest patch of sun. Claw when you were Maggie-ish, swirl around ankles when life was good.

And cats get run over all the time, so a person wouldn't be stuck there all that long if she got to feeling rested and ready to battle the human mess again.

Struck by the notion, I pulled over and shut off the engine, then lifted her up and stared like my life depended on it. "Sister?" I whispered. "You there?" I heard my heart going *ga-lump, ga-lump*, air swishing real loud through my nostrils. I rolled up my windows to be sure I wasn't missing anything. "Sister, I swear I'll take as good a care of you as you did of me—better, even. I'll do it all right this time, every last thing, and I'll make you happy you decided to come back. I'm so sorry I failed you, Sister," I said. "I need you to know that."

But Isis only stood up and started pawing at my hair, so I understood that Sister wasn't there but I just couldn't crank the car up yet. I realized I could be on the wrong road. It could be the wrong time of day. I could miss Sister by seconds and never get the chance—

Staring down at the skirt I had made from scraps, tier upon tier of bright colors, the patterns wavered in the blur. Isis glanced up after a drop plopped on her head, then started climbing up my halter top.

Needle-sharp claws pricked one breast. I jerked out of my slump, grabbed the cat and rescued my flesh from Isis's love. Or maybe just her sense of adventure, of what's-over-the-next-hill. Whatever it was, that little scrap of life yanked me back from the swamp in which I was about to put one size-ten foot.

Did I think this would be easy? Had Madame Eva promised such? And what about faith? What about the-universe-will-bring-you-what-you-need? *Open your mind to the highest good*, she had counseled. Sister had put it a little differently, *Worry don't change nuthin'*.

Fate didn't always speak up when called. "All right," I said to Isis, who was wiggling in my grasp. "So you're not Sister. She would never stand for eating cat food, anyway—what was I thinking?" I pulled her close under my chin and rubbed her against my throat and stared ahead for a bit.

"It's too dang hot in here." It was nice to have someone to talk to again, even if she was a little light on answers.

Isis raced across the seat, batting at my tissue box. I turned on the engine and discovered that the A/C was back to frigid.

Sign enough for me. "Hang on, sugar. Here we go."

Site of Community of Nameless

First surveyed in the 1850s, this area attracted numerous settlers by 1868. A community grew up, and in 1880 townspeople applied for a post office. After postal authorities rejected six names, the citizens replied in disgust, "Let the post office be Nameless and be d----d." The implied "name" was accepted.

SISTER'S MOJO

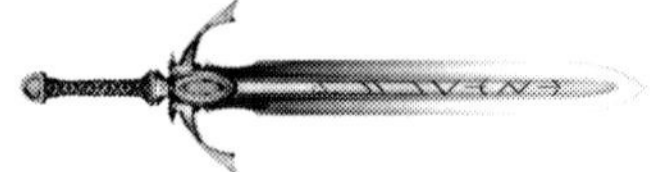

"Heaven in Texas is as close as I'll get—" I sang my heart out with Tanya Tucker, while Isis chose to remove herself to the back seat. Not that I blamed her; though I gave a song my all, no one would ever delude themselves that I had talent.

But I needed a little distraction. Night was creeping in and with it, that shadowy sadness that hits you when you're far from the familiar. The countryside seemed huge and menacing all of a sudden, and I wondered if Mama ever got scared those nights we would leave in the wee hours to escape the landlord or the bill collectors. She never said she was, but sometimes when I was supposed to be asleep in the back seat, I'd catch an odd expression on her face in the green glow from the dashboard. There were times you just knew to leave Mama alone, and night was one of them. Maybe that was why she brought home men even a child could tell were losers.

At that moment, I wished I could go back and give Mama a hug. I did the math I'd never bothered with before and realized that when I was born, Mama was years younger than me, only twenty-four and had two kids depending on her for everything. She worked as a waitress most of the time; she never finished high school, having gotten knocked up with Sister when she was fifteen. She ran off with Alvin, but that marriage didn't last five years. Casper was never her husband, only one in a series of stopgap boyfriends. God knows Mama never met a worthless man she didn't like.

That first night out on my journey, I only had a little kitten to care for, and I was scared spitless. I kept nodding off, though, getting too tired to be safe. I wanted a motel or a truck stop, any sign of civilization, but there seemed to be nothing around for miles, not even the distant glow that indicated a town on the horizon. What I needed to do was to find a place to pull over and nap a little for the sake of that kitten, but I was never real good at dealing with the dark, and that had only gotten worse once Sister was gone.

Finally I spotted an old gas station that looked left over from the Forties, and I pulled under the canopy, right beside two rusty pumps with the old rounded contours. The windows were coated with grime, and through them I could see a beat-up metal desk and empty shelves on the wall behind it, one of them hanging off its bracket.

Tell Me would have come in real handy right then, but my mind seemed as dried-up as my spit. The whole place reeked of hard times and sorrow.

I decided it would be foolish to be sleeping out here in plain sight, so I moved the car around back, keeping carefully to the concrete, dodging the odd fifty-five gallon drum leaking heaven knows what. "It's only a nap," I told Isis. "A catnap, pardon the pun." And smiled so she wouldn't be nervous.

I couldn't get comfortable, but I was afraid to climb in the back seat in case I needed to make a quick getaway. I told myself Isis would be my alarm system; animals sense things we don't, after all.

But I kept checking the locks. Picturing Freddy Kruger or that hockey mask guy. Wondering if I heard a coyote. I turned on the key and listened to old country, the twangy guitar and fiddle kind, that's how desperate I was to forget that an axe murderer could be giggling right then and sharpening his blade.

Then I thought about my great-great-grandmother's brother, Bob. He just walked away one day and no one ever knew where. That was well over a hundred years ago, and Brother Bob didn't have a key to turn or a flashlight to switch on. He couldn't play a radio or make a quick escape. He walked off into the world all by his lonesome and probably spent a lot of nights sleeping under the stars, complete with scorpions and snakes and guys with six-shooters.

Of course, since no one ever knew what happened, he might not have made it through that first night. But I was not going to think about that. Not right that minute.

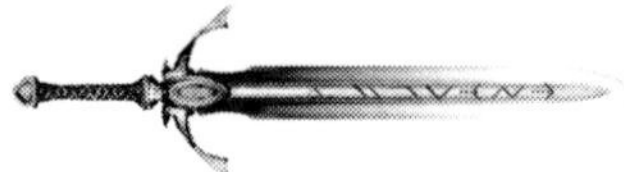

I got a snooze or two in somewhere along there, to my surprise. But by the time morning arrived, I had discovered something about cats that made me almost wish I was allergic. For all that Isis slept so soundly during our drive and was next to no trouble, night seemed to be her time to prowl. While I lay sweating, unwilling to roll down the windows even a crack, she held an all-hours kegger. She even knocked Sister's picture out of the ashtray and scared me to death it was damaged. I scolded her and put it in my billfold for safekeeping, but she didn't seem one bit sorry. We had ourselves a Maggie moment or two.

At first light, I was back on the road with her once again curled up innocently in my lap, a Halloween-colored little dab of fur, and I could almost forget what a hellion she'd been.

But to be fair, I had never slept all that well. I wanted to, never assume I didn't. I used to stare at Sister and wish I could be her, dropping like a rock into slumber as soon as her head hit the pillow.

But me, I go down hard and wake up easy. The slightest noise. The faintest worry. Sister used to tell me if I didn't lighten up, I was going to burn out early. That no child should be so serious.

But Mama never worried at all, just drifted from one man to the other. Sister was forever focused on the path ahead, on charging through the swamp of Mama's mistakes, only looking back to be sure I was still in her wake.

It was up to me to be the rear guard. Neither of them ever seemed to see all the demons lying in wait along the path, blowing on their fresh-manicured nails and whistling until we got past, fixing to leap up and chomp us the second I relaxed.

So I didn't blame Isis, really. I wouldn't have slept soundly even if she were conked out.

But I sure needed a shower. Bad.

I kept my eyes peeled, and sure enough, a half hour later, salvation popped into sight.

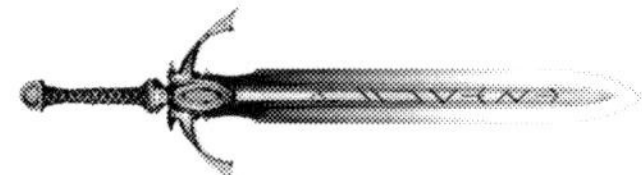

"You're not our usual customer," said the guardian of the truck stop showers outside San Saba. Above his shirt pocket was stitched his name, Vernon. "Truckers only back there." The tattooed fireplug of a man was probably used to juggling guys on the jagged edge of enough, loner guys, lords of the highway. A skinny Viking girl wasn't going to impress him.

So I tried being a girly-girl, something I was never very good at, but I had learned a thing or two watching other women while serving drinks at Fat Elvis. "I know," I said. *Sweep my lashes up and down real slow. Utter a breathy sigh.* "And I wouldn't want to be any trouble. It's just that—" *Down sweep. Pinch my nostrils together as if to stem tears.* "He hit me, and I was so scared that I took off running and—" *Little hitch of breath.* "I spent last night in my car on the side of the road, terrified every second that someone would murder me in my sleep and I just—" *Pin him with an earnest look.* "I have to keep going, but I just can't bear being like this. I don't have much money, though, 'cause he always took what I earned—" *Soft sob. Mouth covered with hand, eyelashes batting like there was no tomorrow.*

"Hey, there . . . " Dubious brown eyes turned nervous. "Aw, don't—come on," he said, pointing behind him. "We're not that busy right now. But make it quick, hear?"

"Oh, I will!" Genuine tears of gratitude filled my eyes then. I zipped 'round the counter and blew him a smooch. "Thank you, Vernon. You'll have stars in your crown for this, I am sure of it."

Down the corridor I spotted a lanky cowboy, straw hat drawn down low over his forehead, slowly clapping, smirk on his lips. "Good job, honey. Vern ain't usually such a soft touch."

I sailed on past him. My tips had shot right up at Fat Elvis once I learned to ignore the cynics.

"Need someone to wash your back, sugar?" he said before I got out of range. I just shook my head and bit my tongue near half in two to keep from saying the wrong thing. I was never that good at flirting. Mama was, I think, but I was too young to pay attention. Sister, she didn't hold much truck with men as she got older, with the odd exception. Not that she was a lesbian or anything—though mind you, I don't have a problem with women who prefer women. I think they're actually smarter than the rest of us.

Cowboy was gone when I emerged from the women's shower half an hour later, hair spreading a wet spot over the back of my tank top—homegrown air conditioning. I felt more human. Teeth brushed, body bathed, clean clothes . . . amazing what we take for granted. All that was on my mind as I headed outside—trying real hard to ignore the seduction of frying bacon—was making sure Isis was still okay in the car parked in a patch of deep shade I'd found behind the building, windows rolled down as far as I dared.

Until I heard the screaming.

Halfway around the building, a girl's voice from out by the gas pumps intended for passenger cars. Not a squeal. No giggling. Anger—abruptly cut off. Then it turned to unmistakable fear.

I whirled and saw her, small and pulling away, one wrist caught in the grip of a young man with shaggy, greasy blond hair, dangerous and gorgeous. Despite her loose black T-shirt and tight black jeans ripped at the knee, her rows of earrings, spiky too-black hair and troweled-on eye makeup, she seemed a girl playing dress-up, much too fresh-faced and well-fed. I would have bet the farm her mother had never seen that outfit before.

I looked around, expecting someone else to notice, but no one reacted. I wasn't unfamiliar with domestic violence—one of Mama's boyfriends used to like to knock her around, and I still had a scar from where his big fat ring connected with my forehead when I jumped him.

I wasn't five anymore, and I would always hate to see a man use his size against someone smaller, so I hollered, "Hey, cut that out!"

He didn't hear me. He was too busy yelling at her, towering over her while she shrank away.

"Let her go or I'll call the cops." By that point, I was within ten feet and juiced up from fear.

His head whipped up, and gorgeous blue eyes narrowed. "This ain't your business, bitch. Get the fuck out."

A smart person would have left it to the cops, but nobody ever called me a genius. Not when I could see her lip bleeding. Not when her fear rolled over me like fog. "I don't think she wants to go with you."

She froze. He yanked her along, storming up, getting right in my face. "Nobody asked what you think." He whirled on her. In a voice cold enough to freeze blood, he said, "You want to tell this ugly bitch how wrong she is, Alexandra?"

When she didn't speak, he jerked her up against his side. Tears rolled mascara rivers over her skin.

I looked at her, ignored him. "You don't have to go with him, you know." I wanted to pour strength into her the way I never could with Mama. "I'll call someone for you. No one has the right to treat you like this."

His fist shot out and slammed into my ear, knocking me sideways. I kept my balance, but just barely. My ears rang, and I couldn't see so good. Then I caught a glimpse of him rounding on her again.

And I charged. I don't know why; I just lowered my head and barreled into his chest. All three of us hit the pavement.

I tasted blood. I grasped for him and felt the roughness of his jeans, then the telltale softness beneath. Dizzy and desperate, still I knew I had the family jewels in my hand.

So I squeezed. Hard.

He let out a shriek that just about poked a hole in my eardrum.

But his vise-grip fingers lost their hold on me. I rolled away, staggering to my feet. Grabbing the girl's arm, I ran. Beat feet toward my car while she was sobbing in my ear and jerking away. From somewhere I found the strength of ten and held on, my voice tight with how high the stakes were. "Come on!"

We reached my car, and I all but tossed her inside. I jumped into the driver's side and turned the key, tires squealing as we fishtailed our way out of the parking lot. People stood around, mouths open, wondering what on earth was happening.

I sort of wondered that myself, but it was a good ten miles before the adrenaline faded enough for me to stop shaking. For my fingers to relax the death grip on the wheel.

Finally, I had to pull over because I was shivering. My passenger had fallen deathly silent. The day was already at least ninety, but I was freezing to death. After a minute, I looked over to see her a small ball in the seat, knees under her chin, staring forward, with her face blank.

"Are you okay?"

She remained utterly still, except for one fist clenching and releasing the leg of her jeans. She said something too quietly for me to understand.

"I'm sorry. I didn't get what you said."

No response except for the relentless clenching. Her nails were bitten down to the quick, flakes of black polish clinging to them.

"Are you hurt?" I asked. "He hit you hard. Let me look at you."

Finally, she lifted her head. Her pupils were huge, her blue eyes dark in that delicate face. "Take me back."

"What?" I blinked. I could not have heard her right.

"I said, take me back."

"Are you crazy?" I laughed, harsh and hysterical. In the rearview mirror, I saw Isis, claws still clinging to the seat back, and I just laughed harder. Like a loon. Like I escaped from an asylum.

"I have to go." She gripped the door handle.

I still couldn't believe what I'd done, and my astonishment made me slow to respond.

When the girl—whose name I couldn't recall—cracked the door to get out, though, reality smacked me in the head. "You can't just leave."

"I have to. He might not wait for me."

"Why would you care? He was beating the tar out of you."

"I need him. He loves me." Suddenly her entire frame crumpled. "He just hasn't gotten used to the idea of having a baby."

Baby? I pretty much lost the power of speech then. My gaze dropped to her belly, and I realized that her t-shirt hid a small mound beneath.

"Ohmigod." I swiveled in my seat to face her. "You're pregnant? Are you okay? How far along are you?" As if I had the faintest clue about the fine points between one month and another.

"Five months, I think. And I'm fine."

Fine, oh yeah. "He hit you. Dragged you. Something could be hurt. You need to see a doctor. Where do you live, and I'll—I'll—" I couldn't seem to make my mind work. "I have to take you home."

"No way."

"But I can't take care of you."

"Nobody asked you to." Her voice was shaking. "You should have left me and Nicky alone." She was tensed up, desperate, and I had absolutely no idea what to do with her.

Then she burst into tears, dropping her face into her hands.

I patted her awkwardly, and she flinched. The hunch of her slim shoulders made her look much too young to be having a baby. "How old are you?"

"What does that matter?"

Having spent a whole lot of years running from the laws

governing the fate of children, this was one angle I did understand. "Because I think you're underage, and The Authorities—" The words were always capitalized in my mind, my own private bogeyman "—won't let you keep your baby without a support system. If you want to keep it, you need to go back home to your parents."

"I can't." She scrabbled at the door handle, then jerked it open. "Never mind. Just leave me alone. I'll hitch."

I was out the other side just as quick. I finally remembered what her tormentor had called her. "Alexandra . . . "

"Don't call me that!" She whirled and started walking fast, her thumb sticking out.

I squeezed my eyes shut and sighed. Charged after her.

She sped up, but my stride was longer. She was just a little bitty thing, barely more than five feet. "Alex—" When she didn't fuss at the nickname, I went on. "Alex, it's hot out here. You don't have any water or a hat or sunscreen."

"You're not my mother."

"Thank God. But she's got to be worried."

"No." She whirled on me. "She's not." Her chin was jutting, but it was also trembling, and her eyes were pure devastation.

So I treaded lightly, improvising as I went. "Listen, you might have trouble getting another ride. This road isn't that busy, I don't think."

Her eyes popped. "You don't *think* so?"

"I'm not exactly sure where we are."

"You're *lost?* You just, what, took off from the truck stop without knowing?"

"I was a little bit busy," I reminded her. I tried for a smile.

Wrong move. One fat tear rolled down her cheek. "You have to fix this."

As if I had the faintest clue how to do that. "What do you suggest?" Before she could answer, I spoke. "Besides take you back to him."

She shrank into herself, looking exhausted. As lonely and scared as anyone I'd ever seen.

Thinking madly, I spoke again. "Okay. Let's get back in the car, and I'll find us a nice air-conditioned place where we can have a bite and just talk. Figure out who to call. Your family and friends have to be missing you."

"There's no one—" Pride clamped her mouth shut. She glanced

away, but not before I saw an instant of pure terror.

Oh, lordy. What if she really didn't have anywhere to go? No one who wanted her? I didn't sign on for this. What on earth was I thinking when I laid into Pretty Boy? I could barely take care of myself, much less her. But I saw how her shoulders were rounded, and I had to do something. "Listen, we're both tired and hot, and I don't know about you, but I'm hungry." Like someone talking to a wounded animal, I kept my voice slow and quiet. "Ride with me that much farther, would you?"

She clasped her elbows, arms crossed over her middle, and stared at the ground, but her shoulders eased just a little bit. "I guess," she said in barely more than a whisper.

Why I felt relief, I cannot begin to imagine, since my head was whirling with so many questions that I was fixing to get a sick stomach. "Okay." I started to reach out and hug her, but I wasn't sure she would consider me any kind of comfort. "Okay. Let's—let's get back in the car." I turned but waited for her to follow. Over my shoulder, I saw her brush at her eyes. I whipped my head around quick, so she wouldn't know that I saw. In an act of pure faith, I started walking. It took a minute, but I finally heard her steps behind me.

We got back in the car. I started the engine and tried real hard not to think too much about what I would do next.

Alex quickly fell asleep like an exhausted child.

As I drove, I wondered just how insane I was to be doing this and what the detour would do to my journey. First a cat, now a girl . . . a pregnant one, at that.

Pregnant. Wait a minute—my heart literally skipped a beat. Holy cow—what if—

No, it couldn't be.

But babies were the most common method of reincarnation, most every source I'd read agreed.

Sister? I glanced at Alex's belly. Had this sudden urge to touch it. To put my ear close and listen. What were the odds that Sister had chosen this child?

Not good. A long shot, surely.

But why else had I been at that truck stop, just in time?

I gripped the steering wheel hard. There were too many variables, and the world was full of babies.

I could be doing everything wrong. The uncertainty chilled me to the bone.

Sister was so much braver than me. Her life had changed in an instant—in the space of one car wreck, she'd been saddled with me. She hadn't sat around whimpering, though; she'd taken action. Not that she hadn't wished things were different. I remember hearing Sister and her friend Carla late one night right after Alvin skedaddled. *I was this close*, Sister said to Carla, and I imagined her finger and thumb only a breath apart, *to being free, but—*

In that moment, something huge and scary had stood just outside the back door of the tiny, scrubbed-within-an-inch-of-its-life trailer. It mushroomed real fast, casting its shadow over the front door, too, and all the windows. Like how the Stay Puft marshmallow man in *Ghostbusters* smothered everything in goo and squished all the air out.

I leaned my ear closer to the crack of the door with my eyes squeezed shut, wishing I knew how to pray. Understanding that from then on, I would have to be better than good.

Please, Sister. I'd heard the whispers: *foster care . . . ward of the state . . . no living relatives.* Even with only the vaguest idea of what those phrases meant, their threat was clear, and only Sister stood between me and that unnamed fate wrapping slimy tentacles around my throat. *Sister, please*—Terror locked a stranglehold on my voice.

Then the quiet words. *What can I do? She's my sister.*

I collapsed to the floor, my head ballooning so fast from relief that I thought it was fixing to pop. I must have knocked against the door and slammed it shut because the next thing I knew, Sister and Carla were pounding on the door and shoving at it. *Pea, what's wrong? What happened?*

As the knob rattled and turned and the hard edge of wood jammed into my shoulder, all I could think was this:

Sister had mojo. And with it, she saved me.

So I kept driving, pregnant teenager and cat in tow, hoping like crazy that a little bit of Sister's mojo would rub off on me.

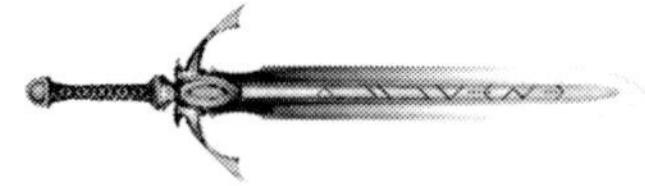

You have to fix this.

If I hadn't felt so much like crying, I'd have laughed. I was not the best of fixers; Sister could have testified to that. When her disease put me in charge, the results wouldn't exactly make your chest puff out.

Mama's approach to life was to dream of better times, then run when reality reared its ugly head. Sister stayed on point, never letting reality out of her sight, but my very existence stacked the deck against her, so in the end, she, too, had to run.

Me, I tended to get right up in reality's face and dare it to pop me one, back in the days when I knew Sister had my back.

But since she'd been gone, well, my report card wouldn't have won me any medals. I hadn't dreamed like Mama or faced things all that well, either. Mostly I'd just kept putting one foot in front of the other, sometimes landing myself in a mess. Like moving in with Jelly Davidson and thinking he was any kind of solution.

I heard Alex's stomach growl then, and the sound snapped me right back into the present. Soon I spotted a tiny store with one lone gas pump outside. A glance at my fuel gauge made the decision, and I hit my blinker to pull over.

"A bait shop?" Alex's nose wrinkled.

I hadn't noticed that part, but I wasn't going to tell her. I pointed to the cooler outside. "We can at least get us something cool to drink, and they might have snacks inside. I don't know how much farther it is to a real restaurant, but this will tide us over."

Her eyes rolled. "Whatever."

I locked my jaws down hard. If there is a phrase more certain to drive a person around the bend than that callous *whatever* that delivers a stinging slap of *screw you I couldn't care less you are dumber than dirt and beneath my notice*, I do not know what it is.

But she was twisting her t-shirt hem in that fist again, so I sucked in as much compassion and patience as I could muster and didn't slap back. "Go on in and pick out what you want. I'll be right there once I take care of Isis."

I resisted the urge to panic. Alex had nowhere to go yet, and that was my fault. I had interrupted her life, and now I was in charge, like it or not. She was hungry; so was I. One thing at a time. I pulled the car closer to the building under the straggly shade of a mesquite tree. I let Isis out to do her business, then scooped her up and started for the store. With every step, she yowled louder. *Oh, yeah. Bait shop. Fish. Cats who love to eat them.* "Alex—" I called.

Her head popped out the door. "What?"

"It's too hot. I can't roll the windows high enough to keep her inside without frying her. Let me give you the money, and you get me something, okay?" I walked closer, digging in my purse, with Isis straining and screeching to get down. "Ow!" I practically threw the bill at Alex as I struggled to keep the kitten from leaping down.

But even over the caterwauling, I heard it.

A giggle.

My head shot up, and there she was, the young girl beneath the Goth. "Very funny," I retorted, and her head jerked up, a frown already forming.

So I smiled. "Quick, before she turns my stomach into hamburger." And I chuckled, hoping she'd see that I was only joshing with her.

She picked up the bill. Returned her face to careful neutral. "What do you want?"

I cannot tell you to this day why I got wise all of a sudden, but for whatever reason, I remembered what it felt like to be dragged around and have no control over the littlest thing about your life. Here was one thing I could give her. "Something cold to drink and something salty to snack on. Surprise me."

A sideways glance, a frown. Finally a nod, then she went back inside.

I returned to the car and opened the doors to let in a breeze. I set Isis in the dirt and let her sniff around, though I had to grab her every time the wind shifted and she got a whiff of the bait shop.

At last Alex returned, an icy-cold orange drink and a bag of peanuts for each of us. The only thing I liked less than orange drink was grape, but I would have cut out my tongue before I told her. "Thank you." I popped the top and practically inhaled the liquid.

"I got us some water, too." She proffered a bag in one hand and change in the other.

"Wow, great idea." I started to take the money, but something of that better impulse lingered, and I shook my head. "Why don't you keep it." When pride stiffened her spine, I added, "For the next stop."

Her eyes narrowed. "What will that be?"

I blew out a breath of air. "I honestly couldn't tell you, but if you'd keep an eye on her, I'll find the map."

Alex settled in the dirt beside Isis, and I dug into my glove box. While I unfolded it, I noticed that she'd found a leafy twig and was dragging it around for Isis. Isis had forgotten all about fish and was arching her back and leaping and pouncing like she was all that stood between us and the barbarians. I couldn't help chuckling, and Alex's head rose. Her eyes were shining, and she was grinning, too.

"Never occurred to me that she needed something to chase," I said.

"They love this, especially when they're kittens. It's how they practice hunting."

"I don't know anything about cats," I admitted. "I'm allergic—or I thought I was."

"Oh, you'd know in a heartbeat. My stepwitch's eyes would swell up and water like crazy." Her voice tightened. "That's why my dad made me get rid of Spanky."

"I'm sorry."

She tried for that *Whatever* shrug but didn't quite make it. "No big deal."

But it clearly was. "Do they hurt you? Is that why you were with Pret—um, Nicky?"

Her head was down. I could see blond roots at the base of her black spikes. "I don't want to talk about them." She sounded younger than ever.

I pressed my lips together to keep from arguing and focused on the map. "The truck stop was near San Saba," I said aloud as I traced my finger. "I turned off the road to the right, and when we left, I . . . " I turned the map upside down to see if it would face the right way, but then the words were upside down, too, and my head started spinning and my chest felt tight. "I don't have the best sense of direction."

I reversed the map and tried to think about where the sun had been, the way Sister used to tell me to do, but . . .

"Here." Alex snatched the map. Spread it out on the hood and scooped up Isis. "Where were you headed?"

"New Mexico. I thought I'd go through Lubbock."

Her shoulders went rigid, and I wondered if Lubbock was where I'd find her family, but I didn't push it. She kept her head down and perused the map, then finally stabbed a finger. "I think we're somewhere around here."

I bent over her shoulder. My long hair swung down and gave Isis a new toy. She latched on and started to climb. "Yow!" I leaped back, and Isis came with me, but this time Alex didn't laugh at her antics.

My mind was racing while I disentangled the kitten from my hair. I couldn't keep Alex, but I couldn't just dump her, either. What on earth was I to do?

"This doesn't count as a meal or air conditioning, either," she said.

I glanced up at the sudden demand and saw both desperation and plea. Ten months would soon be eleven and time was slipping away. Maybe I had an answer here and maybe not, but what would it hurt to let things play out a little longer? I looked at Alex, saw her twisting her t-shirt and gnawing her lip, and what else could I do? "You're right. And I am a woman of my word." The instant relief on her features wiped the *Whatever* teen right out of my head. "What's the next town that might have a real café or such?"

"Nowhere close, not the direction we're going."

"You be the navigator," I said.

"I could drive." Hope danced over her face.

I doubted she was old enough to have a license, but even if she did, it wasn't with her. All she had was the clothes on her back. I grimaced. "Well, thanks to me, you don't have a purse, so I'd better drive so we'll be legal."

A pause, in which I waited for some reminder of how I'd interfered in her life, but for whatever reason, she seemed to think better of it. I braced for *Whatever*. But she said, "Okay."

Our second successful negotiation concluded, she got inside, and so did I. Maybe she felt a little hopeful, too, but I wasn't going to ask.

"We'll need to turn in about fifty miles or so, but until then, just stay on this road," she advised.

"Thank you." Teamwork at last. Imagine that.

About a mile down the road from the bait shop, I spotted a marker and pulled in. Alex looked at me funny. "When I'm on the road," I explained, "I like to stop to read what they say. You learn a lot that way." I got out and waited to see if she would follow.

Amazingly enough, she did. She read alongside me, and I suspected she was mostly humoring me, but I didn't care. It was one more moment of peace, and I would tiptoe through it.

And mentally apologize to Sister. I'd still been a sweet little girl when Mama died, but Sister had been forced to endure the teenager. Doing so was harder than it looked.

The Crash at Crush

A head-on collision between two locomotives was staged on Sept. 15, 1896, as a publicity stunt for the Missouri, Kansas & Texas Railroad. Over 30,000 spectators gathered at the crash site, named "Crush" for MKT passenger agent William G. Crush, who conceived the idea. About 4 p.m. the trains were sent speeding toward each other. Contrary to mechanics' predictions, the steam boilers exploded on impact, propelling pieces of metal into the crowd. Two persons were killed and many others injured, including Jarvis Deane of Waco, who was photographing the event.

EVERYONE NEEDS A LITTLE ADVENTURE

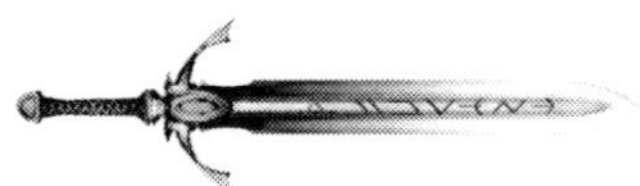

A semi blew past with such force that Valentine Bonham reconsidered his new resolve to go straight. He'd been sweaty before—broke, too—but never for this long. In the past he would have been in the bed of some sweet thing whose house was air-conditioned to a sub-Arctic degree.

At least until her husband was due home.

The sweet thing would have a big smile on her face—Val never left a woman any other way—and she would insist on making plans for the next day. He'd tell her that he had to leave town on business. There'd be a request for him to call when he returned, a promise he would duly make because it wasn't really a lie. He seldom revisited any town.

Then he'd spend a few more minutes putting that smile right back on her face before he left.

With one on his own.

Along with a piece or two of her jewelry—plus maybe some of

her cash—in his pocket. A fair trade, he'd always thought, for services rendered. He never picked a woman who couldn't afford him. He didn't take anything of sentimental value to her. He was careful to give her time to get presentable before her husband came home.

He never, ever, got his heart—or hers—involved.

The Valentine Bonham Code of Ethics.

Not the commonly accepted standards of proper behavior, maybe, but far beyond those of the uncle who'd raised him. Who'd first used a small boy to slip into places an adult couldn't fit and open the doors from inside. Uncle Paul—who'd turned out not to be related at all—had gone on to tutor Val in all the finer arts of thievery and cons: picking a pocket with small, nimble fingers; garnering sympathy, when needed as a distraction, as the poor child separated from his mother; disabling a security system in ten seconds flat.

Uncle Paul had no scruples about whom he preyed upon. Val, raised outside the mainstream and now with no way to enter without raising suspicion, had developed stricter standards. As a child, he'd been terrified of the officials who could part him from the only safety he knew, so he'd cooperated with Uncle Paul's demands.

He'd never been to school, never left the tracks of his existence others took for granted—no drivers license, no Social Security number. If there was a birth certificate with his name on it, he hadn't seen it. He had vague memories of a gentle older woman rocking him against her soft bosom, but the only life he'd known had been with the man who called himself Uncle Paul, who'd been kind to Val, in his own manner.

But Paul Armstrong was long gone, and Valentine had made his own way, mostly content with the life he led.

Until last week's mistake. A husband home early. With a gun in his truck.

So here he was, after a hasty retreat from East Texas, out on the wrong road in hotter-than-Hades temperatures, already regretting his impulsive decision to Go and Sin No More.

Not a car had passed for two hours. The next one he saw would stop if he had to lie down on the road to accomplish that.

Val used his forearm to wipe the sweat off his brow.

And smiled when he heard the sound of an engine approaching.

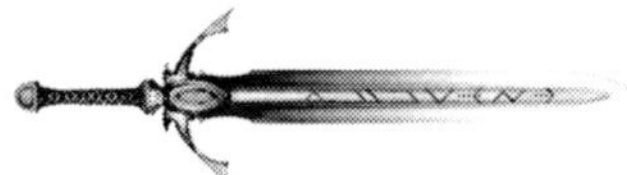

I was really feeling the effects of the lousy night's sleep and the events of the day, so all my efforts went to staying awake. Alex hugged the door and stared outside, tucked into a shell of silence and pretending to be asleep so well that she fell right into the real thing. The dark circles under her eyes made me believe the best plan was just to keep driving as long as possible.

That was all right with me. It wasn't a big stretch for me to imagine how scared and alone Alex must feel. Or to see a crack in my blessed assurance about Mama and Sister. I'd wished many a time to be the one with the steering wheel in her hand, positive I would make better choices than either of them. Things didn't look quite so simple on this side of the front seat.

The highway was so hot the pavement was doing that shimmering oasis-just-ahead trick. Even the trees seemed to droop under the assault. I saw a bunch of cows gathered in a patch of shade, and I couldn't help thinking they'd probably change places with me in a heartbeat, especially since the A/C had gone North Pole again. I cast a glance at Isis and Alex, now all curled up together, and saw goosebumps on Alex's arm. I reached across her to adjust the vents so she and Isis wouldn't turn into popsicles—

Something popped into my side vision. I jerked back, yanked the wheel and swerved hard to miss it, but—

An unmistakable thump. Not likely my heart.

Which had stopped flat. "No—" I moaned. *It's an animal. A really big one. Not a person, oh please God not a person.* Little scatter-shots of terror pelted my brain.

"Wha—" Alex jerked up to sitting. "What happened?" Isis yowled in protest.

I couldn't speak. Could barely hear over the clamor inside my head. How hard was the thump? *Not bad. I don't think it was bad.* Somehow I managed to shift the car to Park and shut off the engine before yanking the door open. "Stay here," I hollered to Alex and charged outside.

It was a man. Oh, mercy, a man. Lying very, very still.

"What's going on?" Alex asked through the window.

"Don't get out of the car," I ordered. If I'd killed him, I didn't want her to see a dead body. No telling what that would do to someone so young, to say nothing of marking her baby.

I dropped to my knees, shaking and more scared than I'd ever been in my life. "Oh, lordy, mister, I'm so sorry. Please be okay. Please . . . " Frantically, I searched for blood and tried to recall the first aid tips in the manual under the front counter of my last job.

Before I could think of a single one, he groaned.

Then his eyelids twitched.

And finally opened. "Wha—?"

Relief burst through me so hard my whole body rocked.

Then he stirred.

"Oh, no, don't move!" I started to clamp him down, but I was terrified I'd injure him worse. "Where do you hurt?"

"Everywhere." He grimaced. "What happened?" He began to rise to his elbows, and pain chased over his features.

"Please don't." My hands wanted to flutter, but I forced them to still. "Please just—" Then I realized that he was lying on asphalt that was egg-frying hot. "Oh! Oh, let me—but wait—try your legs. Wiggle your feet."

"Lady, what the hell—"

"If you've got a spinal injury, we can't move you."

"If I don't move, my spine's going to melt to the pavement. Get out of my way—unh!" He gasped as he rose to sitting, but his legs stirred, thank goodness.

"Here, let me help you." I wrapped his left arm around my neck and grasped his waist. "Alex," I called to her as she stood wide-eyed next to the headlight. "Open the back door and take everything out." I turned back. "Ready?"

"I guess."

I let my knees rest on the scorching pavement just an instant before I shoved myself upward. He threw his own muscles into the task. We rocked to a stop.

Then his eyelids plummeted. He swayed on his feet.

"Easy there. Just rest a second." The sun beat down on us, but I didn't see any choice but to pause. Sunstroke wouldn't help him, though. "If I hold on, can you walk?"

"I think so." He straightened, and he was an inch or two taller than me.

"Are you positive nothing feels broken? I can't see any bleeding, but inside do you . . . "

"I don't know. Maybe if I just rest for a minute."

"I better take you to a hospital, but I'm not sure how far it is to the next one."

His eyes flared wide. "No hospital."

"But—"

"It's not that bad," he said, but his expression didn't reassure me. I'd have liked to believe him—my six hundred dollars wouldn't go far at a hospital, if I could even find one here in the back of beyond. I had no idea if my car insurance would cover his expenses.

"Oh dear mercy!" I blurted as realization hit. "I have to wait for the cops."

He tensed. "Cops? Why?"

"To turn myself in, of course. Vehicular homicide or manslaughter or . . . "

His lips curved. "I'm not dead." His eyes slanted toward me. "Unless you're an angel?" He wasn't model gorgeous like Pretty Boy, but that smile, faint though it was, had definite potential.

"I don't think angels run down innocent strangers on the road."

He grunted. "How about I go horizontal for a while first, then I'll perform a citizen's arrest if I don't get to feeling better."

Relief duked it out with my conscience. Regardless, I needed to make amends. "Of course. Listen, I'm sorry as all get-out. It was all my fault. Wait, you're limping."

"My knee. Damn, it's hot."

"Sorry. Let's get you inside." With slow steps, we made it past the mounds of my belongings, but I couldn't spare any concern for them. The trunk could handle more, and I wasn't going anywhere that it would hurt if my clothes were wrinkled. I settled him on the seat. "We'd better look at your knee."

He shook his head. "Just a sprain, I think. The bumper—"

Oh, God. I bit my lip. "Are you sure?"

He nodded.

"We'll stop for ice as soon as possible." His eyes were closing, but he nodded again. "I'm going to close the door now. Sorry there's not more room for you to stretch out."

"Don't worry on my account." He paused, inhaled raggedly, and I could barely resist the urge to wring my hands. "I only need to sleep a little."

"Car's getting crowded," Alex complained. "I'll hitch."

"No!" I whirled to face her. "Hitchhiking is dangerous, Alex. And you have your baby to think of." I was ready to read her the riot act when I noticed that her hand was fisting in her shirttail, and it hit me that our passenger, being male, might make her nervous. I lowered my voice. "We can't just leave him." I bent closer. "Are you worried because he's a man? I don't see what else we can do, do you? No telling how badly he's hurt."

She stared at him, then back to me more than once. "I guess not." Her voice didn't carry a lot of conviction, though.

"Alex, I'll keep you safe, I promise."

"I can take care of myself." She frowned. "What's your name, anyway?"

Oh, good grief. In the uproar of our meeting, I guess she never asked, and I hadn't noticed. "Pea. Pea O'Brien." I waited for the usual snicker. "Actually, my name is Eudora, but everyone calls me Pea." I jutted my chin, daring them to laugh at either name.

But they didn't. Then Alex and I both looked expectantly at him. "Val. Valentine Bonham," he answered. "Try having a name like Valentine when you're going out for the football team. Eudora's a strong name. You should use it."

I stiffened. "My sister called me Pea. For Sweetpea," I mumbled.

He shrugged. "Your choice, Red." His tone made me feel foolish. Then he flashed this killer grin that probably had women of all ages slobbering.

But not me. It was none of his business what I chose to be called. "I'm aware that Pea sounds ridiculous for someone my size," I responded frostily, "But for this trip, I'd appreciate your cooperation. I have to go by the name that would get her attention, or I might not find her."

He cocked an eyebrow. "You're looking for your sister?"

"Yes." No need to explain more. "Where were you headed? If it turns out you don't need a doctor, tell me where to drop you off, so I can be on my way."

"Where to?"

"New Mexico."

"What part?"

I resisted a sigh. "I'm not sure."

"Why not?"

"That's my business." He'd never understand, and neither would Alex. I busied myself tucking his foot inside. "We'd better get a move on before the day turns any hotter."

Another shrug, then he looked past me at Alex. "What about you?"

Alex's mouth was tight with mutiny. Her tough act was back. "Doesn't matter where I want to go, not to Hitler here." She yanked open the passenger door and got in, slamming it for emphasis.

I thought of all the times Sister probably wanted to wring my neck for sassing her. I counted to ten while carefully closing the back door.

The counting didn't do diddly. I marched over and yanked her door open. "Look, you deserve better than to be knocked around by a loser like Pretty Boy, no matter what he looks like. Your baby certainly deserves more. I'm only trying to help you. Needing a man too much is a recipe for disaster, Alex." I cast a baleful glance back toward Val to put him on notice that I would be watching. "You don't raise a hand to women, do you, Valentine?"

"Nope. No self-respecting man would."

I turned back to Alex. "Exactly what do you suggest I do with you, then?"

"I'm still hungry," she said in a small voice.

She was young and scared. He was hurt. I rubbed the spot between my brows. "Okay. I promised you that." Food I could manage, though not for long, not with my pathetic bankroll.

I closed Alex's door and sucked in a deep breath. A few more of them and the top of my head felt more settled on my shoulders and less in danger of exploding. I walked to the trunk and loaded the rest of my belongings plus the duffel that must be Val's.

Then I rounded the car. And prayed that the A/C was still in Eskimo mode, since Maggie already had her claws sunk way too far into me.

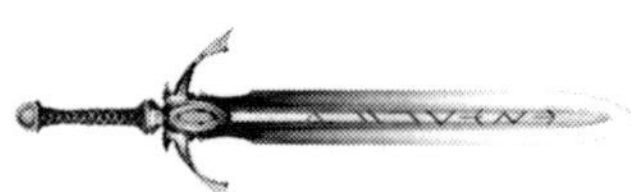

Three people plus a cat were too many for a night in my car, and my stomach was gnawing on my backbone. We needed a place to stay and a real meal, but Alex had no purse, and Val was injured, so the solution was up to me.

Thanks to Alex's map reading, I had an idea where we were, at least. Problem was, there were a lot of miles to go to find a main road.

I kept looking for signs and prayed that I could find a place that was clean but also in my budget.

Budget. Hah. Maybe I should have taken Anwar up on his offer. I was going to need money soon, unless Val could help out, and I couldn't ask him right now. He was sound asleep in my back seat.

Asleep. Ohmigosh. I jammed on the brakes and slid to the side of the road, then leaped from the car and yanked open his door. "You have to wake up."

"Hunh?" He blinked at me, then his lids descended again.

"You can't sleep. Concussion." I dragged at him. "Let me look at your eyes," I snapped when he resisted. I shoved him to sitting. "Wake up, Val. I mean it."

He frowned. "Go 'way." Started sliding back down.

"Alex, please get back here and prop him up. Oh, God, I knew we needed a hospital."

She opened her door, but Isis beat her outside. "Wait!" she cried. "I have to catch the cat. Oh no!"

I glanced up just in time to see a tiny furball skittering toward the road. A truck was barreling down the blacktop.

I let go of Val and charged. Launched myself at the kitten as an air horn wailed.

Tires screamed, and a wall of wind knocked me backward. I landed on my butt, then smacked my head on the ground—

People always say *my head rang*. Or bystanders talk about the roof-jumper's head splitting like a watermelon. I was caught inside the watermelon, and the meat of my brain slapped hard against my skull with a dull gong.

For a second, I was lying in Kentucky blue grass with sunrays winking in and out, darting into my eyeballs, then dancing away behind the leaves of the elm tree I'd bailed out of, holding onto a dish towel for a parachute. Mama was bent over me, her lips moving without sound, her eyes wide and panicked. *Are you all right? Breathe, honey. Breathe.*

I didn't want to. I wanted to stare at her longer. Feel her touch as she pulled me into her generous bosom. Let me linger in that green, fresh-mowed grass scent of heaven.

Breathe, Pea.

Obedient as always, I did.

And sound rushed into my silent movie.

It took a second to realize that a few of those needles in my chest were coming from the outside.

"*Mrowr—*" Isis sank her claws deeper.

One rock poked hard into the back of my skull. A whole host of others jammed into my back. But Isis was alive, and so was I.

Just then the world exploded into voices.

"Lady, what the hell do you think—"

"I didn't mean to let her out—"

"You are one crazy woman, you know that?"

Faces crowded around me; a crusty old cowboy with a gimme cap that said *Truckers Do It In The Road.* Alex, looking not at all tough and very much terrified.

And Val. Grinning.

"You're not unconscious," I managed.

"Kinda hard to sleep through a daring rescue attempt," he drawled. He nodded at Isis. "If you'd loosen that death grip, she'd probably unsink those claws."

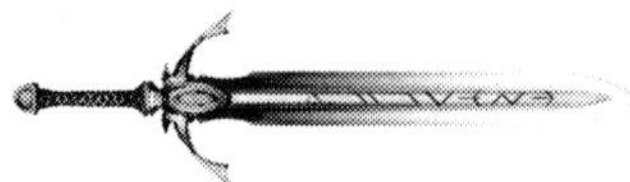

I woke up in the back seat sometime later, sweaty and sticky with a mouth full of fur. The car was stopping. "Where are we?"

Val spoke from the driver's seat. "The kid's hungry, and I need some sleep."

"He won't let me drive," Alex complained. "And I'm not a kid."

Both turned to me, scowling.

I glanced around. The little burg was barely a spot in the road. No other choices than the old-fashioned motor court with the empty cracked pool and a sign proclaiming *HBO.* Good thing I didn't need hi-speed internet.

The sign said thirty-nine dollars. I winced. "I guess that's not so bad if we're splitting it."

His shoulders sagged. "If only I could. I was robbed right before you hit me."

I flinched. "I'm so sorry. Don't worry. I'll handle it."

"I'll pay you back." His expression was earnest. "The first second I can." Sorrow lined his face. "My grandma . . . she died. I'd been taking care of her, and when she was gone, I just couldn't stay there anymore. I quit my job, withdrew my savings and set out on a pilgrimage to visit all the places she wanted to see but never managed." A muscle in his jaw jumped. "I'd gotten to the first three, and then someone . . . " His lips tightened.

"You were robbed."

He nodded. Looked away, ashamed.

"Every cent?"

Another nod.

"That's terrible. Where had you planned to go next?"

Wearily, he rubbed at his eyes. I felt horrible for ever worrying about money. "Taos. She was there once when she was young, and she always wanted to go back to visit the pueblos."

Oh. My. God. *Taos.* Sister's people. Pueblo Indians. "That's where I'm thinking about heading." I hesitated. I didn't know him that well, but he'd been nice so far, and he'd certainly had me at his mercy for however long I'd been conked out. Alex didn't seem nervous around him anymore. What if his arrival was another sign from Sister, and I let him leave? "Maybe you could ride along."

He took a long time to answer, which made me feel better still. "I don't want to be trouble. You don't seem to have much money yourself."

Resolve flooded me. *I'm listening, Sister, as hard as I can.* "I don't, but I'm a hard worker. I can find jobs along the way, if need be."

"That's too generous, Red. I'll pitch in, too."

He was trying. And the company would be nice, especially after I got Alex settled. Full up on optimism, I smiled. "Let's go check in, then we'll eat something."

"Better yet, I'll go next door and scrounge up food while you're checking in," he said. "So you can have first dibs on a shower."

"How's your leg? Should you be walking that far?"

"It's sore, but it's not bad." He looked over the seat at me. "You didn't hit me that hard."

I couldn't help wincing. "I'm really sorry." Not to have to pay a hospital bill or wrangle with my insurance company, though, was a huge relief. I dug in my purse and handed him a beat-up twenty, then realized it might not be enough. I got out one more.

He took it hesitantly, clearly uncomfortable taking my money.

"Alex, you want to stay with me?"

"I want to pick out my own food."

Are you okay with him? I tried to ask with my eyes.

Her brows knit together, but Val got it. "She's a little young for me, Red," he said with a grin. "And forty bucks isn't enough to pay me to take her off your hands."

"Hey!"

He held up his hands. "No offense, kid."

"I'm not a kid."

To forestall the brewing argument, I interrupted. "Get milk," I said. "Make sure your food is nutritious."

She rolled her eyes. "Yes, Mom." Then followed after Val with the slow, shuffling steps of a chain gang.

Oh, Sister, I thought. *I owe you. Big.*

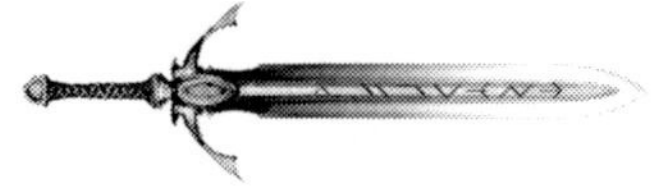

I was in the shower, ignoring the cracked tiles and missing grout. The ancient dun carpet and cowboy-print drapes. Some Hollywood designer would probably have paid big bucks for the scarred wagon wheel headboards and the ceramic horse table lamps.

Isis was outside the bathroom, flinging herself at the door and howling fit to beat the band. A little hard to block out, especially with the trickle of water. *We might have just a little attachment problem, Kitty Girl.*

But she was so young. I closed my eyes and concentrated harder on the relief of being clean. A few minutes wouldn't kill her, surely.

The howls became an eerie scream. I leaped from the shower, skidded on the spatter-print linoleum floor and yanked open the door to scoop her up.

And looked straight into the grinning face of Valentine. The O of Alex's mouth.

The next screech was me. *Slam door. Breathe deep.* Maybe Val would suffer amnesia during the night, and Alex's baby wouldn't be scarred for life.

Oh, crap. I dumped the cat on a pile of towels, where she licked her behind, yawned real big and curled up, instantly asleep. *Thanks a lot, girlfriend.*

Back in the shower, I wished for instant blindness so I could block out that there were two people, one wall away, whom I would soon have to face. I stuck my skinned elbows under the water and instantly forgot everything but the urge to scream.

Hunger drove me out, finally, along with a pang of conscience because I'd used so much hot water.

Finally, there was no choice but to put on the T-shirt and pair of Jelly's Tweety Bird boxers I decided to wear to bed. My wet hair was rapidly soaking my shirt, but one thing you learned as a Naturally Curly Girl was never to blow dry or brush unless you wanted your hair's volume to increase to a scary degree. I already had hair out the wazoo. I left the sleeping cat on top of the toilet in her nest, figuring I'd retrieve her when the next person was ready to shower. I grasped the doorknob and sucked in my courage.

Open door. Walk through, head high. Nothing happened.

Wet shirt. A/C. Instant nipples. *Oh, crap.*

I wheeled around and headed back.

"If I had boobs like that, I'd go naked everywhere," Alex said.

So much for *nothing happened.*

I glanced over at her and understood that she was making an effort. "Thanks," I responded, vigorously avoiding Val.

"Don't mind me," he said. "I can take it. My heart only stopped twice."

My eyes shifted to him. He was smiling, yes, but it was a nice smile. Mischievous, sure, but not . . . leering. Not a Fat Elvis fanny-pincher.

"They're just breasts," I said. "I'm not going to be mortified."

"Yes, you are," Val responded. "But you can take heart that we know you're a natural redhead."

I grabbed a French fry to throw at him just before the scent of them hit me. Then I could think of nothing but food. Like a locust horde, I devoured my hamburger and fries to the last pickle, the final dab of ketchup. It was all I could do not to lick the paper they were wrapped in.

"Here." Val tossed the second twenty at me and began to dig into his jeans pocket, hauling out coins and small bills. "The kid and I did good."

"Stop calling me kid," Alex said, but there was no heat in her words. Their mission seemed to have worked something out between them. "Even if I have to drink milk," she muttered.

I was relieved to see that she had a salad instead of fries to go with her burger. "Baby Alex thanks you," I said.

An expression of wonder crossed her features. "Baby Alex," she repeated softly, as if she had never considered the child to have anything of her.

Val was regarding Alex with bewilderment, like she was some sort of foreign creature. Mixed into it was something almost . . . fond.

I couldn't blame him. I'd seen pregnant women before, of course, but I'd never had anyone in my life who was carrying a child. It seemed at once the most terrifying risk I could imagine, the heaviest burden . . . and yet the thrill of it, the unknowns, the possibilities took my breath away.

Alex was no longer alone. If she handled things right, she had years ahead when there would be a home and someone who loved her. For the rest of her life she would have a bond, a special connection to someone who shared her blood, who would be part of her forever.

Except I knew only too well that life and Fate could rip all that away. That someone could be so much a part of you that you got reckless and took them for granted.

If Sister was right about the do-over, I could have another chance to be with her, and my heart hurt, actually hurt, I missed her so much.

But what if—I closed my eyes, clenched the neck of my t-shirt and twisted it in my fingers. Dared to think the words.

What if Sister was wrong?

"Are you okay?" Alex asked.

"Yes," I answered quickly, shaken to my soul. Stumbled as I made my way to the bathroom, each step feeling like I was slogging through molasses. I picked up towels, folded them, cleared away all the red hairs I seem to drop like some molting bird. Brushed my teeth and grabbed Isis. Walked through the bedroom and straight out the door, which I carefully closed. Across the parking lot to the scrap of what might be called a lawn bordering the empty, cracked swimming pool.

But I felt too exposed there, in the center of the horseshoe of rooms, so I rounded the edge of the last building.

There was a field. Trees. I settled beneath the sheltering arms of an ancient one, tucked between two massive roots. I cuddled the purring kitten and fought not to crush her as I sought her warmth.

I wished for a blanket in the cooling wind. I wished for a place of my own, for the luxury of belonging.

For my sister and the home she'd always been for me.

I couldn't let myself think Sister was wrong. If I did, I was completely lost. Yet what did I really know for certain? Yes, she might be right back there in that room—or she might be across the planet, for all I knew.

The magnitude of what I was tackling socked me right in the gut.

Like a story I'd once read about the Spanish explorer Cortes, I'd burned my boats behind me. I was too far gone to turn back, and anyway, I had nothing to return to.

I kept trying to catch my breath, but there was no air.

When things seem too big and scary, you got to pick just one thing you can handle and focus on that, Sister would tell me on those worrying nights. *Just one thing. Tell me your one thing, Sweetpea.*

I hunched in my shoulders and cuddled the cat close, wondering exactly what it was I thought I could handle.

Driving, I decided. I could manage driving. I would keep heading for Lubbock and see what the next day would bring.

And try to believe.

I believe I believe I believe.

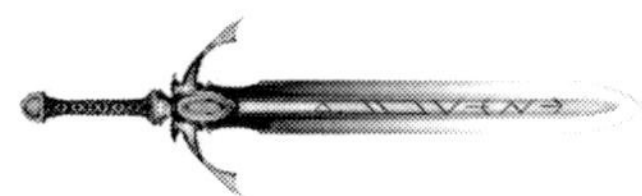

Val cursed under his breath. Her purse was right here. Money. Car keys. Freedom.

"Well, don't just stand there," Alex said. "Go get her."

Red should know better. A second-grader could skate away with all she had.

"Hey! Are you listening to me?"

"What?"

"You can't just let her walk out like that."

"Of course I can."

"You gonna steal her purse?"

"I look like a thief?"

"Maybe."

"Well, I'm not." *Not exactly*, he added silently. And not anymore. Women liked to buy him things. Who was he to resist? He kept his part of the bargain; he made them happy.

"You embarrassed her, talking about her . . . you know. Pubes."

"You brought up her boobs first. I was trying to keep her from feeling self-conscious. She's the one who opened the door when she was naked. And anyway, that wasn't what upset her."

"What did, then?"

"How the hell should I know?"

"You still need to go after her."

"You do it."

"I'm sleepy. Anyway, I'm not big enough to carry her back. You are."

"She'll come back when she's ready."

"Coward. You're scared of her."

"There's not a woman alive I'm afraid of."

"Keep telling yourself that. But you still hurt her. She might be bossy, but she doesn't deserve that." The last words slurred as sleep claimed Alex.

Val remained in the ancient aluminum kitchen chair beside the formica table for several minutes, staring at that purse made of crazy quilt pieces of tapestry and velvet. Thinking about a woman foolish enough to be ready to turn herself into the cops after falling for a con. Wondering if her head still hurt after the spill she took, saving that scrawny cat.

Damn it. He never asked to be picked up by a Mother Teresa with a killer rack.

With a sigh, he rose and walked out the door.

Mrs. Angelina Bell Peyton Eberly (About 1800-March 15, 1860)

A Tennessean, Angelina Peyton came to Texas in 1822. With her husband, J.C. Peyton, she operated an inn in San Felipe, capital of the Austin Colony. Peyton died in 1834; in 1836 the widow married Jacob Eberly. She and Eberly had a hotel in Austin by 1842, when Angelina Eberly discovered men secretly removing records from the capital. Firing a cannon, she started the "Archives War," and rescued the original records of the Republic of Texas. Later she lived in Indianola. Her burial place and marker were destroyed in a flood in 1875.

GUNS 'N' GLORY

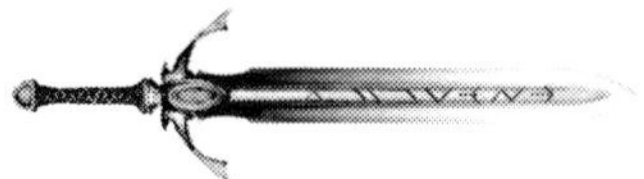

I was used to waking up in strange places, but I was usually alone when I did. That next morning, I couldn't place all the noises that crept into the edges of my grogginess, but I'd long ago learned to approach morning with caution. No moving, just listen. Then feel what's around you very slowly.

I was on a bed, but I was close to falling off. The mattress was lousy, but I'd had worse. Light was starting to leak around the drapes.

I heard purring. A sob.

And somewhere below me was a definite snore.

I went rigid. Stifled a yelp when tiny claws anchored themselves in my thigh. Isis, I remembered, and smiled. Gently pried her away while glancing over to see the small shape in the next bed, shoulders shaking.

A loud snore. *Val*, I remembered. I rolled in the opposite direction to get nearer the other bed. "Alex," I whispered. "Are you okay?"

She only curled tighter. Sniffed hard and burrowed deeper into the covers.

I didn't dare talk any louder. And anyway, I needed to pee something fierce, and if Val was awake, I wouldn't be able to, thinking about him listening. As it was, I wouldn't be able to flush for fear of waking him, but if he got up to go in there and I hadn't, I'd just . . . die.

My cheating ex-boyfriend Jelly could never understand my thinking on this; I suspect most guys can't. They have to do it in front of others all the time. I have no idea how they survive without stalls. At Jelly's, I'd go down the hall to the second bathroom, a luxury if ever I'd seen one, after so many years of sharing bathrooms with Mama, her various boyfriends and Sister. Sure, I'd been naked with a man while having sex, but that was nowhere near as intimate. Letting a person into the base creature moments, the ones that could never be glossed over, was a whole other level of trust. My life had contained too few private corners, and this was one I clung to.

To scout out the terrain, I leaned over the edge of the bed to see how asleep Val was.

Oh, lordy. He was awful good-looking. Lean and kinda sleek even in worn blue jeans, shaggy black hair almost to his shoulders. I didn't exactly remember the color of his eyes, but I thought they might be green. His eyelashes were an injustice, that was for sure. No man should have them so thick and long. He wasn't pretty, but he was striking, even the nose which looked to me to have been broken at some time.

In my former life, I could have been attracted to him. Good thing this was my new life. My do-over, and not just with Sister.

He stirred, and I froze, but I couldn't wait any longer. Slowly, holding my breath each time the lumpy mattress squeaked or the wagon wheel headboard scraped the wall, I inched off the other side of the bed and tried not to think about Alex being awake.

It wasn't just men I didn't want to have listening, see.

Once in the bathroom, I took care of the essentials, still undecided over flushing or not. Then I spotted something tucked back behind the door that made me sad.

Alex had washed out her minuscule panties and skimpy little bra, then put them to dry in the most inconspicuous spot possible. She might have a lot less practice at this no-privacy thing than me, I thought, but what really got me was realizing that here I'd been feeling all alone and scared, and that little dab of a girl was pregnant and had only the clothes on her back.

I would have to do something about that. I mentally ran through the clothes stashed in my car, pondering what on earth I would have that might fit a fairy. Shoot, my shirts would be dresses on her, but maybe that would be okay until we got someplace to buy her new clothes.

There was so much to think about when you were responsible for someone else. When Mama and Sister were alive, I just scrambled along and did my best to keep up with them. I knew a lot more about following than charting courses, but what good had the paths either had chosen done for them?

When you're the caboose on the train, you never think about how the engine feels. Okay, yes, a train has a track it has to follow, so that wasn't the best example. The lead wagon in a pioneer train, maybe, trekking across foreign land, wondering when the savages would attack or the rattlesnakes would strike the horses—

I brought myself up short. I had all sorts of problems to tackle this day, enough to make me want to burrow back under the covers, but that was Mama's way, and it couldn't be mine.

I might not know every step of my journey, but standing still wouldn't accomplish a thing. Sometimes you just had to take a step, whatever the direction, and see what happened.

Okay, I thought. *Step one: Be Brave.*

Flush.

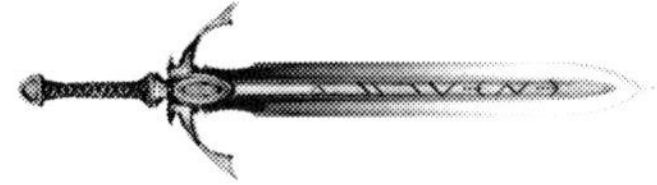

Alex, dressed in a tight aqua belly shirt of mine, which was baggy on her, looked sort of sweet. Colors suited her much better than Goth black. She still had the low-rise black jeans on, but she'd ditched some of the excess hardware on her ears and wrists.

I had the unexpected urge to dress her up like a doll, to find out how she'd look in a cute little sundress.

Like she would stand for that. Anyway, she was too busy sulking because I'd said we were going to Lubbock. If there was a chance in the world Alex's baby might be Sister, then I was in no rush to shed myself of her, but how did I explain that to her? I felt a little shaky around her that morning, not sure how to treat her. Wondering if

Sister was listening and watching my every move. Trying to figure out how to be positive that she was in there.

The list of what I wasn't sure of was so long it could have made me real tired if I'd let it. I tried to look on the bright side—I didn't have the money to support both of us until her baby was born, but I could earn it. If I hedged my bets by taking her with me to Taos, then, either way, my odds of finding Sister would have increased.

As for Val, this morning he seemed restless and, well . . . grumpy. He'd lost his grandmother recently, though, so that was understandable. Alex kept looking at him funny while he was ignoring her, but I was not going to play intermediary in whatever their problem was. Best to just keep going and let Fate play her hand.

Just then, I saw a sign for a historical marker, and some of the tightness in my chest eased. I pulled over just past the marker.

"Why are we stopping?" Val asked.

"It's this weird thing she does," Alex answered.

"I beg your pardon—" which my tone should have made clear I did not "—but this was a favorite activity of my mama's and it's also educational. Education is something everyone can use."

She didn't look at me, but I swore I could feel those eyes rolling.

"Takes all kinds," said Val. I couldn't tell if he meant it nicely or was making fun, but whatever, I was in no mood for critics right then, so I simply left the car with as much dignity as possible and proceeded to the marker.

Val came to stand beside me. He seemed real ill at ease, hands in his pockets, jingling change. "You okay, Red?"

No, I was not, but I didn't want to discuss it. My innards felt about as limp as cooked spaghetti.

Another jingle. "Want me to drive?"

He was trying, I had to give him that. I merely shook my head.

He faced the marker, his shoulder only an inch or so from mine. I was very tempted to lean, just for a minute, but I was not Mama, and I would not let myself be.

"We're on an old stagecoach route, huh?" he said. "You like this one?"

I merely lifted one shoulder, then relented a little. "It's not one of the best, but you can learn from any of them. Makes me think about how this country looked to folks back then who didn't know what was ahead, but they still kept going without any assurance that they'd make it, that their children would survive, just the hope that what they were traveling toward was better than where they'd been." That kind of courage left me breathless. They were like Brother Bob, these people.

"I know that feeling," he said quietly.

That got to me because I did, too. Where did he come from? Where was he going, once his pilgrimage was done? I wanted to ask him all those things, but his face was full of a longing that was too private to intrude on. We barely knew each other, after all.

Still, that look of his made me a little more patient somehow. More ready to stop thinking so much and let events play out a while longer. I recovered just a dab of my sense of adventure, but it was enough to tide me over. I stepped back. "You ready to move on?" I asked him.

"Sugar, I was born ready," he answered.

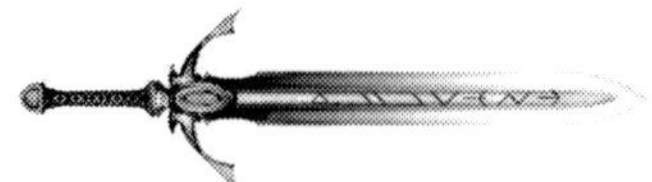

In times of uncertainty, I couldn't help missing Jelly's mom. Not that she was any June Cleaver, not one bit. Big Lil Davidson—all five-foot-one of her—had probably never worn an apron in her life. She was a former Kilgore Rangerette (*Beauty Knows No Pain* was her motto), one of those country club ladies always turned out to a tee, every perfect, champagne-blonde hair in place, shoes and purse to match any outfit. She was tiny compared to her husband and three giant sons—not a one of them under six-foot three—but she was the acknowledged queen of their universe. Mighty Mouse in a tennis skirt. A gen-yoo-wine steel magnolia.

I was certainly not her pick of the litter when it came to a match for her baby boy. Our first meeting could hardly be called ideal: Jelly had left to meet some buddies, and I was in front of the bedroom closet buck naked, looking for clothes while singing Garth Brooks, "I got friends in low places—" A noise in the hallway caught my attention mid-croon.

I had no idea his mother had a key to his house. I'm not sure which of us was more shocked, but I'm positive which of us could speak.

"So," she said, in that prom queen voice of hers. I asked Jelly once if she'd been prom queen, and he acted like I was some kind of genius. It was easy to see how she ruled the roost. "My son's taste has taken a turn."

I thought about that for a minute, wondering if I ought to cover up, then decided that horse had already barreled out of the barn.

Her gaze did a quick two-step over me, and it was sort of like going to the gynecologist, how you're feeling all awkward and embarrassed and the guy acts like you're a 327 Chevy engine, only a whole lot less interesting. She looked me down then up and said only, "Well, at least this time the boobs are real."

Big Lil might flutter and flatter the men in her life, but it was just part of her game plan. She was a realist to the core, a take-charge woman. If Big Lil had been my mama, no telling where I'd be now. Big Lil wouldn't have run from a landlord, that's for sure. She would not have picked loser boyfriends the way Mama did—or the way I did with Big Lil's sweet but worthless baby boy. She tried her dead-level best to bust me out of Jelly's life before I got hurt, I swear I believe that. She understood men in a way I never had. Big Lil would never have let her life revolve around a man. She understood that things worked better if everyone revolved around her.

Now seemed to be one of those times when my motto should be: *What Would Big Lil Do?*

I was puzzling over my current situation in light of the Big Lil standard, when suddenly Alex cried out from the back seat. "Stop right now!"

I jammed on the brakes, swerved to the side. "What's wrong? Are you sick?" I was half-climbing over the seat, all sorts of scary possibilities racing through my head. "Is it the baby?"

She frowned at me. "Are you trippin'?"

My racing heartbeat slowed. "Why stop, then?"

"I want to go over—" She pointed across the road and back a bit "—there."

I swiveled my head and saw a portable building, very small, with burglar bars all over it, and a sign on the front.

Guns 'N' Glory Firearms. Buy Sell Trade. A gun shop? In a portable building? How on earth could that be secure, even with burglar bars? I looked back at Alex. "Whatever for?"

"I'm on my own now." She crossed her arms over her chest. "I need a gun."

Miriam A. Ferguson Birthplace

A five-room log cabin on this land was the home of Miriam A. Wallace (1875-1961) from her birth until her marriage to James E. Ferguson in 1899.

After her husband had been twice elected governor, Mrs. Ferguson became the first woman elected governor of any state. She served two terms, from 1925 to 1927 and from 1933 to 1935.

The property was inherited by Mrs. Ferguson and about 1917 was mortgaged to support her husband's political career. The home was destroyed by fire in 1926.

STEEL SPRINGS AND WHALEBONE

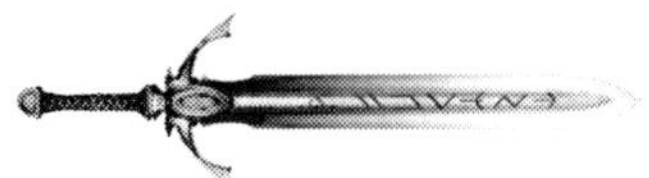

"Are you crazy?" I screeched.

Even Val looked unsettled, but he opted for a different tack. "Alex, honey, if you're worried about whatshisname . . . "

"Pretty Boy," I supplied.

"Nicky," she corrected. "If *you'd* had a gun, he couldn't have gotten close enough to hit you."

"You don't know that, and anyway, you're too young. I will not have—"

A sharp glance from Val stopped me. "Alex." His was the tone of reason. "Guns are expensive. I'd take you inside, but we can't afford one."

I glared at him. "You are not taking this child in there. Alex, you're not all alone. You have us."

"I do not. For all I know, you're just waiting to ditch me as soon as you can. I have a baby to protect, and I need a weapon."

"I'm not going to ditch you." Though I didn't really have a clue what on earth I would do with her. Nor did I think explaining my theory about Sister and the baby would help matters right then. "Anyway, you don't have any money," I pointed out.

"The sign says *Trade*. I have something to offer."

I sucked in air to holler at her until she got some sense, but Val's expression clearly told me to back off. "Make a U-turn."

"I will not."

"Fine." He opened his door, then hers. "Come on, kid."

"Valentine, if you do this, I'll—"

Both faces turned to me. "You'll what?" he asked. "Drive off and leave us? I sincerely doubt it, or you'd have done so already."

Oh, how I would have liked to prove him wrong.

Except, of course, he wasn't.

"Fine," I snapped. "Get in. You're not dragging a pregnant girl across the highway. You both could get splattered on the pavement."

He laughed. Closed her door. Slid onto the seat beside me. "Red's got a temper on her, Alex. Nice to know."

"I could have told you that," she muttered. "How do you think I got in this mess?"

"Mess?" Before I lost it altogether, I clamped my mouth shut. Barely. Hit the gas, painted a rubber arc on the asphalt with a squeal of tires. Screeched to a halt in front of the stupid beige building. "Hah—all locked up." I pointed to the padlocked gate that barred our entry.

But they were not one iota discouraged. Val vaulted over the barbed wire, then lifted Alex. They approached the building, and Val took a peek into one window. "Whoa, dude. Interesting place."

Alex kept jumping, trying to see in. *Stop that,* I wanted to tell her. *You might hurt the baby.* But before I could, Val boosted her up. She leaned against the window. "Oh, wow!"

Just then, a blast went off. I launched myself from the car, but Val had already grabbed Alex and dragged her behind him.

Two huge dogs appeared from behind a big silver propane tank at the side of the building, barking and frothing, strings of rabid-dog slobber flying from between enormous and deadly teeth.

I screamed, "No!" Scrambled over the fence and charged.

The dogs reversed their direction and headed for me.

As I skidded to a halt, another blast rang out. "Gary! Frakey! Stay!" a voice yelled.

Huh? Not exactly your basic Killer or Bubba, Texas-type dog names.

Both dogs' butts hit the dirt right in front of me. Their barking stopped, but a scary growl took its place.

Then from around the building emerged an old woman with white hair cascading from beneath a battered bush hat, ancient work pants over what appeared to be combat boots. She wore possibly the rattiest Grateful Dead t-shirt on Planet Earth, a tattoo twining around one bicep and—

I squinted. Pearls? A strand of . . . *pearls?*

"Shut your mouth, girlie. Flies'll get in."

"I, uh—we don't mean any harm."

She glanced from me to Val and Alex. "You just snoop on private property because you think it's your God-given right or something?"

I glared at Val first because, after all, he was the one who encouraged Alex.

The jerk had the gall to chuckle.

The woman frowned at him. "You there—what's so funny?"

He took one step toward her. The dogs' growl became a low roar. He paused. "Ma'am, Pea's right. And please don't blame her. She didn't want to stop here."

"Pea?" She snorted. "Someone's got a nasty streak, calling you that."

"You should talk." I pointed at the dogs. "What did they do to deserve those names?"

One eyebrow arched. "You display your ignorance." She made me wait, and I started steaming, but she was the one with the shotgun, after all.

"G-E-R-I. F-R-E-K-I." She spelled them out for me slowly, like I was a first-grader. "They're Odin's wolves. You know who Odin is?"

Val and Alex were watching with interest.

I shrugged. Being a big reader can come in handy. "The king of the Norse gods, of course. Any idiot knows that."

Her brows snapped together.

"Ma'am, we owe you an apology," Val intervened before I could get us into worse trouble. "We were only trying to get close enough to see what your hours are," he said. "We're interested in your merchandise."

Alex spoke for the first time. "I'm the one who's interested."

The old woman frowned. "You, little girl? You're not even close to legal. Anyway, pistols aren't cheap."

"Your sign says *Trade*."

"Don't care what you want to offer, not that I believe you have two nickels to rub together amongst the three of you."

"But you have to help me," Alex insisted.

The woman cocked her head. "Why would I?"

Alex approached her. The dogs growled. At a sharp command from the woman, they stopped. Alex leaned close and murmured too softly for me to hear.

The old woman snickered. Cast a quick glance at me and smiled really big. She slung one arm around Alex's shoulders and led her to the door of the building.

"Hey!" I shouted.

The dogs rumbled.

Things were spiraling out of control fast. I hadn't bargained for any of this. I ignored them. Stepped forward.

They leaped to their feet.

"You just go right ahead," I told them. "Bite me, and I'll buy my own damn gun. Blow you to kingdom come."

Val snorted.

"You—" I stabbed a finger in his direction. "Shut up. You started this."

He held up his palms. "Hey, I'm just along for the ride."

The old woman entered, with Alex close behind.

"Hey, you!" I called.

The woman's head reappeared. "You're not only big, you're noisy. What?"

Sometimes you gotta go along to get along, Sister used to say.

I exhaled loudly. "I want to see, too," I mumbled.

"What's that?" But it was hard to hear her over the dogs and Val's chuckle.

"I will deal with you later, buddy." I jabbed a finger in his chest.

He only grinned wider. "Ooh, I'm shaking now, Red."

"Speak up, big girl."

I wanted to have a hissy, a real conniption fit, but my mad had gotten me in hot water before. *No style points for hissies, hon. And the woman, after all, is armed.* Okay. All right. I had resolved to let Big Lil be my guide, after all. "Call off the dogs and let me come in," I said.

The shotgun was pointed at the ground, and for a second I wondered if I could cross the space between us quick enough to yank it from her.

"Don't even think about it," Val ordered. The man was spooky sometimes.

The old woman spoke up. "Your mama should have taught you some manners, girl. What do you say?"

Alex was smirking, Val was staring. Even the dogs seemed to be waiting for the magic word.

Oh, just do it, Big Lil snapped. *She can call the cops on you, you know.*

I wanted to slap Big Lil right off my shoulder. *I didn't say I wanted you ordering me around.*

I'm keeping you out of jail, hon. Use your head.

I never said Big Lil couldn't be aggravating. Especially when she was right.

I huffed out a breath of pure frustration. "Please," I relented.

The woman cupped one hand around an ear. "That the best you can do?"

I stifled the urge to scream. Stomped my foot hard enough to send Val back a step.

"Come on, Red. We need to get in there before the kid does something crazy."

"She's gone way past that," I muttered.

"Geri—" the woman said.

Geri's ears perked. He bared his teeth.

"*Prettypleasewithsugaronit*," I shouted. And bared my own.

"Hmmph." The woman seemed disappointed. "Geri, Freki, down."

The dogs looked at me as if to make certain I understood that if it were up to them, I'd be toast, then they plopped in the dirt.

"Welcome to Guns 'N' Glory." The woman gestured us inside with a shark's smile. "I'm Glory."

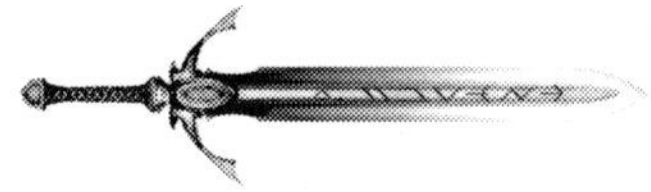

I strode past Val without a pause, certain he still had that grin on him. Glory preceded me into the dim building. I crossed the threshold and glanced around for Alex.

She had stopped six feet in, right smack in the middle of the space, and stood stock-still. I nearly rammed into her back before I realized that she and I occupied the only clear spot in the whole place. Val and Glory were still in the doorway.

"Wow," she said. "Cool."

I couldn't argue. The outside might have been plain and the windows barred, but inside, well . . . words failed me.

We were bathed in rainbows. Crystals hung inside the four windows, shooting arcs of red, green, blue, purple . . . the full spectrum of colors shimmered and danced in the air around us. I could barely focus on Alex, much less what lay past her.

And then I could. And understood a little better why the old woman wasn't worried about the safety of her merchandise.

The walls were lined with safes of every size, from taller than me to short and squat, mostly in shades of black or gray or dark green. But massive, all of them. Other safes and cases of ammo created a maze, and there was barely enough clearance between for a person to walk, much less to open a safe door.

Behind me, Val whistled. "This slab must be dug way down to handle this much weight."

"Five feet," the old woman said. "Rebar at two-foot spans."

That seemed to impress Val even more, though it meant nothing to me. Anyway, I was too flabbergasted by what else I saw. On the walls, between the expected animal heads, stuffed and mounted, there were scattered several paintings of women, fierce ones, all of them armed. One of them, sporting a horned helmet, looked exactly the way I imagined the Valkyrie would. Another figure, part of a group draped in flowing short gowns and clasping swords, might have been an Amazon, best I recalled the Greek myth.

But that wasn't all Glory had on display. On top of the safes, there were lunch boxes of every imaginable era, some old metal ones with Roy Rogers or Howdy Doody, some in plastic with Miss Piggy or Hulk Hogan. Barbies of all stripes. *Baywatch* Barbie caught my eye. There was even a new, screaming-yellow soft-sided one bearing SpongeBob SquarePants.

I stared in amazement, itching to climb up and look through all of them for my personal favorite, the Bionic Woman. I had owned one once, and I would never forget the day Sister had brought it home, long after I'd given up hope.

You did real good on your report card, she'd said.

I guess. As usual, I'd had my head in a book and hadn't even looked at her.

Pea, I got you something.

What? I put my finger on the page to mark my place, but then the next sentence captured me.

Pea!

I yanked my head up. Slowly, she'd pulled one hand from behind her back, and for a minute there, I couldn't catch my breath.

I'm proud of your grades. She extended it to me, all bright plastic glory, and I barely managed to close my book before I leaped. I cradled it to my skinny chest and rocked it like the long-legged woman in the picture could show me how to jump off a house or race a hundred miles away from the snotty kids and the dumpy apartment and the school full of strangers.

Not until this minute had I stopped to think what Sister must have sacrificed to buy me that lunch box when we could barely make the rent. It got stolen within two weeks, but soon after we were gone, anyway.

I always believed, though, that the Bionic Woman could have made me stronger, if only I could have hung onto her. Eager to see if she was there at Glory's, I took a step forward. Blinded by yet another rainbow, I smacked my hip right into a sharp metal corner. "Ow!" I jerked back and stepped on Glory's toe.

"Big girl, you are about to get on my last nerve." She not-so-gently yanked me back to standing. The woman might not have been a lot taller than Alex, but she was strong. Wiry. Might not even have needed that shotgun to handle most people.

I, however, was not most people. "And where do you get off trying to sell firearms to a minor? Maybe I'll just turn you in."

"I'd like to see you try it." Her chin jutted, but she didn't have room, with four of us crowded into a space that two would have a tough time maneuvering through, to lift the shotgun and point it at me.

"Red . . . " Val warned.

"Oooh . . . " Alex's cry of delight interrupted whatever might have happened next. "Beauty and the Beast!" She began to scale the safe in front of her to reach it.

Val squeezed past me to stand guard, in case she fell.

I saw my opening. I leaned down and stared into the old woman's pale gray eyes. "You're right—we don't have money to buy weapons," I whispered furiously, "So if you help me persuade her to drop that notion, I won't call the ATF agent who has the hots for me. And to be fair, I'll scrape up the cash to buy her that lunch box. Now, are we going to cooperate or are we going to duke this out?" She hesitated, and I hissed at her. "You have three seconds to make up your mind."

She glared at me, and I began to have hope that I'd found a solution. Even if the ATF guy was mostly my imagination, patterned on one who was a customer at Fat Elvis.

Instead, she laughed. "Nice try." She brushed past me. "You can't lie worth a damn." She elbowed Val out of the way, set the shotgun on top of one safe and steadied Alex. "You like that, honey?" she asked louder.

Alex plucked it from behind a Teenage Mutant Ninja Turtle and lifted it over the Bee Gees. She turned, cradling the purple plastic to her chest like a well-loved doll, her face, for once, glowing with pleasure. She was suddenly very young. A baby having a baby, lost in some romantic fantasy where a guy like Pretty Boy would morph into a handsome prince who would take her to live in his castle. "I used to have this one. Before..." The dreamy eyes got sad. Lonely.

"I'll buy it for you," I found myself saying.

Her eyes widened, then she hesitated. "Why?"

"Instead of the gun."

Disappointment gave way to rebellion. "I can make my own deal."

"Not and ride with—"

Val's head whipped toward me, warning in his eyes. Then he stepped to her, lifted his hands. "Let me see it, Alex."

She hesitated, then allowed him to lower her to the floor but pointedly gave me her back. They murmured together as if only the two of them existed in this space.

I was sick of being the bad guy. The only one with a lick of sense. I did an about-face and stalked out the door.

Glory followed me.

"I'd like to be alone, if you don't mind." I took another step away.

Her shoulder brushed my arm. I glanced at her, expecting to see triumph, but what I found was sympathy. "Teenagers. And girls are ten times worse than boys."

I was about to respond when I caught a glimpse of something odd through the trees behind her, the curve of some sort of structure. "What is that?"

"What does it look like?"

"I don't—" I stepped to the side, bent low. Then my eyes popped as it dawned on me what I was looking at. "A dome? Is that a geodesic dome?"

"What if it is?"

I swiveled to face her. I'd heard about them but never been in one. "You live there? Can I see it?"

"No."

"Why not?"

"'Cause it's mine. Round up your posse and move on before the girl gets another fool notion in her head. She's worried about you, you know."

"Me? What did she say?"

"That you need a keeper."

My mouth dropped open, but before I could say anything, Val rushed outside, Alex limp in his arms. "What happened?"

"She collapsed."

I leaped toward them, mentally riffling through the first aid manual at the store. "Did she say anything? Did she fall?"

Glory took over immediately, checking her pulse, lifting her eyelids with a confidence that was impressive.

"She's pregnant," I said.

"When's the last time she ate? Has she been drinking water?"

I tried to recall what Alex had had for breakfast but I'd been repacking my trunk, and we hadn't eaten together. We hadn't found anyplace to stop for lunch, but I thought she'd had some peanuts at the last service station. I looked helplessly at Val.

"She said her stomach was queasy this morning. All she had was some toast. She bought a bottle of water, but she finished it a couple of hours ago."

"Nothing serious, probably just fainted. Low blood sugar, maybe a little dehydration. A baby takes up a lot of a mother's resources." Glory glared at me. "Looks like you got your wish, big girl. Come on," she grumbled to Val. "Let's get her out of this heat. Get some water into her."

We made an odd procession up the rutted road, dogs leading the way, Glory behind them, then Val carrying Alex and finally me, all but wringing my hands.

When the structure came into full view, it was far more than a simple dome. There was an unfinished mural painted over halfway up the sides, and it was like no mural I would have expected.

A dragon swooped down from a sky filled with lightning. A man stood between it and a small, peaceful village. There was something about the man . . . he wasn't a knight but someone more primitive. Dressed in a loincloth, furs strapped to his calves, long hair with a headband, huge sword gripped in one hand, shield in the other. All gleaming muscles and sharp, bold features—

"Holy Moley. It's Conan the Barbarian," I blurted. Not the Arnold one but the character from the comics. Billy Simonson, who sat next to me in third grade, kept one in his backpack at all times.

"He was born in Texas, you know," Glory said as she climbed the rise in the lead.

"Conan the Barbarian?"

"Good Lord, no. Robert E. Howard, the man who created him. He lived in Cross Plains. Died there. There's a mural of Conan on the side of the library."

"Where's Cross Plains?"

"Over by Abilene. They have a Conan festival every year."

Visions of cowboys dressed in loincloths but sporting boots and Stetsons were dancing in my brain, but just then we arrived at the dome.

Glory opened the front door, and we followed. "Put her on the sofa," she said to Val.

I glanced around, couldn't help goggling. The . . . room, I guess you'd call it, was basically one big area, except for a walled-off section I assumed was a bathroom. Everywhere I looked were figures or paintings of women, some as ancient as Greek mythology, others appearing to have stepped off the pages of a science fiction epic.

I hurried over to the sofa, where Alex was stirring. "What happened?" She tried to sit up, but she was still very pale.

"Don't you dare move. Why didn't you tell me you hadn't eaten? Alex, you have a baby to take care of. You can't be so careless—"

Glory inserted herself between us, giving Alex water to sip. "Here." She thrust an orange at me. "Peel this," she ordered sharply. Her expression brooked no argument.

I didn't make sure she had water. With shaking fingers, I did as I was told, while I pondered how I could possibly consider keeping Alex with me when I was so obviously unsuited to taking care of anyone but myself.

Oh, Sister . . . and here I swore not to screw up with you again. Did babies have a chance to decide right up until they were born? I wondered. Was Sister watching and judging me to be no more capable than before?

"Hop to it," Glory barked, startling me out of my misery.

I extended the orange sections to her. Looked around for what to do with the peel.

"I'll be outside," Val said.

"No—stay with me. Please." Alex reached for his hand but didn't even look my way.

Glory and Val turned their backs on me, focused on Alex.

Unwanted and useless, I left instead. Started walking the perimeter, examining the mural.

And stopped dead at the painting of a woman nearly Conan's height. With lots of red hair. A sword, a big one. A real warrior woman.

I was transfixed.

"That girl's gonna run away if you don't loosen the reins," Glory said, coming up behind me. "She doesn't belong to you, you know."

Truer words had never been spoken. "I'm only giving them a ride. I just met both of them."

"Well, don't rub her nose in it when she does something stupid. Pride's a teenager's worst enemy, and that girl's supply of it is running low." She paused, then continued. "You're hovering like some mama hen with a brand-new chick. You got to give her some room."

"She was letting some jerk beat the crap out of her," I protested.

"So see to it that you don't browbeat her while you're so busy standing guard." She stalked off and pointed, changing the subject. "That's Red Sonya."

I hurried to catch up. "Wasn't there a movie once with Arnold Schwarzenegger and some redhead—"

"Forget that." Glory dismissed that with a wave. "I mean the real one written by Howard. Or before her, Dark Agnes, the Sword Woman." She looked me up and down. "Both of them your height, gobs of red hair like you."

An honest to goodness warrior woman. My Viking blood stirred. "Where could I get copies?"

"The books are out of print."

"You own either one?"

"What of it?"

"Could I read them? I'm fast." My brain was buzzing over the prospect. This could not be coincidence, I refused to believe that. This was Fate, pure and simple. A sign. I had a great need to be strong, and look what had dropped right into my path.

"I only have *Sword Woman*, but no, I don't think so."

"Why not?"

"It's a first edition. Anyway, you all need to head on out. Where you going?"

"New Mexico. I need to find a place to feed Alex a good meal first. How close are we to the nearest town?"

"About twenty miles, but you won't find anything there until morning. Only café closes after lunch. Pickings are slim until Lubbock. That's about three hours. Abilene's closer, but you'd have to double back."

I wanted real bad to sink to the ground and take a long nap. Maybe sleep until I could wake up and find that all of this had been a dream.

"I suppose I could feed you all supper," she grumbled.

"Really?" My spirits lifted a little.

"I'm not a damn restaurant, though. You'll take what you get. Then you clear out."

"Oh, that would be great. Really great." Hope stirred again. "Thank you so much. I can help. Just tell me what you need me to do."

"Being quiet would make a good start. You're a damn sight of trouble even before you start yapping."

Up yours, you mean old woman, I wanted to say. Longed to flounce off, to gather up Alex and Val and stomp on the gas pedal, leaving behind me a cloud of dust and maybe even the satisfaction of squealing tires.

But just then, I caught the flicker, in Glory's eyes, of something surprising.

Loneliness, I could swear. Given her social skills, was it likely she had any friends? She lived out in the middle of nowhere. Could it be that this fierce woman actually had a weak spot, or had I imagined that one vulnerable instant?

I'd barely met her, but I was pretty sure she'd be ticked to know that I'd seen it. She sure wouldn't like pity. Tit for tat would work best, I decided. "I might, if you'd let me look at *Sword Woman*."

Glory's eyes narrowed, and I braced myself for her fury.

Instead, her lined face split into what some might call a grin, rusty though it was. "You just might have potential, big girl."

"Eudora. Call me Eudora." A strong name, Val had called it. With a rush of confidence, I went on. "You're not as mean as you want people to believe," I said, for the pleasure of watching her jaw drop. "I bet you secretly want me to read that book."

"My ass." She turned to go inside.

But I could have sworn I saw a tiny smile chase over her lips as she did.

Robert E. Howard
(January 24, 1906 – June 11, 1936)

Born in Parker County, Robert Ervin Howard grew up in the Brown and Callahan County communities of Cross Cut, Cross Plains, and Brownwood. He attended Brownwood High School and Howard Payne College, and published his first works of fiction in school newspapers. He later wrote poetry and short stories for popular magazines. His main interest was in science fiction and fantasy. In 1932, he created the character Conan the Barbarian. Howard committed suicide at age 30. His Conan character has become known worldwide through books, magazines, and movies.

A WOMAN WITH A PLAN

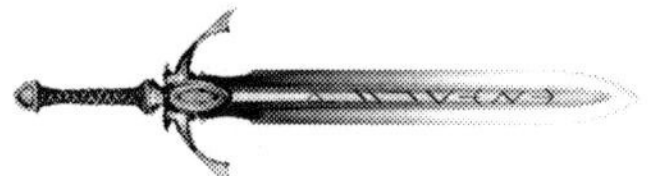

There turned out to be a catch to the offer of supper, though: the meal was freeze-dried rations like military MREs. I am positive now that our soldiers are battle-ready. The food by itself would make a pacifist ready to spray bullets. Val wisely said he wasn't hungry and disappeared outside.

Personally, I didn't blame him for escaping. Our meal consisted of rehydrated powdered eggs scrambled with what could laughingly be called meat loaf. Val might have had the best end of the deal, out there with no food. No surly pregnant teenager. No clingy cat.

"Isis." Suddenly Glory spoke. "Interesting name for a cat. If, that is, you understand the significance of it."

Another gauntlet thrown.

But this time I was ready. "Personally, I think her brother Ra would testify that Isis could hold her own with any warrior goddess."

An arched eyebrow, then a short nod of acknowledgment from Glory. *Touché.*

An answering, very satisfied nod from me. Maybe I was getting the hang of this warrior woman thing. Heaven knows I needed all the help I could get.

Silence ensued for a bit. Glory was not much on idle chit chat.

Then, "There's a sword fighting competition."

"What?"

"At the festival next June in Cross Plains."

A notion occurred to me, based on the mural, the paintings inside the gun shop and the dome. "Are you entering?"

She only grunted, but I could picture it all too clearly, the more I thought about it. "I think you should. Do you know how to use a sword?"

Her gaze cut to the side. "Of course."

Of course. I wasn't actually surprised. "Speaking of which, where's the copy of *Sword Woman*?"

Glory stood abruptly. "You don't have enough time. It's dark, and you need to be on your way." She clomped into the kitchen area with its wood cookstove, the first one I'd ever seen outside of photographs. The woman did have a weird thing for the past.

"We can leave later, drive all night if we need to. I have to wait for Val, anyhow."

"Your young man appears to have skedaddled."

"His duffel's still in my car. He'll be back." Maybe. Not that I was exactly sure I wanted him to. "I'll clear up while you get it." Eating, however lousy the food, had restored some of my energy and spunk. I rose. "Alex, we need to help—" I glanced around for her.

"Sh-h . . . over there." Glory gestured. "Poor kid. Let her be."

I followed her pointing and spotted Alex, a seashell spiral in a papasan chair with Isis nestled in the center. Isis had one eye open, lest she have to remind Freki and Geri why dogs should shy away from cats. Her claws might have been tiny, but applied to a nose, they did the trick, the dogs had discovered earlier.

"Well." I shrugged. "Looks like I have plenty of time." I grinned at her. "Unless, of course, you'd like me to move on and leave Alex with you. Being's how you're the woman with all the answers." I smiled, and I could tell without a mirror that there was more than a little of Big Lil in it.

Her eyes went to slits. "I've been blackmailed by better operators than you."

I waited her out until the silence stretched out to a catgut-twang, like how Jelly would tune his guitar when he was stoned and keep turning and turning the key until your ears were bleeding from the screech.

"Oh, all right." She clomped over to a safe that stood beside the refrigerator. Doesn't every kitchen need its own gun safe?

She returned with a paperback, small and yellowed, cradled as tenderly as any newborn.

I'd expected something more impressive, given the big deal she'd made over it. Still, I reached out for it.

She yanked it away. "Don't touch," she barked. "I told you it's a first edition." Carefully she tilted it upward so that I could see the title. *The Sword Woman.* A stunning creature clad in nose-cone breastplate brandishing a sword, prepared to take off a man's head with one stroke.

I'd wanted to take a man's head off now and again, but this woman was literally about to do so.

I was mesmerized.

She turned the book over. I bent closer.

I drink, fight, and live like a man—said the back cover title.

The great black-whiskered rogue lunged at me like a great bear as he sought to drag me into his embrace, but as I wrenched out my sword he seemed suddenly sobered by what he saw in my eyes. As if he realized at last that this was no play, he gave back and drew his own blade.

He wielded his sword with strength and craft, and well for me that I had learned the art from the finest blade of all. My quickness of eye and hand and foot was such as no man could match. Blackbeard sought to beat me down by sheer strength, but this availed him no better, because woman though I was, I was all steel springs and whalebone, and had the art of turning his strokes before they were begun.

"Bitch!" he roared in swift fury, his eyes blazing. "I'll have you for that! You drink, fight, and live like a man," my enemy mocked.

"But shalt love like a woman!"

"Now *that's* a tough cookie," Glory said.

I had to agree. Shoot, even Big Lil wouldn't dare tangle with Dark Agnes. Suddenly, I went from curiosity to an absolute certainty that I had to read this book. Dark Agnes, I bet, could reconnect me with my Viking blood. She would not have worn ice-pick heels at Fat Elvis—except for the intimidation angle. She wouldn't have let any fanny-pincher slide by because she was afraid of losing her job. She would more than likely have located Sister by now.

And would never have let Sister down like I did.

"Glory . . . " I stared hard into Glory's eyes. "I really need to read this."

"You sure do. You intend to take care of that little girl and her baby, you'll require more than good intentions."

"Where can I find another copy?"

"Well . . . just so happens, I have a photocopy taken from a damaged volume." She waited, with that same smug smile as before. She wanted me to plead some more, I would have bet the farm.

Dark Agnes would never plead.

But I didn't have a sword on me.

That book could contain lessons for me, I just knew it. Here was another sign from Sister, a critical one. Though I could imagine how Sister might be snickering. *Pea, girl, your imagination gets carried away sometimes.* Part of me began to back down immediately. Flights of fancy had always made trouble for me.

But a new, lower voice, solid iron, spoke to me. *So you're going to give up, just like that, Eudora? Play it safe yet again?*

Hey, I was on this journey, wasn't I? I had taken a big chance, just packing everything in my car and hitting the road.

"How fast can you read?" Glory's voice yanked me away before I found a good comeback for what I already knew to my marrow was Dark Agnes.

"Very." I was still staring at the book.

Glory glanced at her watch. "It's getting late."

I frowned. "It's only nine o'clock. Val's not back. I'll hurry, I promise."

"I rise early. I need my sleep." She paused, considered. "Here's the deal. You can stay the night, you and your menagerie. Lights out by nine-thirty, though." She waited for a protest, but I didn't hazard a word. "After breakfast, you help out a little around here and then I'll give you the copy. Once you finish it, you pack everyone up and leave me be. 'Course, I still think your young fella must have split already."

She wasn't going to distract me with Val. I kept my eye on the prize. "I'll grant that someone your age needs her rest, and I don't mind admitting I could use a good night's sleep myself." Triumph was already painting itself on her face, and I couldn't have that. "But—"

"No *buts*, girlie. Take it or leave it."

"Uh-uh." I let instinct take over. I couldn't explain why this woman fascinated me, why her challenges energized me, but they did. She did. "But—" I pointed at a painting. "You tell me a story about one of these warrior women before bed."

Glory did a double-take, then frowned. She was silent for what felt like an hour.

At last, she nodded. "Big girl, you just might be interesting, after all."

I couldn't recall the last compliment paid me, unless you wanted to count Black Dude's long, slow down and up. I finished clearing the table, but it was with a very big smile stretching my chest and wanting real bad to work its way out.

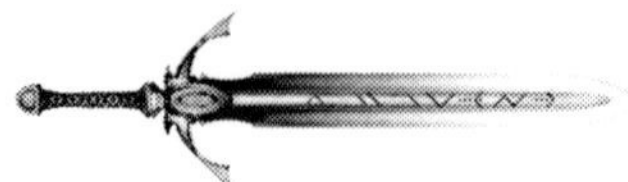

A lot of weird noises crop up in the darkness. Have I mentioned I'm not good with nights?

It was very, very dark in the country.

Alex was tucked in the papasan chair with Isis, who—traitor—seemed perfectly content to snooze the hours away with her.

To distract myself from all that was spooky, I settled back to mull over Glory's tale about Athena, the goddess of invention and wisdom and the female counterpart of the god of war, Ares. Interesting that she created such tools as the bridle, the yoke, the plow and the rake. She came up with mathematics and musical instruments like the flute and the trumpet, along with being the one who taught homemaking skills to mankind and gave humans the ideas for creating civilization.

When she went to battle, Athena liked order and strategy, whereas Ares just liked to fight. He championed the Trojans in that famous war; Athena sided with the Greeks. At her behest, they constructed the Trojan horse, to the everlasting sorrow of Ares and his gang.

I did admire a woman with a plan. If only I had a better one myself. I closed my eyes and tried to sleep, but it was hopeless. Only a few more hours before I got to read Dark Agnes.

Don't bet on it, came her voice. *You are not remotely ready for me.*

Or maybe it was actually Jack Nicholson in *A Few Good Men. You want the truth*? Those demonic eyebrows! That snarling lip! *You can't handle the truth!*

I shifted on the lumpy sofa, caught by a sudden vision of the nosecone breast-plated redhead facing off with Devil Jack himself. The very idea had me stretching in delight—

Something teetered on the end table, a metal sculpture I'd spotted earlier, a skeletal concoction of K-bar knives and pressed tin angel wings. It rattled like a flipped coin, on its edge and slowing, but before I could feel my way to it, it stopped.

My breath did, too, as I waited to see if Glory, tucked away in her pasha's bed hangings, would awaken. That bed was a surprise, I have to say. There was nothing soft about Glory; I could swear she teethed on razor wire.

Yet there she was with a lair draped in silk of so many colors I was flat dizzy, forest green and burgundy, purple and royal blue, a touch of bronze and downright decadent French king gold. Pillows everywhere and a mattress you could surely fall smack into and need a ladder to climb out of.

Of course, with my nine-thirty bedtime mandate, I hadn't actually witnessed her lying down on it. I barely got my teeth brushed before lights out.

My eyes had been open long enough that they'd adjusted, and I was surprised to see just how much the moonlight illuminated. There was a door not far away. Since I wasn't sleeping, I wondered if I could locate the copy and manage one of my tried-and-true read-in-the-bathroom sessions.

Then I remembered that the bathroom door was about six feet from Glory's bed. And Glory knew her way around guns.

Okay, Plan B. I was going outside. I'd retrieve one of my faithful book friends and read in my car by the flashlight I kept in the glove box.

But just before my foot touched the floor, I crossed myself, though I'm not Catholic, and just for good measure, I sent up an insurance plea. *Sister, if you're up there waiting instead of down here where I need you to be, please do not let me step on anything scary or get snakebit outside or savaged by javelinas or whatever else might be lurking out there, okay? Because you know how I get.*

I swallowed hard, my earlier bravado fading. It was night, the worst time to be alone, and that was what I really was, alone. Surrounded by strangers inside and wild creatures out there.

Step One, remember? *Be Brave.* How could I ever succeed in my quest if I gave in to fear now? With my heart thumping to beat the band, I gingerly lowered my sole, touched something skinny and wiggly and nearly screamed—

Until it dawned on me that I had just stepped on the strap of my own stupid purse.

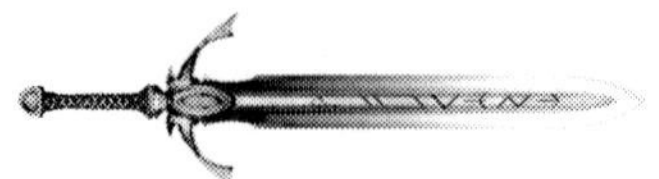

As I rounded my car, I spied Val asleep in the back seat, all the windows down due to the heat. In this part of Texas in the summer, it was only a smidgen cooler at night.

I didn't want to wake him, so that meant I couldn't pop the trunk to get a book, but I knew I'd just toss and turn if I went back inside. I wanted to be on my own turf, among familiar things even just for a few minutes, and if I was really quiet, Val would never have to know I'd been there. I eyed the open window, then wiggled myself through into the front seat, not exactly an easy proposition when there was so much of me to fold up.

Fortunately, I'm quite limber. Something Jelly appreciated, back before the bimbo.

Since Val didn't wake up, I took a minute to just watch him. I might never get another chance before we parted, and I was curious about him. Even in sleep, he seemed a little on guard, sort of like the waking Val was always alert despite his easygoing facade, ready to respond to the moment, to switch course in an instant.

What was it that had made him so . . . temporary? Even though he'd made a strong impression on me, I realized I knew next to nothing about this man, his past, what he wanted from life.

Oddly, for someone so present, so forceful, he didn't seem in a hurry to get on with his pilgrimage. For a minute or two, I thought again about keeping him—only as a companion, of course. A fellow traveler. Maybe I had no interest in romance, but he was good company sometimes, a peculiar mix of cynic and charmer. Funny and kind of thoughtful, like how he found ways to watch over Alex without tipping his hand.

He went toe to toe with me, yes, but he didn't use anger to get the better of me. He wasn't intimidated by my height like a lot of men were, and though he told me when he thought I was wrong, he didn't try to cut me down to size in other ways.

So who was he, really?

His eyelids fluttered as I leaned on the back of the seat, chin propped on my hands. He gave me a sleepy grin, and I couldn't help but grin back.

Maybe this was my chance. "Where exactly is it that you live?"

He jolted. Flung out an arm and smacked it on the door handle, cursing. "Damn it, Red, I was dreaming. You haven't tortured me enough today?" He shoved to sitting.

And we nearly brushed noses.

All of a sudden, the inside of the vehicle got crowded. I was acutely aware that we were alone in the night.

"I was trying to sleep," he complained. "You should be, too."

"I'm usually not much good at that," I admitted.

"Why not?"

I didn't have a simple answer, so I switched topics. "You missed supper. Are you hungry?"

"I hitched into town. Had a burger."

"Glory said there was no place to eat around here."

"Maybe she didn't think you two should be in a honky-tonk."

"There's a honky-tonk? Where? Is it on the way to Abilene?"

"I have no idea. It's outside a place called Jewel. Why?"

"I just wondered. The man who wrote Conan lived in a town named Cross Plains, and Glory says it's somewhere around Abilene. There's a festival."

He barked a laugh. "A Conan the Barbarian festival?"

"Yes."

"Glory's got a thing for old Arnold, doesn't she?"

"That's not the real Conan."

"You're an expert?"

"No, but Glory is." I paused. "There's a competition at the festival. Swordsmanship. You ever handled a sword, Val?"

He settled back. "Never had the pleasure. You?"

"No, but I bet Glory could teach me."

His eyebrows arched. "You thinking about hanging around, Red?"

I snorted. "Of course not. Who fights with swords?" Though now that I'd verbalized it, the prospect taunted me. "Anyway, I have to find Sister."

"You don't know where she is?"

I wished I could see his expression better before I answered, but there was no help for it. "No."

"Where's the last place you saw her?"

"She was—" Suddenly, my throat clogged up. I turned from him. Stared into the darkness as I summoned my nerve. "Don't laugh."

"I promise."

My voice was barely a whisper. "Dead."

He shook his head. "What?"

"She was dead." I faced him defiantly. I was not going to care what he thought.

A very long pause. "Are you hoping to contact her through a medium?"

Maybe he wasn't totally close-minded, but I was alert for a sneer. "No."

He seemed at a loss, but he wasn't making fun of me, and it was a relief to tell someone the truth. "I think she's been reincarnated or will be soon. I have to find her new body."

Another long silence. I wove my fingers together in my lap.

"So . . . " He seemed to be tiptoeing around, like you humored a head case. "How do you know where to look?"

Well, just too bad if he was. This was my journey, not his. "Madame Eva said New Mexico, and that makes sense. Sister believed she was descended from Pueblo Indians. She liked Taos a lot. Said she wanted to live there."

"Red . . . " His voice was so gentle. Too gentle. "How well do you know this Madame Eva?"

"I can guess what you're thinking, but this is too important. You won't discourage me." But he could, I knew he could. "She's a good woman. She was kind to me."

"Red, I've been on the road a long time. People aren't always . . . what they seem." There it was again, that too-careful tone.

"I don't care if you think I'm crazy. There have been—" *Signs*, I started to say. I wanted to tell him about them, but the ice beneath my feet was cracking.

"I don't think you're crazy. I think you're—" He didn't finish.

But I could. "Naïve, right?" *She needs a keeper.*

"Trusting," he responded firmly. "You're trusting. That's not all bad, just . . . " He shrugged. "Dangerous, sometimes."

"Madame Eva didn't make up my mind for me."

He cocked his head and stared at me. "Where's home?"

Good question. "Nowhere, at the moment."

"What do you mean nowhere?"

Enough of the grilling. "I asked you first. Where do you live?"

He ignored me. "You're homeless."

"I am not." I stuck out my chin. "I'm on a mission."

A tiny quirk of his lips. "So how do you figure to recognize her?"

If only I knew. "It won't be a problem."

"How old are you?" He shoved himself forward, intent.

"It's not gentlemanly to ask a lady's age."

"Okay, I'll go first. I'll be twenty-eight in a couple of weeks."

"You're younger than me." Somehow that felt like a betrayal.

"I've got a lot of miles on me. How old?"

"Twenty-nine. Nearly thirty."

He winked. "Older women are like good wine. Age only improves them."

"What a line," I sneered.

"Maybe not." He leaned toward me, his eyes focused on my mouth, and for a second I was tempted. It would have been so easy, so terribly easy to let go. To accept the physical comfort. The wedge against my loneliness. I'd certainly done it before.

No. I jerked away, opened the door. Let the interior light break the mood.

"I have to go." I backed out. Slammed the car door and ran, as fast as my feet would carry me, back to the dome.

Jersey Lilly Saloon

1882-1903 "Law West of the Pecos" courtroom. Named for Judge Roy Bean's idol, actress Lillie Langtry. Awarded Medallion Plate.

THE VALKYRIE

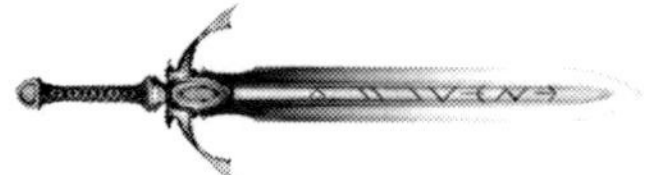

Read it. Don't get it dirty. Put it on the counter before you go.

This was the note that greeted me when I opened my eyes. All the thoughts of near-misses with Val that had kept me tossing vanished. I sat up so fast my head swam.

Sunrise was still a ways off. Alex snoozed in her chair. Val was, I supposed, back asleep in the car, though his long limbs were surely pretzels by now. Glory was no longer in bed, but I had no idea where she was.

Isis uncurled and yawned so wide I could just about spot her tonsils. Did cats actually have tonsils, I wondered? A tiny, elegant leap brought her over Alex's leg and down to the floor to make her way to me.

I couldn't keep my eyes off the stack of paper beneath Glory's note. I scooped up the kitten in one hand, the sheets with the other. The photocopies were terrible, faint and blurred.

"Let's go outside," I whispered to the cat.

As always, Isis was not much of a conversationalist. Her purr brought to mind a lawn mower, first louder, then droning into the distance.

"Alex needs to sleep. We can wait a little longer for breakfast, right?" Not that Glory had actual cat food. Or that I was eager for more MREs.

I located my flashlight, and out the back door we went. Last night, I had seen a porch swing hanging from an old live oak, sheltered beneath its low, spreading branches. Live oaks are more likely to lean than stand straight and are mostly found in clumps. This tree, however, had been there a very long time, judged by its girth. I couldn't possibly wrap my arms more than halfway round its trunk.

It stood all alone, though, and that got to me. I, too, was the last of my line. Whatever centuries of ancestors had made me, all their dreams and hopes, the fruits of their triumphs and struggles would die with me. Mama's family had owned land and played a part in the building of Texas; whatever had sent Mama careening off the path, did they deserve to have their legacy erased? Shoot, for all I knew, even Casper's people might have been salt of the earth folks, worthy of preserving. Every last bit of them could end with me, and I didn't think I could bear that. But even if I managed to choose men better than Mama and Sister, what on earth would I have to give to a baby?

Life, hon, and that's enough. Big Lil seemed oddly kind just then. *Ever occur to you that you should be focusing on the living, not the dead?*

It was a minute before I could argue. *She is living, Sister is. I'm sure of it.*

Are you, hon? A faint sway of the perfect blond coif, the merest hint of a frown in the Botoxed brow.

I clutched the papers and the cat so hard that Isis squirmed to get down. My heart was in my throat as she jumped from what must have seemed like a third-story window. She paused, shook her head as if to restore some sense to it—like that was going to happen—then trotted off.

"Don't you get lost," I ordered.

She stopped and began to lick her butt.

Somehow the sight settled me. Big Lil could think what she wanted. I had Dark Agnes to consult now. I settled into the swing, everything narrowing into one golden circle of light, and began to read.

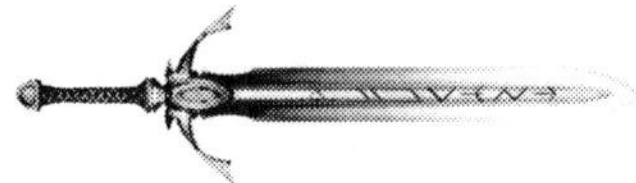

Fate again, in the form of a sister. Agnes de Chastillon was beaten into submission on her wedding day by a father determined to have himself a young man to provide for his old age.

Agnes's sister, bowed already by childbearing and the general lot of medieval women, useful only as chattel and a means to get sons, pressed a knife into Agnes's hand and urged her to escape.

Okay, so Agnes's sister meant her to kill herself instead of her bridegroom. Still, her sister gave Agnes tools. Tools are important. Too many women don't learn how to use them. I'd had a hankering for a skill saw, myself. I put it on my mental list of things to buy when I found Sister and settled down.

Agnes, though, had to leave everything behind, including her hair. Wore a boy's clothes stolen by a helpful wanderer who rescued her in the forest.

Who then tried to sell her virginity to the highest bidder. *Men.* A good example of why I was through with them.

Okay, so I was a little tempted with Val. I like sex. Sue me.

Reading the book was making me realize that maybe I should have been thanking Casper for taking a powder, once I saw how much worse life might have been. He could have hung around, used me for a punching bag and a work animal, then sold me off.

I might not have been any Dark Agnes, but I dared anyone to try that sort of thing with me. I'd made mistakes with the male gender, but the ones I picked were pretty harmless.

I read on, as Agnes stabbed not only the man who would sell her, but the unlucky buyer. This was one bloodthirsty wench. I couldn't help smiling. Jelly was on my mind just then.

You leave my baby alone, barked Big Lil. *He's an idiot, but he's mine.*

I had no trouble believing Big Lil could do a little blade work of her own, if stirred to it. Even if it meant breaking a nail. She'd make you suffer for it, though. A good nail job was a work of art, after all. I was very fond of the stars on my own toenails.

I returned to the story. It was clearly pulp fiction, a swashbuckling tale unlike anything I'd read outside a comic book. Still, there was much to be attracted to about Dark Agnes—she was practical about things, first and foremost, and anything but subtle. If she hadn't been tough as nails, I doubt she would have survived childhood, based on her treatment by dear old dad. I couldn't help wondering what this story meant to Glory. What forces had made her what she was, proud, tough and brittle.

Agnes's father was a warrior who dragged her by her hair to her wedding. Etienne de Villiers, the man who first saved and then attempted to sell her, was handsome—wasn't that always the way?

Why was it that a good-looking charmer could so easily sway you?

There are actions to which we are born, and for which we have a talent exceeding mere teaching. I, who had never before had a sword in my grasp found it like a living thing in my hand, wielded by unguessed instinct, I read. Agnes was no one to trifle with, that was for sure. The body count in the first fifty pages could make you blanch, all the split-open heads and spilling-out bowels.

I wasn't much on violence and sure didn't have her skill with weapons, but I liked her courage and the way she tackled being thrown out into the world all alone. After a life of being a follower and months on my own spent drifting, there sure seemed to be things I could learn from Agnes's example.

I seemed to have been born into a new world, and yet a world for which I was intended from birth. My former life seemed like a dream, soon to be forgotten. Could there possibly be a whole new life out there waiting for me? A new way of doing things I would have never imagined?

Even when she was gravely wounded and outnumbered, she wasn't sorry for the bargain she'd made. *I saw no way out; it seemed I must die there, perish all my dreams of pageantry and glory and the bright splendor and adventure. The dim drums whose beat I had sought to follow seemed fading and receding, like a distant knell, leaving only the dying ashes of death and oblivion. But when I searched my soul for fear I found it not, nor regret nor any sorrow. Better to die there than live and grow old as the women I had known had grown old.*

Wow. I tried to picture myself charging through that world, so fearless and determined. *Swordplay like summer lightning,* one of Agnes's teachers said of her.

I thought about the festival, the sword fighting competition Glory had mentioned. Pictured myself wielding a sword like summer lightning. The muscles I would need for that.

Maybe I could come back, once I'd found Sister. See, someday, how much of Dark Agnes I had in me.

The long day caught up with me, and I drifted off, my fingers grasping the pommel of a blade with such skill and sorcery that I would thrill and amaze them all . . .

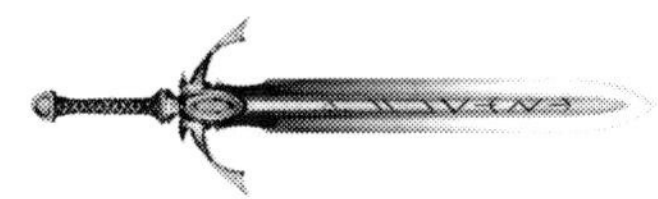

I awoke abruptly, unsure why. Isis was tucked into the crook of my elbow, and my arm was the paperweight anchoring Glory's pages to my chest. The crick in my neck was muttering nasty things to me, and there was a bona fide hitch in my get-along, with no cure but to haul my carcass out of a seat meant for feet-on-floor, head-up sitting. Not for cramming seventy-two inches into fifty.

Then I heard the noise again, but I still didn't know what it was. A whistle of air, too crisp for a swoosh. Then a grunt. An intake of breath.

I inched forward and peered through the trees at a most curious sight, yet one I guess shouldn't have surprised me.

Glory. With a sword.

The woman knew what she was doing.

As I watched, I wondered if Glory was as old as I'd thought. The woman before me was more agile than I would have guessed. Skinnier, too, clad in loose, thin trousers and a cotton top, still with the pearls around her throat. Her hair was a tight French braid. Stripped down, she seemed all bone and sinew. Her face was both intent and deadly, but also serene. Her moves, with a sword that gleamed as it caught the rising sun, were both powerful and graceful. The sword was long and carved on the grip. She swirled it through the shadows, then sliced down in a swift arc that was, I realized, the whistle that awoke me.

It wasn't such a stretch to picture that I was watching Dark Agnes in later years, not charging through the countryside wreaking havoc and taking her revenge, but more settled, more introspective.

But still very dangerous. This woman surely had knowledge I needed for my journey. I stepped forward, eager to gobble up everything she was and all she knew—

When two things happened at once.

Isis yowled at me.

And I heard voices down by the gun shop.

Glory's head whipped around, but not before she nailed me with a glare that clearly said *I'll deal with you later.* Then she leaped for a nearby tree where her shotgun had been resting all along. She fired a blast in the air, then, weapon in each hand, she took off running.

Clutching the pages to my middle, still I wasn't far behind her. Val emerged from where my car was parked, and Alex was catching up. The dogs had beaten all of us.

We converged at the gun shop, where Glory and the dogs were focused on two figures racing toward a pickup parked down the road.

Tires squealed as they took off.

"Get the hell out of here and don't you come back!" she roared. Geri and Freki were broadcasting slobber again, with barks that were pit bull vicious.

Isis was doing her best to climb under my hair and into the neck of my shirt, so it was a minute before I noticed the writing on the wall.

Literally.

Crazy murdering witch. Leave Jewel, you whore, or

And there it had been interrupted.

Murdering?

While I struggled to unhook Isis, Val beat me to the question. "What's going on?" he asked Glory.

"Get out." Her voice was guttural. Defensive. "All of you, just get the hell out."

"Looks like you're in a spot of trouble," Val observed mildly.

But this wasn't the woman who had spared a pregnant teen's pride or decided I could use some toughening up. Not the creature of grace I'd spied on earlier. Her face was dead white, her shoulders hunched, her gait halting. She seemed smaller than before. Defeated.

Yet as I watched, she visibly put herself back together, inch by inch, until the fierce woman who'd brandished a shotgun at us only a day earlier stood before us. "What I am is none of your business. Saddle up and move on." She turned those feral eyes toward me. "*Now*, big girl."

No question Glory could be scary. Possibly unbalanced. But Dark Agnes wouldn't just split. "No. What's this about, Glory?"

When she lifted the shotgun and pointed those barrels straight at me, any resemblance between me and Dark Agnes was too faint to credit. My own voice was shaking, but I tried once more. "Talk to me. Are you in danger? Would they hurt you?"

The woman we'd met yesterday would have snorted. Brusquely waved off my concern. Maybe made me feel like an idiot. I could see that gruff person nowhere in the figure before me. Beneath her ramrod posture, Glory seemed real close to the jagged edge of losing it.

I tried another tack. "I haven't finished reading." I waved the stack of pages.

Yesterday's Glory would have said *too bad.* "Take them," she snapped. After all the time she'd guarded them like the crown jewels.

Something was definitely wrong. "I can't." I felt the need to buy time to understand what was going on.

This earned me a sneer I found heartening. "You promised to pack up first thing," she reminded me.

"After I read the pages."

"Take them or not. I don't care. But you will be off my property in the next ten minutes or—"

Or what? I wanted to ask, since I knew she did care, but suddenly Val was in my face. "Don't," he ordered. "I know you think you have to pick up every stray in your path, but not this one." His voice was serious in a way I'd never heard it. He turned to Alex. "Gather up whatever you have inside."

"But—" I protested.

"No buts, Red. Time to load up."

"It's my car, and anyway, I'm not afraid of her—or you either."

A rueful smile. "Of course you're not. You're too goddamn stubborn and bossy, but there are things you don't know."

"What do you mean?"

He didn't answer, lost in thought.

"Val—" I grabbed his arm. "What are you talking about?"

He wheeled on me, and his eyes were fierce. "In town, last night, I heard . . . things."

"For goodness sake, what? That Glory's weird? Well, look around you. We're all a little off. So what if she's a tad eccentric?"

"They hate her in Jewel."

I blinked. "She's not an easy person to know, but—"

His response was lost in another blast of the shotgun. Leaves showered from the tree above us. Val barely got me out of the way as a branch whistled past my head.

"All right!" I yelled. "Stop that!" Getting shot at could bring you to your senses. What on earth was I doing there, anyway? I was only getting sidetracked from my search for Sister.

Scattered on the ground all around us were the pages I had yet to read, a snowstorm of rectangles. I crouched and began to pick up the pieces. "Get your things, Alex. We'll drop Val at the interstate, then I'm taking you to someone who can help." Forget fool notions about her baby. I had to get refocused. How could I hear Sister's clues with all this chaos around me?

Alex looked like I'd slapped her. I extended an olive branch. "You can have—" *The cat*, I started to say, until I remembered that Alex already had a huge responsibility ahead. I sagged to my knees. "Just . . . put everything in the car and let's get going."

Val led Alex away. Drained and weary, I slowly lifted the branch that had nearly beaned me. Blew dirt off the pages crumpled beneath and ever so carefully worked to smooth them on my thigh. I stood and straightened the stack as best I could, but it was beyond me, at that moment, to put the pages in order.

I met Glory's gaze, but I couldn't read it. Her posture screamed challenge, but something dark and sad peeked out from her expression. "I won't take this with me. It's too important to you." I handed the stack to her, but I had to press my lips together for an instant before I could let go. "The pages aren't in order." When she didn't complain, I worried more.

Nothing was left, though, but the manners Mama had drilled into me. "Thank you for having us." Surely the lamest version of that line ever uttered.

I took one last look at the woman I'd fancied might have so many answers for me, then I turned away before I could do something stupid, like blubber.

In under five minutes, we were on the road again, smothered in a silence as dense as a tomb's but ripe with emotions I could not let myself think about right then.

A moth was clinging to the upper corner of the windshield as I drove off. The wind whipped its wings, frantic and fast—

In a blink, it was ripped away and gone.

The Red River Plunge of Bonnie and Clyde

On June 10, 1933, Mr. and Mrs. Sam Pritchard and family saw from their home on the bluff (west) the plunge of an auto into Red River. Rescuing the victims, unrecognized as Bonnie Parker and Clyde and Buck Barrow, they sent for help. Upon their arrival, the local sheriff and police chief were disarmed by Bonnie Parker. Buck Barrow shot Pritchard's daughter while crippling the family car to halt pursuit. Kidnapping the officers, the gangsters fled. Bonnie and Clyde were fated to meet death in 1934. In this quiet region, the escapade is now legend.

THE WORLD FROM WEED LEVEL

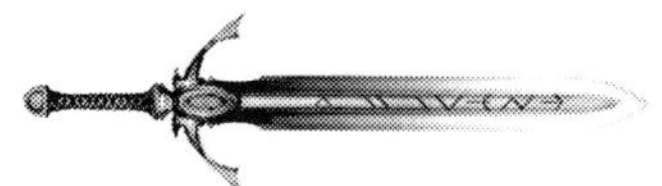

The sky looked just like cotton batting, all cottage-cheese clumpy in spots, stretched thin and wispy in others.

Sort of the way I felt just then. I couldn't get my last sight of Glory out of my mind, whatever threats she'd made. Mama and Sister's way had been to run when things got hairy, but Big Lil never backed off, and Dark Agnes would have simply whipped out her sword and kicked some ass. If I were going to change the O'Brien legacy, I shouldn't be leaving.

"I'm going back," I said, and started to whip a U-turn.

"What? Are you crazy? What part of *murdering* didn't you get?" Val grabbed for the wheel. "Stop this car."

"She's all alone, and I don't believe that, anyway," I said, slapping at his hand.

"You think that woman can't take care of herself? Stop the damn car, Red."

We struggled briefly for the wheel. "Let go," I said.

He did, abruptly. "Hear that?" His face screwed up in concentration.

"What?"

"That sound. Your engine."

"I don't hear anything."

He cocked his head. Shook it. "Never mind." He looked at me. "You have no idea what you're getting into. The woman is obviously nuts, and she clearly doesn't want your help. You barely know her, and the people who do are no fans."

I eased my foot on the accelerator. "What exactly did they say about her?"

"Some guys at the next table just—It's nothing I can put my finger on. Mostly the way her name was mentioned."

"You don't actually buy that murdering claim? It's just graffiti."

"I got a feeling, Red, I'm telling you. When you're in a strange place, you should always trust your gut." He raked one hand through his hair. "It's like they despised her but were scared of her, too."

"They called her a witch," Alex said. "I think witches are real."

Val snorted. "Right, kid. So's Santa Claus."

"I'll have you know that Madame Eva is a witch. A Wiccan, the good ones." I sniffed. "People misuse the term witch."

Val rolled his eyes. "How much did you pay Madame Eva, Red?"

"That's none of your business."

"I figured. It's a scam, you know."

"I know nothing of the sort. You've never met her."

"I've met a thousand of her," he muttered.

"Marker," Alex piped up.

"What?" I yanked my attention from Val.

"You missed one."

Reading markers was the last thing on my mind just then, but as I glanced at her in the rear view mirror, I saw the plea on her face. For Val and me to stop arguing or for me not to take her to Lubbock? I wasn't sure, but she looked all of twelve, piercings and smudged mascara notwithstanding.

As I considered stopping, backing up, going on to Glory's or . . . whatever, all I knew was that I was more weary than ever. *One sign, Sister. Just one.*

The only sound I heard, though, was some sort of knocking.

Coming from under my hood.

If that's you, Sister, do not for one second believe I think you're even a little bit funny.

Val got what he wanted, though. I stopped the car.

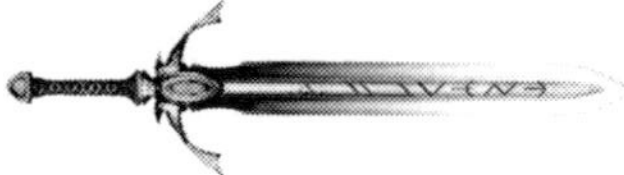

Alex revved the engine. Being behind the wheel had turned her face to sunshine.

Val and I stood before the open hood. The noise had added a dandy little *ker-whap*. "What is it?" I asked as he made manly thinking noises.

"Christ, Red." He turned to me. "How should I know? I look like a mechanic?"

"But you're—"

"A man?" One eyebrow arched. "You didn't get the memo that women can do everything a man can do, only better?"

"Well . . . " I was all for women being strong and independent, but in my book there were some things that men were just better at. I recalled the guys who used to hang around Sister, who spent endless hours in front of wherever we lived at the time, minus shirts and anointing their vehicles with Turtle Wax and Armorall. Shoot, even Jelly liked to go to car shows and discuss the muscle power beneath a hood. A genetic thing. "Don't you work on your own car?"

"I don't have one," he snapped.

"Oh." But that had no bearing on my current pickle. "Anyhow, guys talk about cars all the time in school and well, anywhere. Surely you and your buddies traded repair advice in the locker room or . . . "

"I never went to school."

"You . . . what?"

He tensed, and the moment became awkward and strained. Like I'd found he had a disfiguring scar and pointed at it instead of ignoring it. He wouldn't look at me, and I was feeling clumsier by the minute. I tried to lighten the atmosphere. "Okay. You're right. A woman is perfectly capable of tending to all her own needs."

His shoulders eased, and he reverted to the Val I knew, smiling with pure devilment. "Really?" he drawled. "So I guess you know your way around all sorts of mechanical equipment."

I had probably blushed harder in my life, but I'd have been hard-pressed to say when. "Valentine . . . " I went for stern.

"Eu-dor-a . . . " Somehow he made a dignified name sound vaguely . . . wicked.

Alex hit the horn, and both of us stumbled backward.

"Hey!" I rounded the hood. "What was that for?"

"I need a bathroom," she said. "You done?"

"There are bushes right over there," Val said from behind me.

"Ew! No way!"

"You may not have any choice," I pointed out. "I don't know if it's safe to drive this."

"I'm not sure you have the op—" With a noisy rattle and a shudder, the car died. "—tion," she finished.

At this point, I was rubbing my forehead and wondering exactly what had been so bad about Jelly and the bimbo. There was room enough for all three of us in the house. Sex with him had pretty much lost its flavor, anyway.

Val stuck his head in the driver's window. "When did you last fill this, Red?"

Oh, crap. When did I last look at the needle, was the question. One trigger-happy gun dealer, a smart aleck, one pregnant teenager and a cat ago, best I could recall.

"How far you think it is back to Glory's?" I asked him.

"The town's closer. This is the way I hitched last night." He glanced up ahead. "It's only a couple of miles now, I bet. I'll walk it."

"No, you stay here. I screwed up. I'll fix it."

"Red . . . "

But I'd had enough of people for a while. I dove into the front seat long enough to snag my purse, since money would no doubt be required, and I started walking.

"Red, get your ass back in the car," Val was yelling. Over my shoulder I could see he was charging after me.

I launched into a quick-step. "Go back. Alex can't be left alone."

"Damn it, don't be an idiot."

I lengthened my stride, ignoring, as best I could, the thousand rocks a second digging into my soles. I needed a break from everyone, some time to chew on all of this. If Agnes could take off into a dangerous world all alone, then what did I have to worry about? My virginity was history, so no guy was going to come along to sell it.

Could pepper spray count as a dagger?

"Red!" Val hadn't turned back. He was standing with fists on his hips, glowering. "You're insane. No telling what might happen to you.

A woman shouldn't be on the road alone."

"I worked in a convenience store at night, for crying out loud." I fumbled around in my bag, then brandished my pepper spray. "See? I'm armed and dangerous."

He shook his head. "Let me go."

"Just because you're a guy means nothing. Didn't you see *Deliverance*?"

He didn't laugh, but I could tell he wanted to, just a little. Confident that I'd won, I started to turn back.

"How do you know you can trust me?" Val hollered. "You can't leave me with a kid and a cat," he spluttered.

For the first time, I witnessed Mr. Cool breaking a sweat. He was nearly walleyed.

So it was me who burst out laughing. For a morning that had definitely sucked so far, things were looking up.

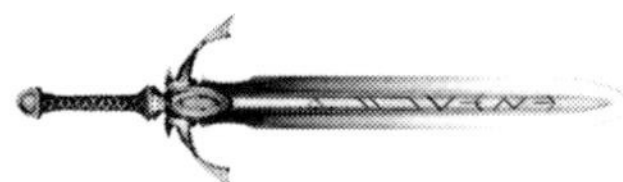

What few clouds there were had broken up; only endless blue remained. The sun was hotter than Hades already, and I had no hat and no shade. I could literally feel the new freckles rising to the surface of my skin. How far was this town, anyway?

A sign ahead. Thank goodness for the world of filthy lucre. Dairy Queens and their kin blared out alerts so you could get in the right lane in time. Surely this one would tell me how much more walking I had to do.

This sign, however, turned out to be different.

Broken Heart

Jesus Heals

With a big red heart painted right smack dab in the center, its double humps between *Broken* and *Heart*, its pointed tail between *Jesus* and *Heals*.

That was it. No directions, no markers. No explanations or hints. Only a simple statement of faith. I was pea-green with envy, pardon the pun.

My religious training was a little lacking. Okay, nonexistent. Mama had been raised in a church, I think, but she'd forsaken it long before I was born. Her faith was more a case of runaway optimism and a diehard belief in being swept away by romance. Sister told me once that my name came from the author of one of Mama's favorite stories, *The Robber Bridegroom,* by Eudora Welty. When I found a copy, I understood Mama better, her unshakable attachment to the notion that there was a good man inside every bad boy, given the right woman.

Too bad she never managed to be that woman. Then again, I wouldn't be here but for her faith that next time, things would be better.

Sister wasn't a big believer in anything up until she discovered reincarnation, and even then, she didn't want to know too many of the details, which is the exact opposite of me. I would offer to look for books on it, but she liked her version just fine. Namely that a lousy life wasn't the end and the next one could be different. Better.

Me, I didn't know what to think about faith. The big picture wasn't something the last in line got to see the way the leader did. When Mama passed on, I followed Sister's lead in just about everything. When Sister was dying, I was doing good to keep my eyes on the next step, then the next, day after day, because the long view was too scary.

And when she was gone . . . well, I couldn't exactly say what I'd been doing all those months. Mostly just getting by.

My thoughts were rudely interrupted by the boom of head-banger music. A faded navy blue pickup neared. Slowed down. I braced myself as every city instinct I ever had reared to attention. *Face forward, keep walking. Hand on pepper spray. Reach for sharp nail file. Wish for Agnes's dagger.* I *knew* I needed sword lessons.

"Ma'am? You need some help?" The window rolled down to reveal a fresh-faced country boy, all white teeth and straw cowboy hat.

But weren't cowboys supposed to listen to country music?

"Ma'am? Are you okay?"

My professional radar told me that this boy was no threat and despite my reluctance to agree with Val on any topic, he was right. Your gut can just about always be trusted. Problem was, most people forgot how to listen. "Is there a town ahead?"

"Jewel's about half a mile around that bend. Hop in, ma'am, and I'll take you there. You have car trouble or something?"

"I did, indeed."

"Where's your car?"

I used my thumb. "Back that way."

He paused. "Ma'am—"

Ma'am. He was eighteen, max. I didn't want to strangle him simply because he was making me feel old. "Eudora. Call me Eudora." I was on a new path, after all.

"Eudora." He pondered a minute. "Well, ma'am, did no one ever tell you it's not safe for a woman to leave her car? First thing they advise you in drivers' education is stay with your vehicle. Not to be bossy or anything, ma'am, but—"

"Eudora," I said firmly.

"Yes, ma'am. Eudora, I mean. Maybe I could take a look at it for you. My dad and grandpa own the service station in town, see. That's where I'm going now, to work. I just finished my chores."

Was he for real? An older Opie, and I would meet Aunt Bea up ahead? "I wouldn't want you to be late."

"Shoot, Pop would whip my tail if I deserted a lady on the road. Hop in, and we'll see what's what." He cleared room, tossing CD cases and soft drink cans behind the seat. "Sorry about that, ma—" My glare must have finally sunk in. "—er, Eudora."

"What's your name, cowboy?"

He didn't answer right away as I climbed inside in my denim miniskirt and was treated to my second long, slow down-and-up of this trip. His neck, like his arms, was very tan, but I could still see the blush rising like mercury in a thermometer.

"Your name?" I repeated.

"Um, Jeremy, m—I mean, Eudora. Jeremy Cashwell." He stuck out his hand.

I smiled at him and accepted it. "Pleased to meet you, Jeremy." I crossed my legs, just for the fun of watching him flush.

Hey, it had been a rough morning. Everyone deserves a little pleasure now and again.

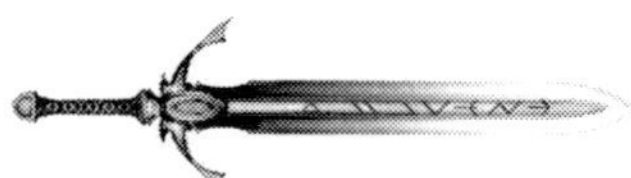

Have you ever spent much time looking at the world from weed-level? Me, either. That I was reduced to it a while later was not much to my liking.

Turned out Alex's daddy had a thing for engines he passed on to her, so she had her head under the hood of my car with Jeremy, and heaven forbid that Val admit how little he understood when a mere speck of a girl could speak the lingo.

So it was me and the cat plopped down on the shady side of my car. Irresponsible of me not to be up there asking questions, I was sure, but I figured I'd find out sooner or later.

I was the only one with greenbacks.

Jeremy had already solved one problem. He carried a can of gas in the back of his truck, which was how he got the engine running again. Just in time for that loud noise to get worse.

I didn't want to think about it.

So I was trailing this stick in the dirt and driving Isis crazy. She was pouncing and darting, and every once in a while, she reared so fast she fell over backward, but in true cat fashion, she recovered before she hit. Landed on her feet every time.

"I think you're my hero, kitty girl," I murmured with her close to my face, so no one else heard. "Seems I can't find my feet half the time now."

She was too busy batting at my hair to clue me in on how she felt about the praise.

"Look at the hawk." Val dropped down beside me.

"Where?"

He pointed to the sky just above a clump of trees. "Man, what must that be like to just glide up high above it all? Don't have to give a shit about anything down on the ground."

The note of longing was a surprise, like that moment earlier when Val admitted he didn't have a car. He wasn't Mr. Cool and Cynical right then, more . . . vulnerable, I guess. A little more open. Maybe I could get some answers. "You never told me where you're from."

He shrugged. "Nowhere." When I hissed, he grinned. "What? Isn't that exactly what you said?"

Grrr. But he was right. You had to give a little to get a little. "I was in Austin last, but we moved around a lot when I was growing up."

"I hear you."

"Was your dad in the military?"

He snorted. "I have no idea who my dad was."

"Really? Me either."

His head swiveled toward me. "No shit?"

"Scout's honor. Except I was never a Scout."

A rueful curve of his lips. "Ditto."

"So it was just you and your grandmother?" No way was I asking about a mom now.

Silence.

Open mouth, insert foot, Pea. "I'm so sorry. It hasn't been that long. You don't have to talk about her if you don't want to."

"Shit." He stared into the distance.

"I'm really sorry. I should never—" I felt awful. I grabbed Isis, started to rise.

"Stop it, Red." His head dropped. He raked fingers through his hair. "You're too soft. Too damn sweet." He swore softly. "This is never going to work. It's the problem with hanging around too long." He stared at the sky again. "I know I'm going to regret this, but—"

"What?"

"It's a long story."

"We're not exactly in a rush here." I settled beside him again.

"My grandma," he began.

"Val, you don't have to—"

"Stop it, Red. I feel like shit already." He faced me. "I don't have one."

"Well, not now, of course, because she—"

"No." His voice was very firm. "I have no family. Never did."

"But—" I frowned. Then it hit me. "Your trip . . . her favorite places . . . your wallet—" I glanced over at Jeremy, who was still tinkering, but my chest was tight and uneasy. "You lied to me?"

His eyes locked on mine. "I'm good at it. And you're an easy mark."

Mark. Wow. "Thanks." I started to stand again. I wanted to keep moving. Outrun what an idiot I'd been.

He grabbed the hem of my skirt.

"Let go of me." But I said it real quiet. I wasn't interested in exposing myself as a fool to anyone else.

"Wait."

"Why should I?"

His hand dropped. "You're right. You shouldn't." He picked up a stone and tossed it. "I knew going straight was a bad idea," he muttered.

"Going straight? Are you a . . . criminal? Is that why you didn't want the cops?"

An amused sideways glance. "Not the kind of criminal you mean. I've never laid a hand on anyone. Wouldn't own a gun if you paid me."

Mark, he'd said. "You're a con man." I retreated a step, but when Alex looked up, I dropped back to the ground, if a couple of feet farther away from Val. "Are you?" I hissed. Then I remembered. No family. "Oh, Val, I'm so sorry. How young were you orphaned?" If he was on his own really young, that could explain a lot.

He stared at me. "You are too much, Red. Do you just forgive everyone you meet, no matter what they do to you?" His eyes were softer than I'd ever seen them. Confused.

Maybe he needed someone to confide in. "Did you have anyone to take care of you?"

He looked down. "I thought I did for a while. Uncle Paul, he called himself. When he wasn't using any of his other fake names."

His voice was tight and a little forbidding. My life had been rocky, yes, but I'd always been with someone who loved me. "Was he mean to you?"

A small, forced chuckle. "I was . . . useful."

Oh, God. I bit my lip. I was afraid of what that implied. "Children aren't to blame for how adults treat them. You're not at fault if he—"

He laughed, but it wasn't pleasant. "Don't drag out your bleeding heart, Red. It's not what you're thinking. He didn't lay a hand on me. I was too effective a tool to risk putting me out of commission." He looked away, a muscle jumping in his jaw.

My imagination was running wild. I touched his arm in comfort. "I'm sorry."

He shoved to his feet, no longer relaxed. "Don't be. I learned everything I know from him." He glared at me as if defying me to be shocked. "I can pick a pocket, charm a woman, play a con, disable a security system before you can blink. What's so bad about that? I might never have gone to school, but I had one hell of an education. If the last woman's husband hadn't come home early . . . "

The last woman. I managed to close my gaping jaw. A con man. Boy, couldn't I pick 'em?

Forewarned is forearmed. I wasn't in the market for a man, anyway, so I was immune to any charming he might attempt, and the plight of the young boy that he'd been moved me. "Mama died when I was eight. Sister raised me after that. We moved all the time because Sister was terrified The Authorities would realize that she was a minor and take me away from her. I went to school, but I'm not very good at making friends. It was too hard, always having to leave them."

I'm not normal, either, I was trying to tell him. *We're both misfits.* The atmosphere between us was charged, and I had a sense of a line being crossed. I felt certain he didn't let his guard down often.

Then Alex giggled, and the moment was broken.

"She'll run, Red, if you just drop her off." Val stared into my eyes. "And then she'll have no one. A kid with a kid, God help her." *We know how that feels,* he was telling me.

"Maybe she'd go with you."

"You picked her up. Stole her from Nicky."

"He was beating her. I couldn't just stand there."

His mouth curved. "I'm betting you can't abandon her, either."

He was right, of course. Even if Sister weren't an issue, how could I let Alex go back into that or even worse? Val was correct in thinking that she needed tending. Heaven help her that her best shot at the moment appeared to be me.

Jeremy rounded the hood. "Ma'am—er, Eudora."

"Pea." What had I been thinking, trying to adopt a stronger name? I was no Dark Agnes. Forget pretending otherwise.

"Um, okay." His forehead wrinkled. I didn't bother explaining about Sister and my nickname. "Thing is, I can't fix what's wrong out here." He launched into a lot of terms that were gibberish to me but seemed to make sense to Alex.

"Your car has to go into the shop," he continued. "Alexandra—" And here his cheeks took on that lovely color again that so perfectly suited a fresh-faced country boy. "She and I can go get the tow truck if you two want to stay here, or you can ride with me, except someone's gonna have to sit in the back. Alexandra says you have a lot of your stuff with you, so I didn't know if you would want to leave the car alone."

I studied Alexandra, who'd insisted on being called Alex, and tried to figure out if I should be worried that Pretty Boy called her Alexandra, too. Was this a signal of some self-destructive impulse of hers regarding men? Except how this sweet boy could ever be a danger was beyond me.

Until I remembered that Pretty Boy was also good-looking and maybe if I'd met him at a different time, I would have thought him sweet. *Oh, hon . . .* I wanted to do my own Big Lil to her. *Men are not the answer.*

Alex piped up. "Jeremy understands you don't have much money."

It was the plea in her eyes that did me in. And what choice did I have, really? "Want to guess what this might run, Jeremy?"

"If it's what I'm thinking, I'll do my best to keep it under a thousand dollars."

I was surprised everyone couldn't hear the thud as my heart took a nosedive. "Do you know any make-do repair that would get me by?"

Jeremy shook his head. "No. I'm sorry. I wish I did, honest." He paused. Brightened. "Maybe Pop or Gramps will have a better idea, though. My Gramps started the garage and taught Pop. There's nothing about an engine the two of them don't know." He waited again for my answer. "The tow is free when we do the repairs." He glanced at Alex and blushed again. "Oh, shoot, ma'am, I'll make sure there's no charge, anyway, but you can't just leave the car here on the road."

I was in a tunnel that kept narrowing and narrowing until the air was close and stale. I shoved past all of them and started walking, gasping for that last breath.

A thousand dollars. After the motel and two meals, I'd still be a good four to five hundred short. I'd also need funds to buy gas to drive to Taos, and if Sister wasn't there, I'd have no place to stay and—

My brain just flat froze up. Rebelled at the thought that I was out in the middle of nowhere with strangers I had idiotically committed to drive—

Someone seized my arm, and I struck out without thinking.

"Hey!" It was Val, but he was part of the problem, the one closest at hand. I smacked his shoulder and jerked away. He only tightened his grip and turned me until he caught the other arm. "Red, calm down." Val gathered me in, and the feel of strong arms around me and a shoulder to lean on was so welcome that for a minute I forgot all the reasons I knew it was wrong.

"I can't afford it," I blubbered.

"Don't sweat it. I'll get the money." He was doing this rocking thing, a soft sway that might have been the single best sensation I'd felt in years, so I didn't hear the words as much as the reassuring tone at first.

Then, however much I wanted to just turn off the brain for good and stay right there with Val's voice a baritone blanket keeping me safe and warm, I finally did hear the words, *I'll get the money.* And remembered others. *I can pick a pocket. Disable a security system before you can blink.*

I pushed away. "What do you mean, get the money?"

"I have a little. I can come up with more."

"How?"

What I was asking was clear to both of us. He was scowling then. "The same way I got this."

"You said you were broke. At the motel, you said it. You—" *Lied.*

"I was broke then. Now I'm not."

"What did you do last night, while you were gone?"

"None of your business. You want help or not?" He wheeled and headed for Jeremy. "Get the tow truck." He glared at me. "Take her with you. I'll stay here."

"No, I will," I insisted.

"I'm not leaving you by yourself on the side of the road, Red." Though he seemed furious about it.

"I started out on this trip alone."

"Yeah. And look how you've managed so far."

My mouth dropped open at his gall.

"You two just stand here and argue," Alex said. "I'm starving, and it's hot."

Oh, God. The baby. What was I thinking? With all the uproar that morning, none of us had had a chance for breakfast. After Alex fainted yesterday, we couldn't take chances. "We should have gotten you something at Glory's."

Jeremy's head snapped toward me. "Glory's?" He scanned all of us. "You're friends of hers?" His expression told me this was not a plus.

"We just met her. She was kind enough to let us stay the night."

His frown deepened. "Kind? She didn't do anything . . . crazy?"

I smiled, but I could tell he was serious. Everything Glory did was odd, but who cared?

The graffiti. Surely this boy wasn't one of them. Didn't actually hate her. "She was fine. We didn't talk much, just ate and went to bed." Somehow I didn't think mentioning Dark Agnes would help me get a good deal on repairs.

"You lucked out, then." He took a protective step closer to Alex. "She's a wacko." His voice was flat and absolutely sincere. "And dangerous."

I wanted to ask why. Crazy, I'd buy and yes, you'd think a woman who'd take us in one minute and shoot to get us off her place the next might be a bit worrisome.

But I'd seen her face when she spoke to Alex, the tender regard. I'd had a sample of her kindness myself.

Alex was hungry, and Val had said he'd help with the repair

expense. Sister or not, an innocent child couldn't be made to suffer while I agonized over how he might do that. I'd just have to keep an eye on him. "Go ahead, Jeremy. Take her with you, but please see to it that she gets something to eat before you come back. She's—"

"Hungry!" Alex practically shouted. She glared at me and all but dragged Jeremy away.

She could not mean to entrap this poor boy, could she? She wasn't showing much, not in that baggy shirt. Still, knowing her straits and the level of her desperation, I couldn't assume she wouldn't latch on to whoever could help her. At the moment, though, I had all I could handle, so I let it go.

"Val, please. Would you go with them? I think he's a good kid, but—"

"You can trust me here with your car, you know. A con's no fun if the mark knows it."

I stared at him. "You're going straight, you said."

He shrugged. "Trying."

"Why? The husband?"

"Not just that." His exhale was long and weary. "I'm not sure I can explain, even to myself." He jerked his head in the direction of Jeremy's truck. "Sure you don't want me to stay?"

Alex was probably safe with Jeremy, but still . . .

"Go ahead."

He turned. Looked back. "You'll be all right?"

"Frankly, I could use some time alone."

He nodded. "I hear that."

I watched them drive off, then settled back on the shady side of my car. What a troupe we were, this ragtag band of strangers who felt a little more like friends, if weirdly complicated ones, with every mile.

Sister, am I ever going to have some stories to tell you. Unless, of course, you're already with us.

I leaned my head back against the car door.

And just started to laugh.

Edith

Settled by cattlemen who ran herds on open range, and stock-farming homesteaders.

Development began in early 1880s after Winfield Scott, rancher, fenced his spread.

Area had three schools, lodge hall, tabernacle, general store, cotton gin and blacksmith shop.

The post office, established in 1890, was named for Edith Bonsall, an admired young lady of Ballinger. It closed in 1955. Dwindling schools combined, then consolidated with those of nearby Robert Lee.

As trend toward urban living increased, Edith declined.

THE TEXACO MAN

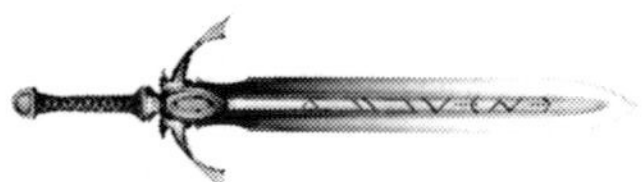

Less than an hour later as we made our way down the road in Jeremy's tow truck, my car hooked behind, I was looking around for signs of life. All I saw were mesquite trees, the occasional live oak and, oh boy, countless more goats and dottings of cows. All this open space could make a person nervous. I knew my way around cities just fine, but what did people do with themselves out here?

Then, just ahead of us over the crest of the hill, came a sight that made me practically get whiplash doing a double-take.

An old man on a riding lawn mower was pulling a little trailer. The trailer sported a flagpole, American flag waving. In a basket hooked to the back of his seat was a beagle, ears flapping faster than the flag.

I burst out laughing and pointed.

Jeremy pulled up beside the man and waved out the window. "Hey, Gramps!" The old man waved back.

Oops. "I'm sorry. I didn't know—"

Jeremy turned to me, neck and ears bright red. "Gramps doesn't see so good anymore, but he wouldn't listen to anyone. Finally, Gran turned him in to the Department of Public Safety and got his license pulled. He hasn't spoken to her in nearly six months." He flashed a quick grin. "He figured out a way to get around, though. You don't need a driver's license to operate a mower. He and Rascal can cover some ground. This spring, he drove all the way to Brownwood. Gran was fit to be tied."

Before I could summon a response, we arrived in Jewel.

Not much to it didn't begin to describe the place. The city limits sign said *Population 973*, but if a hundred people lived there, I'd have been astonished.

There was one main thoroughfare, the highway we were on, if a two-lane road can be called such. Maybe a dozen side streets, a couple of which seemed to actually be farm-to-market roads with a handful of houses closer together on each one, until you started running into exactly what we'd been seeing for hours.

A whole lotta nothing.

But I was riding in a tow truck, which was a seriously amazing piece of machinery, with all its levers and stuff. I wondered what it would take to get Jeremy to let me drive it. First, though, I'd have had to get his attention, which was glued to Alex. We were all jammed in the front seat together, and I was nearly on Val's lap.

He'd suggested exactly that, but I had declined. After our conversation, I knew he was only hitting on me because . . . well, that was part of his trade. *A con man? What kind of sign is this, Sister?*

I would soon have to explain to him about me and men and what was going to happen between the two, which was zip, zero and nada. Being a little too attractive for his own good, he would likely argue. Men like Val weren't used to women turning them down.

But that was neither here nor there at that moment. I was much more concerned about Jeremy's reaction to the fact that we'd been at Glory's. His pickup was different from the one that sped away after her shotgun blast, but was he one of them, the people who called her a whore and a witch? And why?

She was different, yes, and humans have a hankering to cut misfits from the herd. She was gruff and cranky; I doubted she bought a lot of Girl Scout cookies or contributed to bake sales, but that was a long way from being a righteous target for vandalism.

As a fellow misfit, I was more than a little concerned about entering the town that likely harbored the vandals.

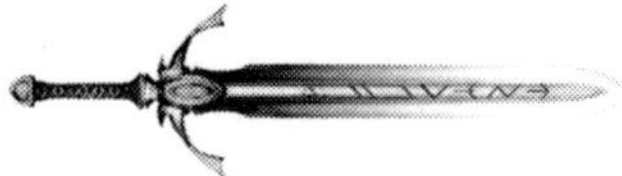

"The backside of beyond," Val muttered, and I couldn't disagree. Jeremy pulled into an old-fashioned service station in what was literally the center of town.

How could I be sure of that? Well, when you can see both ends without craning your neck, hey, can you say middle?

We pulled around to the bays at the side of the stucco canopy, and I spotted what was next door. The sign said *Cashwell's Grocery*, but it looked like a kissing cousin to a convenience store.

And it had a *Help Wanted* sign in the window. Where on earth they'd find applicants was beyond me. How much business could there be? "You folks own this town?" I asked Jeremy.

That fair coloring of his reddened easier than mine, poor kid. "Not really. Well, not exactly."

"Gas and groceries power the economic engine, my man." He was so dang cute, I could have just slurped him up like an ice cream sundae.

He shrugged. "Gramps owns the service station, and Pop worked for him until Gramps got his license yanked—then Gramps flat quit for a while. Pop had to take over, so I'm helping him after school and all summer, though Gramps has started showing up again. Gran still operates the store and café, but it's hard on her. Sometimes Aunt Millie helps out, but she's about to have another baby, so she can't anymore. Pop and his brothers and sisters think Gran should close the store down, but folks around here depend on it." He ducked his head and sighed. "Things were better before Gramps and Gran stopped speaking. They've always been pretty hot-tempered together, but this is new." He paused. "And weird."

Val chuckled. "Marriage will do that to you."

I elbowed him in the side. "What do you know about it?"

"I have known my share of married women, Red." His glance recalled for me the husband who'd come home early. "We don't have time for me to tell you all I understand about marriages."

Time. I was feeling the press of it. I wanted to be on the road with plenty of daylight left. "Out," I said to Val as I looked at Jeremy.

"How soon can your dad check out my car?"

"Right now, I expect." He nodded out the windshield.

An older version of Jeremy, only stockier, stepped out of the nearest bay. Though he was probably only in his late forties or so, he was wearing a uniform like the ones I'd seen in really old magazine ads.

For a while after Mama died, I went on a kick of trying to recreate what her world was like when she was my same age. Mama was born in 1954, back when a service station provided real service. Pumped your gas, washed your windshield without holding you up for spare change the way the homeless guys do at intersections. Mama used to talk about those days with reverence, telling me how her mother wore white gloves and a hat to church and how men used to open doors for women and such.

But no matter how many old movies I watched or *Life* and *Look* and *McCall's* magazines I read back then, I couldn't seem to figure out what Mama would have done with herself if she were me.

I couldn't picture Mama with a mother who wore white gloves, anyway. Mama was more prone to wear cha-cha slides, tight skirts and low-cut blouses. Just this side of trashy, I guess, but I didn't see it that way back then. I just knew she was real pretty, not like her skinny daughter. When I was tossing out our past like crazy after Sister died, I do recall seeing some photos and thinking that Mama pulled off the look, with her doll-baby face and cute curves. Men couldn't get enough of her.

Her people, though, weren't like that, best I could tell. They were serious folks, Sister told me, even a little upper crust. From what I've been able to piece together, Mama just went off the track real bad when she discovered sex and boys discovered her. I guess she could never find her way back. But I think she must have been a little homesick for the life she'd left behind, based on the stories she'd tell.

The world Mama grew up in might as well have been on Mars, but I couldn't get enough of it. The magazine ads, with their dainty references to female troubles and their notion that a woman's life should be built around pleasing her man, were interesting in a sick sort of way. And I'll admit right now that I really liked those Betsey McCall paper dolls in each issue. She was so wholesome and she had a real dad and all these great clothes.

I might not have figured out what Mama would have done at my age, but I sure got an eyeful of why she waded through an ocean of men and tried to please even the most worthless of them.

The man before me in his dark gray uniform pants and shirt wasn't all that much younger than Mama would have been. Maybe they read the same magazines, only he was missing the sharp cap and bow tie.

And he didn't much look like he was itching to give me the sparkling Pepsodent smile.

"Pop, this is Pea—" Jeremy frowned at me as if just then noticing he didn't have my last name.

"O'Brien," I supplied. "Pleased to meet you." I held out a hand.

"Tommy Cashwell." His dad nodded but just kept wiping his hands. Then he looked at Val. "This car been acting up long?"

Hey, I wanted to say, but Jeremy was shuffling his feet, so I answered politely. "No, it hasn't—"

Just at the same instant Val said, "Yes. Been running rough for a good fifty miles."

Hoo boy. If he—any of the three *hes* standing there—thought I would just hang back and play the simpering little lady, they were severely wrong.

"Longer than that," Alex piped up before I got a chance.

I whipped my head in her direction and glared.

She merely folded her arms and shrugged. "You never noticed, did you?"

I tried to look stern, but Jelly could have told all of them that cars were not my strong suit. He thought it was funny, the time I drove off with the nozzle still in my gas tank. Like to busted a gut laughing, and it wasn't just that he'd been drinking beer at the lake all afternoon.

Shoot, except for the cashier who came screeching out the door, I thought it was pretty funny, too.

If I'd been around back in the Fifties, a shined and pressed service station man would have been pumping my gas, and my husband would have made sure my car was always running. It wouldn't have mattered that I tended to daydream instead of having my ears always tuned to the zillion noises a car can make, even when it was doing just fine.

But everyone was staring at me, and I was nailed.

Any fool knows that women get taken advantage of by mechanics if they act like helpless maidens these days, however. "I noticed," I said and cast Alex a withering glance. "But I had a few other things on my mind." Making it clear by my pointed looks at her and Val that if I hadn't been so busy with pregnant girlfriend beaters and con men, I would've been right on top of whatever noise they heard that I wouldn't have in a million years.

I swore I would make Val pay for the snort that followed.

"I have an excellent mechanic back home," I said, to put the disapproving station owner on notice. "If you can just do something to get me by, I'll see him first thing when I get back." There. I hoped that would save my pitiful grubstake.

"We'll see." He turned to Jeremy. "Stick it in bay two, and I'll take a look."

At that moment, Jeremy's grandfather putt-putted into the drive. His dad sighed, cast a rueful glance next door at the grocery, then back at Jeremy's grandfather, who was dressed just like his son and looked much more authentic.

The phone rang. "I'm expecting a call from Charlie," Jeremy's dad said to him. "Just be a second."

"Charlie's my uncle." Jeremy kept his voice low. "Been refereeing between Gran and Gramps all this time. My dad says he's an idiot. That if he'd just quit relaying messages, they'd give up and talk to each other and leave the rest of us out of it."

"Don't whisper, boy," said his grandfather, approaching us. Mama would have swooned. This was the Texaco man come to life. Except for no smile. "Won't do you no good. I still got the ears of a bat."

Jeremy flushed. Shuffled his feet. "Sorry, Gramps."

"You just remember, boy. What's between me and her—" Here, he shot a baleful look next door "—is our business."

The tips of Jeremy's ears were bright red. "Yes, sir," he mumbled.

Face still a little thunderous, his grandfather turned to me. "'Mornin'. I'm Ray Cashwell. What seems to be the problem?"

Everyone but me chimed in on symptoms and solutions. All of them seemed tickled pink by the discussion.

Not me. I was seriously depressed. I drew Jeremy aside. "Are you sure there's nothing you can do to get me back on the road right away?"

"Sorry. Wish I could." He glanced over at Alex with a calf-sick look. She smiled back ever so sweetly.

Uh-oh. Was the boy blind? He didn't stand a chance, not being in full possession of the facts relating to that little ball of dynamite who'd ensnared him. "May I speak to you for a minute, Alex?"

She didn't budge. "Jeremy was just going to take me over to his Gran's. They serve breakfast here, and you want me to eat well, right?"

Son of a gun. I'd thought I was channeling Big Lil, only to

discover she'd taken up residence inside that little dab of a girl.

Small women just cannot be trusted. The more helpless they look, the more you'd better be on red alert. I toyed with the notion of blowing her cover right then and there, except that Jeremy might only have turned the hots he had for her into some sort of chivalry.

Val grabbed my arm. "Breakfast sounds good. Let's go, Red." He turned to Jeremy's grandfather. "We'll look forward to your verdict." None too gently, he drew me away before I could plant myself good.

He'd better at least be buying, was all I could think.

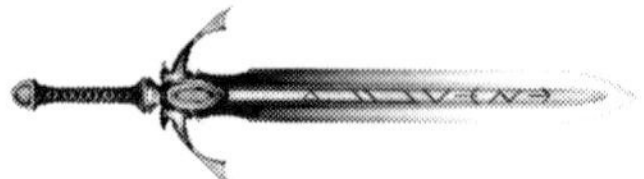

Once inside the small rock building, there were smells that immediately sucked me in. There was coffee—just plain coffee, mind you—and Lysol and Windex. Standard convenience-store fare.

But then there was bacon frying and toast on a griddle. Pancake syrup.

To one side were wooden shelves of groceries, but these were more staples than grab-and-go midnight items. No walls full of refrigerated cases for beer and soft drinks. Instead, I saw one standing case with milk and eggs and a glorious old red metal Coke machine beside it.

Along the front wall on the other side was a series of orange formica booths, and several sets of tables and chairs standing between the booths and a long counter. Behind the counter was the kitchen.

"What you got there, sugar lamb?" A voice came from back that way.

"Some hungry friends, Gran."

A woman emerged, silver hair in a scraped-back coronet, her face lined, her eyes interested and kind. She was wearing a shirtwaist dress with an apron over it, the old-fashioned type with a ruffle around the edge. Her only jewelry was a plain wedding band and two tiny pearl studs.

She wasn't Aunt Bea, she was better. Aunt Bea was a little ditzy and way too helpless. There was an air about this woman that said *Rock-Solid Steady. Warm Cookies and Hot Chocolate. Bedtime Stories and Real Big Hugs.*

Grandmother with a capital *G*. Just like I always wished for.

"You're a long, tall drink of water, aren't you?" She looked up at me with a smile.

It didn't matter that I'd have to bend down a ways; that wistful child in me wanted to step into her arms and claim one of those hugs.

When I couldn't seem to speak, Jeremy did. "This is Pea O'Brien," he said. "And this is Alexandra and Val. They had car trouble. This is my grandmother, Lorena Cashwell."

Isis picked that moment to awaken and stir inside my purse. Her head poked over the edge, and she yowled at the smell of food.

"Can't have a cat out here." His grandmother held out a hand. "I'll take her."

I clutched Isis. "She won't get on anything. I won't let her."

"Give her here."

"I'll just wait outside."

"I'm only going to get her a drink," she said, then winked. "Not make tacos out of her." With surprising quickness, she nipped Isis from my hand and stroked the cat's tiny head.

Isis, the traitor, started purring.

"Grab a seat. I'll be right back."

"Wait!" I charged after her, heedless of *Employees Only* signs and Jeremy's quick intake of breath.

I followed her into a storeroom, its walls lined with jars of home-canned vegetables, their colors so vivid they might have graced a cookbook photo. Lower shelves held boxes and tubs and ancient kitchen utensils, some of which I'd swear I recognized from old magazines. A chest freezer on one wall and two refrigerators on another.

I smelled grapes, and spotted jars of jelly cooling on a dishcloth. It might have been the single best scent I had run across in years. My stomach growled.

"Hungry, dear?" She filled a bowl with milk that Isis was already trying to dive into. She set the bowl and the kitten on the floor.

"I have some food for her in the car," I offered.

"No need for that. I don't mind a bit." Then she looked up. "But I was talking about you. You look a little peaked. Why don't you go on, now, and look at a menu. Figure out what you want to eat."

The bell over the front door rang, and she shook her head wearily. "Drat. I'll take your order as soon as I get done."

I remembered the *Help Wanted* sign. Had a notion about how I might be able to offset the expense of my car repairs and breakfast.

No, not breakfast. Val was going to buy that much, I decided, with his suspicious windfall. But my car repairs . . .

Sister, I apologize. I was about to give Fate the back of my hand.

You just hang on now. We'll be together before you know it.

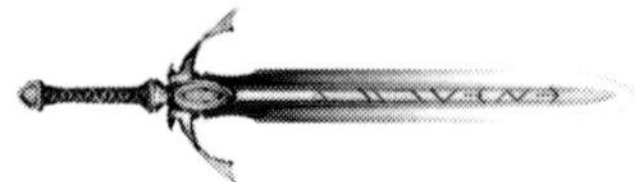

I was pretty sure we'd died and gone to heaven, and the others probably felt the same, but we three were too busy stuffing our faces to discuss the matter.

The woman could cook. Lord have mercy, she could cook. The pancakes were fluffy and golden with the slightest crispy edge, and she had these amazing little Fiestaware pitchers brimful of maple syrup and melted butter so that you could just pour rivers of each over your stack. The bacon was perfectly browned, the coffee fresh and strong, and there was even honest-to-God cream for it. None of those teeny little plastic containers of fake cream that would last through a nuclear war, nossir.

Alex was even drinking her milk without complaining. "This is seriously amazing," she said.

"Practically orgasmic," I responded. "Oops." I saw Mrs. Cashwell and clapped my hand over my mouth as Val snickered.

She only smiled. "Y'all want more coffee?"

"Mrs. Cashwell, this is quite honestly the best meal I ever had." Val clasped her hand and ostentatiously kissed the back of it.

"Oh, go on with you!" She retrieved her hand, but her cheeks took on color. "Just plain country food."

"Ma'am, Val's right. I would give my right arm to cook like this," I said.

"Anyone can cook, dear. It's merely a matter of patience and practice," she said. "Along with a little sense of adventure. Some of the best results come from taking a chance."

"Did your mother teach you?" I asked. Both Mama and Sister came up a little short in the cooking area.

"She did. Now there was a woman who could work a miracle with only a cast iron pan. She had me helping from the time I was knee high to a grasshopper. Mostly I just learned from watching her."

I could just picture her, a little girl with long braids standing on a chair as her mother showed her the ins and outs of the kitchen. They would roll pie crust together, the little girl with her face all screwed up in concentration as she worked the rolling pin, a smudge of flour on her cheek. Real *Little House on the Prairie* kind of stuff. It had me all but sighing in envy. "Did you always live here in Jewel?"

"Oh, yes. My people go back to the Republic of Texas. They're all buried here." She began gathering our dishes, and I jumped up to help her. "No, honey, you just let me do this."

But I was too eager to hear more. And too nervous about the verdict in the garage next door. I didn't stop stacking plates. "Did you have brothers and sisters?" When she moved toward the kitchen, I followed.

"One sister who died young, another still living and two brothers, both gone now. What about you, dear?"

"Just one sister." I didn't want to think about the true barrenness of my family tree, so I pressed on. "How many children do you have?" I cut my eyes toward the door.

"Three boys and two girls. Tommy and Charlie live here with their families, as does our daughter Millie. Our son Jeff is in Omaha, and our daughter Janie is in North Carolina."

"How many grandchildren?" Smoothly, I sidled up to the sink and began running water.

A line appeared between her eyebrows, but I just smiled and went on. I kept thinking about what I might need to do if the bill was as bad as Jeremy had estimated.

Before she could answer, the door to the store opened, with its jangle of sleigh bells. "I'll be right back. You are not to do those dishes."

She left, and I kept going. Dishwashing was not high on my list of enjoyable pursuits, but whether or not I needed a job, I could see what Jeremy meant about her seeming tired.

She was back in a minute. "You need to come out front, dear." Things had gotten very quiet out there. I continued washing. If it was the verdict on my car, I wasn't sure I was ready to hear it. Then someone cleared his throat. "About your car—"

I turned to see Jeremy's grandfather in the doorway, Mrs. Cashwell frozen like a statue about six feet away, scrubbing a countertop as though her life depended on it.

He addressed me, but his gaze kept straying to her. "Electronic parts—" He harrumphed. "Got no use for 'em."

"What does that mean?" It was all I could do not to squeeze my eyes shut and stuff a finger in each ear.

"Means we practically have to tear out everything under the hood to get to what's wrong, and the part has to be ordered."

"Ordered? How long will that take?"

He shrugged his shoulders. "We could get it in maybe two days if you wanted to pay extra for it."

"What kind of extra?"

"Another fifty bucks, I'd guess."

Fifty bucks? Just for shipping? "What kind of total are we looking at?"

"'Bout eleven hundred, more or less."

"Dollars?" My knees wanted to buckle.

"Damn foreign cars, all those electronics. Man used to be able to work on his own vehicle under a tree, swap out parts in the salvage yard. Not anymore."

"How long, once you have the part?"

"Couple of days, maybe three."

"And without paying extra for fast delivery, how long will the part take to get here?"

"At least a week."

I felt sick. I whirled and went back to the dishes, trying furiously not to cry. I knew he was waiting for an answer, but I didn't have one to give just then.

"Perhaps you could ask him to allow you a little time to think," Mrs. Cashwell suggested.

"Perhaps I ain't deaf," he responded. "You might tell her to mind her own business," he said to me. But despite the sarcastic words, there was no heat in his words.

She only scrubbed harder.

While he stared. At her, not me.

I had to wonder just how much their children and grandchildren were paying attention. They might not be speaking, but there was a lot more than a feud swirling in the air around us.

"If I could have a few minutes, I'd be grateful," I said to him.

He didn't respond immediately. Finally, he heaved a large sigh and removed his focus from his wife. "Come over to the garage whenever you're ready." He waited a few beats longer, but she never looked his way. At last, shoulders sagging, he left.

I went back to washing dishes. And started trying out arguments to convince her to save my hide.

But there were no magic words, so once I finished the last dish, I dried off my hands and turned to her. "Ma'am?" I said. "Mrs. Cashwell?"

"You can call me Lorena."

I hesitated just for a second, but what real choice did I have? "Um, I noticed your sign in the window. See, I don't have enough money to pay your, er—Jeremy's, um, grandfather—"

"Just call a spade a spade. My rat bastard husband."

I couldn't help it. My mouth fell open. *Close your mouth, Pea, you'll catch flies*, Sister always said. But that sweet little old lady had just said *rat bastard.*

"Close your mouth, honey. You'll catch flies."

Okay, now I was flabbergasted. I had been at the point of asking Fate some hard questions. My faith had wavered now and again, I had to admit.

But when that woman, who held the keys to getting me back on the road with money left to find Sister, spoke to me in my own sister's very words I had just that moment been recalling, well, there was no way it was not another sign. An honest-to-God bolt from the blue. "Er, yes, ma'am. That is—" And here I considered that the aforementioned rat bastard had my car and an equally important role in sending me on my way. "If you say so. I just met him, after all."

She laughed, and eyes that she'd bequeathed to Jeremy sparkled. "Now there's a diplomat." Then her expression grew a little wary. "What was it you wanted to talk about?"

Okay. Deep breath. "You're shorthanded, I hear. Your family is worried about you."

Her brows squashed together. "My family needs to mind its own business."

Uh-oh. Put my foot in it. "I guess. Thing is, I have experience running a place like your store. I could help you out."

"For a week?"

Make it good, Pea. Problem was, a person doesn't get a lot of practice at salesmanship in a convenience store. Folks already know why they're there, so there's not much chance to sell them on what they should want to buy. "Maybe a little longer. I guess it depends on how much you'd pay me and how long it would take me to work off the repairs." The very thought of an indefinite delay in my journey made me want to howl. To sit on the floor and suck my thumb.

"I couldn't pay more than minimum wage," she said. "Assuming I would want to employ someone at all, especially someone who I know won't stay."

She was right. But I was desperate. "I swear on Isis's head that I'm honest and hardworking and you can trust me."

She studied me for a minute that strung out forever. Finally, she spoke. "Isis?"

Okay. Detour. "Egyptian high priestess. Only person to know the secret name of the sun god Ra."

"Mighty important name for such a little speck of a thing." Then she switched topics. "What will you do if I say no?"

"Honestly, I have no idea. I didn't expect car repairs when I left Austin. I have some money, but not a lot. First, I'm going to ask Mr.—er, the rat bastard if he can just do something temporary and, well, cheap."

"Cheap is his middle name," she muttered. "Knows his vehicles, though. No one better. If he could do it cheaper, he would have already suggested it."

My slim hopes for a repair I could afford vanished in a puff of smoke. "So . . . will you hire me?"

"I have to think about it." She looked me over, though that scan had nothing at all in common with a long, slow down-and-up. This was more like a microscope, and I was the germ squirming under glass.

"You're worried that I'll rob you blind."

"Not really." A pause during which my heart shivered in fear and hope. "You strike me as reliable."

Oh, wow. I pictured myself in a uniform. Sort of the female version of the Texaco man. Someone people depend on and know will never steer them wrong.

Nice. Okay, boring, but people don't give routine enough credit. They take it for granted. You should never, ever assume life won't slap you upside the head with a surprise or two you'd just as soon have passed on.

I sweetened the pot. "I'm a quick learner, and you're right, I am reliable. Maybe I won't be staying, but you might be able to take some time off in a few days, once I get familiar with your system and you're comfortable with me. Have yourself a little vacation." I waited, barely breathing, to see which way the scales would tip.

"Don't get ahead of yourself, young lady. I haven't even agreed to try you out."

I opened my mouth to plead, but her expression said I'd best leave her alone to ponder.

The wait was a long one while she rearranged some items in the refrigerator. "I suppose we could try it. A trial run only, mind you."

Yesss! It was a chance I desperately needed, but I managed to nod soberly and keep my happy feet still. "Thank you. I won't disappoint you, I promise."

"If you do, you won't be the first." But she smiled just a little. "So where will you stay?"

Oh, lordy. "Is there a motel?" The very notion of more expenses was more than I could stand.

"In Jewel?" She didn't roll her eyes, but she might as well have.

"Ah, is there one down the road, then?"

"And how would you get to work?"

"I'd walk. I'm strong and not afraid of hard work."

"Child," she said, eyes soft. "There's not a motel for a good sixty miles."

"Oh. Well," I said, thinking frantically. "Maybe we could . . ." *Sleep in the car*, I started to say, but that was just dumb. There wasn't room for two, much less three plus a cat.

She touched my arm. "There's an RV parked behind my house. You could stay there, you and your sister."

"My sister? Oh—you mean Alex. She's not—I don't really know her. I just, um, picked her up." At her slight frown, I continued. "She was in some trouble, and I couldn't just stand by."

"So where will she go?"

"Beats me." I wanted to confide in her that I wasn't sure what to do with Alex, but I was on thin ice here, and explaining my theories about Sister might not further my cause. "I'm working on that." Anyway, I wanted to get back to the subject of the RV. "You wouldn't mind us staying there?" Then, though it just about choked me to ask, I went ahead. "Would you want me to pay rent?"

"Of course not." She looked scandalized. "I would never do that. Back in my grandparents' day on the frontier, hotels and boarding houses could be days' ride apart. Folks left their houses unlocked, and if a traveler passed by and the owners were gone, the travelers would just go in, stay the night, fix a meal, then clean up after themselves before they continued their journey. Good country hospitality. You would be my guests and welcome to it."

I could not imagine that world she'd described, but gratitude blew through me like a cool breeze. "I would pay for our meals."

"Nonsense."

"Then you would have to let me help you prepare them. Let us help," I amended. Val and Alex could pitch in.

She nodded. "That would be fair."

I was getting more encouraged. She didn't know yet that I would do one whale of a job for her, but I did. Then I remembered that she'd only spoken of two of us staying there. "Is there room in the RV for three?" Though sharing more close quarters with Val was not high on my wish list.

"Your young man can bunk with Jeremy. I don't hold with unmarried couples sleeping together."

"We're not a couple," I said.

"Even more reason to be proper. He's a friend of yours, then?"

"Uh, well, actually, I don't really know him either." That was an understatement.

"He's not part of that little girl's trouble, is he?"

"Oh, no." But I could just imagine her reaction if I said *He's a con man, but he's trying to go straight.*

"You picked him up, as well?" She peered at me closely. "Did no one ever talk to you about the dangers of picking up strangers?"

It had been a long time since someone had taken the time to lecture me. Mrs. Cash—um, Lorena, was looking very grandmotherly to me, but it felt, well, kinda good, actually. "He's . . . um, it's hard to explain."

Lorena glanced over toward the storeroom where Isis had given up trying to bat her way out of the door. "She one of your strays, too?" Her eyes were twinkling.

I ducked my head, smiling. "Well . . . "

"Child, you have taken a good slice of the world on your shoulders, haven't you?"

My chest was full of warm honey that spread through my veins and made me as happy as I'd been in quite some time, simply because this woman made me feel cared for. Abruptly, tears threatened. I shrugged but couldn't speak.

"Come on," she said gently. "Let me show you where you can stay, and you rest up a bit before you come to work."

"No, ma'am, I couldn't do that. Let me tell Val and Alex what's going on, then maybe you could show Alex where to put our things. I'll go talk to the, er, your husband. Once I'm done, I'll come back here and get to work. I can sweep the floors or something until you get finished. I know how to work most every cash register ever made, so you don't worry about that one bit, unless there's some code you need to give me."

She smiled and shook her head. "No, we don't run much to codes and security systems around here, dear." She studied me, then relented. "All right. We'll meet back here in a jiffy."

Barely, I resisted the urge to hug her and left the kitchen to talk to Val and Alex.

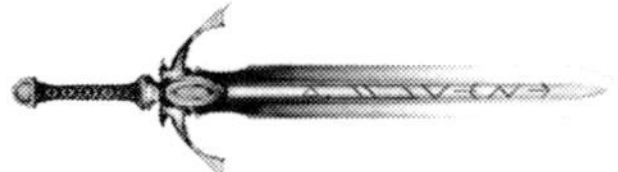

The cash register was ancient. And unbelievably cool. Ornately carved metal with tall round keys you had to push down hard.

And a drawer that went—hand to Jesus—*ka-CHING*! when it opened.

I was in clerk heaven. Even if this place closed at six p.m. and there was no possibility of a night shift. I could have played with that register all day. Could, literally, because—get this—there was no monitoring tape or file to track money in and out. I could punch keys to my heart's content.

Unfortunately, there were also no customers after the ones Lorena handled while I was still on pins and needles about asking her to let me work.

I wanted a customer so bad I could taste it.

Since there were none, I made Alex play pretend with me. She wasn't real happy about that, but mostly because Ray wouldn't let her hang out at the garage. Jeremy was supposed to be working, see, even though, best I could tell, he was spending half his time out on the driveway casting moon eyes at Alex.

Val, however, was allowed to hang out. Men only, seemed to be the deal. Even though Alex understood way more about cars than Val, testicles were the ticket for admission.

"I'm tired of this," Alex whined.

I glanced at the clock. Ten fifteen. "Good idea. I'll put the groceries away this time." A lot of trouble to keep returning them to the shelves, yes, but we did, after all, need to make this realistic for proper training. "Then you can go rest. Nap a little."

"Nap?" Alex shrieked. "I'm not a kid."

"No, but you're having one. Rest is good for you." As least, it seemed like it would be.

The pout was already forming when Lorena came out of the kitchen and hijacked it. "We need to finish getting ready for the lunch rush. Alexandra, would you please fill the salt shakers?"

Lunch rush? I'd barely even seen any cars drive by.

"Come on over and slice me some green tomatoes," she said to me. "I'll work on the okra."

My ears perked up. "You serve okra? Not boiled and slimy, right?"

"Of course not. Fried, just like the green tomatoes."

Pitty-pat, pitty-pat. My heart was warming up for a little happy dance. If Lorena's fried okra was as good as the pancakes she made us, then life was definitely looking up. In my book, fried okra was manna from heaven.

Didn't even have to be a sign from Sister, though I defied anyone to tell me it wasn't. Nope, good fried okra was reason enough to rejoice, all on its own. And if the green tomatoes were decent . . .

Well, no call to get too carried away, now. I could take or leave them, except if by chance she made them with a dab of brown sugar the way one of our neighbors used to.

But I was getting ahead of myself. "Just let me put these groceries back," I said.

"Then wash your hands, both of you."

I had to smile. She really did sound exactly like a grandmother should. How did I know that? Well, I had had a little taste of a grandmother myself. Only one, of course, since Casper—well, he had a mom, I guess, in whatever sense ectoplasm can have ancestors—but since I never met him, the concept of a mother for him was a little fuzzy.

Mama's mother, though, I only saw her once that I recall, and what struck me most was this: She smelled of lilacs.

And she ordered you around in a way that felt real good.

Like you were worth the trouble.

Mrs. Cordia Sloan Duke
(Jan. 10, 1887-July 23, 1966)

Chronicler of a unique era in the history of the Southwest.

Born in Belton, Mo. At 17, taught school in Indian Territory (Okla.)

In 1907 she married Robert L. Duke, a ranch hand who had risen to division manager of the XIT Ranch (then world's largest). In addition to her own family, she "looked after" the 150 cowboys who worked the 3,000,000-acre spread. Kept a diary of everyday events in ranch life around here and successfully encouraged 81 others to do likewise. Thus was preserved an authentic account of a passing phase of American life—the cowboy and his work.

THE ZEN OF FRIED OKRA

By afternoon, I would have sworn I had met all nine hundred seventy-three inhabitants of Jewel. Helped serve lunch to every last one of them.

At last I was off my feet, nearly too tired to eat. Except that Lorena made the best fried okra that had ever crossed my lips, and her fried green tomatoes did indeed have brown sugar in them. Not too much so they were sicky-sweet, just exactly enough to offset the pucker.

I sighed again, in between shoveling mouthfuls like a longshoreman, and Lorena smiled real big. Not one hair on her head the slightest bit ruffled, I might add.

"You are amazing," I told her.

Her cheeks pinkened, and I couldn't help but stare. She was so in charge and together, that seeing her flustered was . . . fun.

"I mean it. This is the best food I have ever put in my mouth. No wonder the entire town showed up for lunch." Then I frowned. "But you won't be able to take much time off, after all." I glanced at my adored cash register and sighed again.

"Why not?"

"I could never in a million years cook like this. I can manage the store just fine, but—" I waved my hand over my plate. "This is way past me."

"I told you any fool can cook."

"Not like this, I assure you. I'll run the store for you, though."

"I appreciate your help with lunch. Usually I'd still be in there working for another hour, at least."

"I'm glad." There was something about working together with other women. I felt closer to her already.

"But back to the cooking. A body should know how to prepare meals from scratch. It's a crying shame how many folks rely on prepared foods or junk from a fast food restaurant. You were right that you're a quick learner, and there's no reason you can't start out with one dish and expand to more." One eyebrow arched. "Unless, of course, you're a coward?"

Well, that shut me up. Dark Agnes stirred and stretched a bit, like she might wake up. "No, I'm not." Not that cowardice didn't have its appeal, but how would I ever find Sister if I was too chicken to tackle this?

Her lips twitched as if she had just watched the hook catch in my mouth and was already reeling in line. "I sort of cotton to the idea of a little vacation. Based on what I've seen so far, I'm optimistic that you can manage. We'll give it a while and see."

"But—" Why hadn't I kept my mouth shut? Had to go and talk her into hiring me, didn't I? The very thought of cooking for people used to Lorena's miracles had me stone-cold terrified. "Um, it's not that I don't want to help you . . . "

"Oh, pish. You're plenty smart enough to handle this, Eudora." She called me Eudora—got the story of my name out of me before I knew what was happening—and from her, it actually sounded right. Fitting, as if I could lay claim to that sort of dignity. That kind of strength.

So . . . courage. Maybe I'd exercise a little of it and ask her the question that had been bugging me. "So why exactly are you two not speaking? Six months is a long time, you know."

"You're telling me. Man was never much for words, but I like a good chat of an evening. House is real quiet. He doesn't make much noise. Even quit belching. Never thought I'd miss that."

I goggled. "You still live together?"

She looked at me like I was a half-wit. "Only got one house. Already told you there's no motels around here." Her mouth pursed. "Not that I'd set foot in one, mind you. I'd sooner start selling cigarettes and beer."

Oh. I was definitely not in Kansas anymore, Toto.

But back to the point. "Isn't it . . . awkward?" I was trying to picture day after day sharing a home that way, living in a state of . . . what? Armed truce? Could they leave notes? Were there separate bedrooms?

She chuckled. "You get used to it. Oh, I'm not saying it wasn't miserable at first, being so mad at each other. The air was like a tornado back then, whipping around so full of bad energy that a body could barely get a breath, but—"

"What?" I dared.

"It went from full-out, can't-be-in-the-same-room kind of mad, all I-leave-when-you-show-up, door-slamming fury to, I guess you'd call it an armistice."

Armistice. I'd never heard a human being use that word before. It's a World War I throwback, the stuff of Victorian novels and a bygone sense of chivalry. Of elegant manners.

Not one thing in common with *rat bastard*. "You declared peace?"

"You ever spent much time around the two of us, you'd know better." Then she smiled. "No, it was more a rock-hard *you-are-beneath-my-notice* kind of thing. On my part, at least. Him, well, I think it was mostly just rock-hard head. Which hasn't changed in fifty-three years, I might add."

"Fifty-three years. Wow." I couldn't even begin to imagine it.

"Yeah."

And then I had her. A note that could only be called fondness, tinged ever so faintly with regret. "You still love him."

"Of course I do. Changes nothing."

Okay. I thought I was beginning to grasp this, but—"Why not?"

One eyebrow arched. "Life isn't that simple, girl. He's wrong. He . . . hurt me. And he'll choke on his pride before he'll admit it."

"A driver's license is worth going so long not speaking?"

She seemed taken aback, maybe that I knew so many details, but she didn't comment on that. "Not just a license. A woman. A betrayal."

A woman? Okay, now I was behind her one hundred per cent. One hundred ten. "Rat bastard." Then, for good measure, "Slut."

"Man won't apologize. Not that I'd accept it."

"Of course not. *I'm sorry* won't begin to cut it." I was enraged on her behalf.

But she only stared at something I couldn't see, her face filled with sorrow.

How would I feel about Jelly in six months? Would it still hurt? Probably not. It really didn't hurt all that much already. "Men and sex. Too much trouble," I said.

She gasped. "Bite your tongue. I never said I was done with sex, and you certainly better not be."

Oh, lordy, I was not at all ready for that mental image. "But—"

"The point is not the sex so much. It's that he chose Glory. Nothing could hurt worse."

Glory. The woman was *Glory????* I couldn't even begin to picture the warrior I'd left being involved with the Texaco man next door. *Eww.*

"Enough of that." She rose. "Finish up, and we'll get started preparing for tomorrow." She glanced over at Alex, who had already cleaned one plate and started on another, though I had no idea where she put it. Baby Alex must have been hungry. "You, too, Alexandra."

"Huh?" Alex was, as she had been except for when Jeremy was over for lunch, staring out the window. When Jeremy meandered out of the bay, you could practically see her melt, as though she was merely a teenager with a crush and not a mother-to-be who was far from home.

I wanted to remind her about the perils of the male of the species, but if she hadn't learned anything from Pretty Boy, I wasn't optimistic. And, to be fair, Jeremy was his polar opposite. Also cute as all get-out. At lunch, Alex had dreamed up any number of reasons to stray by the booth where Val, Jeremy and his dad and grandfather sat right across from the kitchen.

Speaking of which, did no one around there notice how often the not-speaking grandparents stole glimpses of each other?

"You'll help Eudora."

"Help with what?"

"Earth to Alex," I said. "Breakfast tomorrow. Lunch."

"What about them?"

She was so gone. Jeremy was toast.

"You'll assist Eudora with the prep for tomorrow's meal."

"Are you kidding? Does anyone cook anymore?" She caught herself. "Besides you, I mean. This stuff is fantastic."

"You cannot rear a child properly without home-cooked meals."

"What makes you say . . . " Alex's voice trailed off as she noticed me shaking my head.

"Jeremy may be clueless, kiddo, but you can't hide that baby forever. I'm surprised you've done so this long."

"I wasn't exactly . . . "

My snort didn't make her one iota happier.

Lorena placed one hand on Alex's forearm. "My grandson has a good heart, but he's only eighteen. Still a boy, while you are a woman now. Years aren't the benchmark," Lorena said. "Motherhood is. It changes you forever."

So Alex was more mature than me? Lorena had a point, though. I was dependable and conscientious, however unglamorous that made me, but I hadn't even signed a lease since Sister died, still waiting to find that perfect spot . . .

Home. Not that I'd know much about staying in place.

"But what if I can't keep it?" She had tears in her eyes.

"Where is your family?" Lorena asked.

"Doesn't matter. They don't want me." I saw in her desolation that she really believed it. Maybe even a grandchild might not change that?

She was like me. Like Val. Alone. Her relatives might be living while mine were not, but the world was full of families who hit wide of the Brady Bunch mark.

"Do they know?" I asked her softly.

She nodded. "My stepwitch and my dad wanted me to get rid of it." She blinked several times, then lifted her chin. "I wouldn't."

"Is he the father?" Pretty Boy. I couldn't call him Nicky.

"He says no, but he's wrong. I've never been with anyone else." The tears she'd been battling spilled over.

And it was me who was toast. I was far from the ideal savior for this girl, but it seemed I was all she had. "It'll be okay, Alex." I covered her hand with mine across the booth. "We'll figure out something." I didn't know how, but that was for later. "You just go take your nap, okay? For the baby's sake," I hastened to add. "Got to keep your strength up."

"Come with me, Alexandra," Lorena said, and wrapped her arm around Alex's thin shoulders. "There's plenty of time to decide." She glanced back at me and nodded as if she approved of my behavior.

When they were out of sight, I let my head sag against the back of the booth.

But when Jeremy popped out of his bay for his ten-times-an-hour check of the store windows, I managed a convincing smile and sign language to reassure him that Alex was indeed fine.

Then I got up and went back to work.

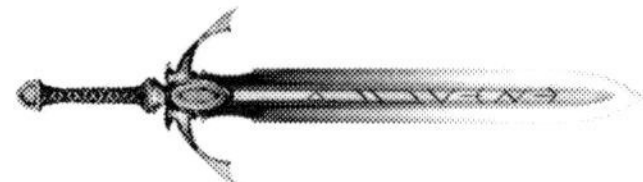

Ohmigosh. The RV. How freaking cool it was.

Okay, so it was really more of a trailer that had to be towed behind a truck than some streamlined house on wheels, but it was our own little abode.

Except its tires were flat. And even if they weren't, I didn't have the truck to haul it, but still . . .what I couldn't have done with something like that.

I had to give Alex credit. While I was running the store that afternoon, she had taken a little nap, but first, amazingly enough, she'd made a stab at some cleaning. There might be hope for us.

The place dadgum sure needed it. Lorena and the rat bastard hadn't used it, she said, since they'd stopped speaking. They used to take it to the mountains in New Mexico, she told me. Boy, did my brain start clicking over that. Sister just kept those clues coming.

The store and station were closed on Sundays—something I could not imagine—and sometimes, she said, they would just lock up on Saturday, too, and go fishing or to see their grandbabies who lived out of state.

The dust in this trailer and the flat tires told the whole tale. Glory had a lot to answer for. More, it seemed to me, than the rat bastard. I could not imagine what he saw in her. Not after comparing fried okra to MREs.

I stopped dead in my tracks. Could Lorena still be cooking for him at home? Oh, surely not. Surely . . . I couldn't ask. I didn't want to know that a woman I had begun to admire deeply could be so foolish.

Men. They are the undoing of us. I certainly couldn't hold myself out as a shining example of wisdom.

Isis liked this place, I could tell. She'd already sniffed out the kitchen area, though we would be having a chat about where cat paws belong. Which was not on top of the counters—such as these counters were, about all two feet of them. Okay, eighteen inches.

This was the playhouse I used to think I would give up my dreams of a pony for. Stove, refrigerator, booth table that made into a second bed. Bathroom—with a shower!—and, way up high, a double bed.

Perfect for one person, okay for two if they were close. Which, of course, Alex and I were not.

"Pea."

"What?"

Alex emerged from the bathroom. She'd changed her clothes and looked . . . cute. Odd, yes, in a denim jumper Lorena borrowed for Alex from her daughter Millie, but sweet. Elfin, not some Goth wannabe.

"Jeremy wants me to go with him to meet some of his friends." Her face was strained with misery. "You have to tell him I can't. That you need me for—" She shrugged and scanned the trailer. "Something. I can't go."

She'd been so excited earlier. "Why not?"

"Look at me!" she nearly screamed. "I'm dressed like a dork."

"We'll get you something else soon, I promise, but you can't expect to look like you used to before." Bless her heart. It had to be hard, all the changes in her body. "Anyway, Jeremy would find out sooner or later. He deserves better than to be lied to."

"What do you care? You won't be around long, anyhow," she muttered. "And I don't know where I'll end up once you ditch me. I don't know why you couldn't have just left me alone." She wheeled, grabbed the door handle. "I was doing fine with Nicky, no matter what you thought." She was halfway out the door when she paused. Looked back. "He loved me once. He could have come around in time, once he saw his son."

"You know you're having a boy?" I asked, since I didn't have the first idea where to begin explaining all the ways in which she was wrong about Pretty Boy.

But only empty air was there to hear me.

I refused to sit down. Nothing good ever comes of sitting still in troubled times. All you do is think your way into a funk.

Meanwhile, dust awaited me.

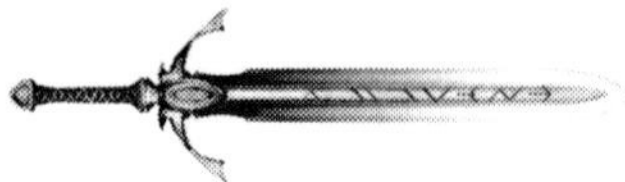

By the end of my second day, I was flat worn out. Even being a cocktail waitress on stilettos was nothing compared to what a woman twice my age managed every single day.

Lorena was a revelation. Patient, kind, an excellent teacher . . . and tough to the bone. She might have been quiet and reserved, but the woman did not know the meaning of the word quit. I couldn't begin to imagine what she'd been like when she was young; even though she moved more slowly than me, it was all I could do to keep up with her. I was ready for a nap before we even served lunch.

So by all rights, I should have had no trouble falling asleep that night. Alex sure hadn't, curled up with Isis on the short bed made from what would have been the RV's kitchen table. As for Val, I'd seen little of him except that he showed up at the café in time for every meal. I had also spotted him over at the station now and again. I'd have worried more, I think, about what trouble he might be getting into at the station while everyone else was under a car or a hood, but I'd actually seen him with grease under his fingernails before he cleaned up at lunchtime today. Unlikely con man behavior, I'd say. Looked to me like he was really trying to go straight.

I'd caught sight of him earlier joking around with Jeremy, the rat bastard and Jeremy's dad, seeming more relaxed than I'd known him to be since I'd met him. An extended version of that one vulnerable moment I witnessed when he spotted the hawk.

Just because he learned how to pick a pocket as a boy didn't mean he did that anymore. Okay, so he still hadn't explained where he got whatever money he was carrying, but he appeared to be working hard now. I couldn't help but feel sorry for a little boy brought up that way.

I flipped over yet again and punched the pillow.

I could not lie there pretending to sleep one second longer, or I'd scream. I got up and crept out quietly. Over my shoulder, I saw Lorena's house, darkened, and I wondered about the silence.

I had a mind to have a chat with Ray.

Or, better yet, to go see Glory and ask why she did it. Although the image of her shotgun pointed my direction did put a damper on my yen.

But I kept thinking about that sword competition and wondering if I could get her to teach me. Not that I would be around for the festival, but the mental image of a sword in my hand, of being a woman who could wield one, had stuck in my brain and didn't appear to have any interest in leaving.

Past the house, gray with hot pink trim, and the heart-shaped handrails on the front steps. I couldn't help smiling every time I thought of them or the metal silhouettes attached to the side of the house. Two snoozing cowboys book-ending one of a couple dancing close, her skirt flaring at the knee like she was wearing petticoats. The house sat back halfway between grocery and garage. Ray and Lorena should remember that its position meant something.

Love lived there, you could feel it. In a world filled with woe, there is no excuse for wasting love. Somehow, before I left, I would get to the bottom of their situation and fix it, I hoped. I had to try. I just didn't think I could bear to walk off, knowing their standoff might last for heaven knows how long.

People do not seem to understand how easy it is to lose those you love.

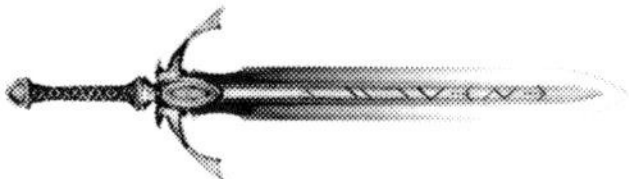

I wandered outside in the light from the big lamp on a pole in the middle of the yard. Moths were dipping and diving, and the drone of cicadas was punctuated by the croaking of frogs. I slapped at a mosquito and pondered going back, but I was tired of tossing. It was dark, though, out past that circle of light.

Then I heard footsteps crunch on gravel. I shielded my eyes to peer at the road and began edging backward, out of sight. Who would be walking down this road in the middle of the night?

The figure stopped. "Red? What are you doing out here?"

"Val?"

"Yeah." He skirted the edge of the light to reach me. "You okay?"

I shrugged. "I guess."

"Why are you out here so late?"

"Can't sleep." All too aware of him standing so close, I was grateful that I'd taken the time to slip into some shorts and a tank top. "What are you up to?"

"Headed back to Jeremy's. Didn't want to wake anybody, so I had my ride drop me off a ways back."

"Where were you coming from?"

"The Rough and Ready." He paused. "You should come with me sometime."

"Thanks, but I'm not that big on bars. For a while, I was a cocktail waitress at a topless joint."

His eyes lit. "Short skirt? High heels?"

"Four-inch stilettos."

"Tell me there was cleavage, and I'll die a happy man."

I couldn't resist teasing back. "A peek of nipple if I wasn't careful when I bent over."

A guttural sound from his throat. "Red—" He reached for me.

I side-stepped. "Nuh-uh."

"Fine." His hand dropped, but his eyes held a glitter that should have had me running. "But you're missing out."

It's only fair that I let him in on the secret, that I am Through With Men and thus immune. "Val," I began "I don't want to hurt your feelings, but I'm not attracted to you."

His eyebrows rose nearly to his hairline. "Sugar, that can't be right."

"Oh, really? You're that irresistible?"

He shrugged. "Hey, no bragging, just simple fact. Women like me. A lot. Even when I don't exert myself."

"But if you do, they fall at your feet?"

"I don't ask for things to be that way." A quick flash of teeth. "Just how it is. I know I'm lucky." He leaned toward me, his voice sliding low. "But I'm also real good, sugar."

I couldn't stifle the laughter that erupted, part amazement at the size of his ego and part pure amusement as I contemplated taking it down a notch.

He laughed with me, and the moment sang with something shiny and bright and . . . fun.

I crossed my arms and shook my head slowly. "I truly do hate to dent that fragile ego, but I won't be viewing you from shoe level anytime soon, and you can forget feeling bad about breaking my heart because you won't."

"Oh, really?" That devil's grin again. "How do you figure that?"

"Because I'm finished getting attached to the male of the species."

The grin widened, but it didn't deter me. "I come from a long line of women who make poor choices, and I have carried on the tradition admirably up to this point, but there's one thing different about me."

"And what would that be?"

"That was Pea. I am now Eudora, and Eudora is Through With Men." I enunciated clearly, to make sure he understood. Then I relented a bit. "Except for their obvious uses."

"Which are?"

"Hey, I appreciate a good orgasm as much as the next woman."

"There are appliances to deal with that." He shook his head. "A poor substitute, you ask me, but okay in a pinch."

"I couldn't agree more, and I did not come unprepared."

His eyes went hot. "Well, well, Red, you surprise me. Can I see it?"

"I'm not finished," I said primly. "There are occasionally other uses for men."

"Not as much fun, I don't imagine. Let me guess—opening jars."

"Please. They make little rubber pads for that."

"Killing bugs?"

"Snakes, maybe. I murder my own bugs, thank you."

"Car repairs, I know that about you already. You can't even remember to fill your tank."

"I could, if certain people hadn't been distracting me."

"Wanna see how distracting I can be?" He leaned so near that I could feel his breath warm on my cheeks.

I stood my ground. And yawned.

Val chuckled. "Okay, okay." He studied me. "Tired but can't sleep, huh?"

"I've been trying."

"I have a remedy that never fails." He held out a hand, started towing me along.

"Where are we going?"

"You'll see." He led me to a small clearing at the far side of the grocery, away from house or RV or garage. He tugged me to the grass. "Stretch out."

"You must think I'm an idiot."

"Don't be so paranoid." He settled himself on the grass beside me.

"I'm not going to roll around on the grass with you, Val. I told you—I am Through. With. Men. Period."

He simply snorted, then tucked his hands behind his head. He couldn't have looked less concerned. "I didn't ask you to roll around. You can't count stars that way."

I frowned. "Count stars?"

"Anyone can count sheep. You good at math, Red?" He nodded toward the star-drenched sky above. "'Cause we got our work cut out for us."

For the life of me, I could not seem to figure him out. The endless faces of Valentine Bonham drew me in deeper than I knew it was wise to go.

But he didn't scare me. Unh-uh. No sir.

I lay back and started counting. The sky was like Lorena's pastry board when she'd spread flour all over it. I never knew there were so many stars up there.

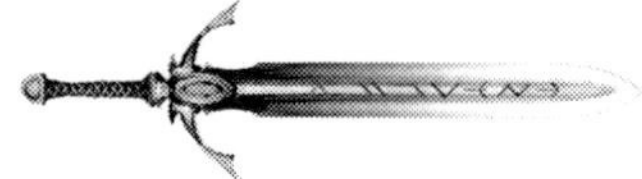

"Some people believe the stars are pathways, you know," I told Val after a while. "Portals where you can communicate with the departed."

Hmm was all he said.

"You have anyone up there you want to contact, Val?"

"Not really."

Okay, so he wasn't feeling talkative. Suddenly I was. "Guess what?"

"With you, the possibilities are endless. Care to narrow it down?"

"Lorena and Ray, the reason they don't talk. It's not just the driver's license. He cheated on her with Glory."

A flicker of a frown, but he didn't say anything.

"I wonder if there's something I can do. I like Lorena and I feel sorry for Glory. Ray . . . I don't know. He's so closed in. He doesn't seem the type. Anyway, I don't get Lorena and Ray wasting what they have by refusing to speak to each other. Living like strangers."

"You think infidelity's no big deal?"

"Absolutely not," I said. "That's part of how I got started on this trip."

"You were unfaithful?" He stared at me.

"Of course not. My boyfriend and I disagreed on whether being faithful meant all the time or just if you didn't get caught."

"Ouch."

"It's okay. I really only miss his mom." I waited a beat. "And his bathroom. It was a seriously great house. Big whirlpool tub, the works."

"No wagon wheel headboards, I bet."

I had to giggle, remembering his face as I'd tried to hide behind a kitten. "Nope. His mom decorated his place. She's a Dallas socialite."

"I get the picture—equal parts Botox, silicone and money. Met a few in my time. Doesn't seem like you'd go for the son of one."

"I had no idea when I met him. Jelly's her wastrel, but he's also her baby. She keeps thinking she'll reform him."

"What's his dad think?"

"Whatever Big Lil tells him to."

"Poor sap. Fall for the glitz and pay forever."

"You ever been married, Val?"

"Are you kidding?" He was clearly horrified. "You?"

"Nope." I hesitated. "No one has asked. Not sober, anyway."

"Don't tell me. While you were wearing stilettos."

His playfulness removed some of the sting. "My customers liked me a lot."

He patted his heart. "Can't blame them."

"But no proposals except from drunks."

He clasped my chin and turned my head to face him. "Then you've been going out with idiots."

I had a silly urge to cry. "Thanks." We lay there in a comfortable silence for a while.

"It's not a stupid risk, you know," I said finally.

"What?" He swiveled his head toward me.

"Searching for Sister."

His lack of response was damning.

"It's a gamble, yes, and I know that." I fixed my gaze on the stars once more. "But I have to try. I—"

When I didn't finish, he prompted me. "What?"

Another step would have led me into treacherous territory, for I was not proud of how I'd handled things with her at the end. Val's listing of his past sins, though, had made me feel like not such a freak.

"I was mad at her." I shook my head. "Mad isn't right. I was furious." My throat tightened, just remembering the last time I'd really lost control.

It was the day she fell and snapped a femur honeycombed with cancer as she was stalking away from me after an argument I'd provoked. A stupid one, at that. One I wouldn't have dared to start in the early years when I was still terrified that Sister would abandon me if I wasn't a perfect angel. Over time, though, she made me believe that we were stuck like glue.

Mostly, we were. So I became a teenager with a mouth full of sass. And Sister, God love her, still didn't toss me out on my ear. Or strangle me before I grew up. We had some rough times, but we weathered them, due in no small part to Sister's patience.

Then cancer came to visit and decided to make itself at home. I was mad, then, you betcha. I used that fury to propel me through the doctor visits where I'd demand answers to questions Sister was too scared to ask. I was full of myself then, flexing my muscles, sure that if I pushed all the right buttons, yelled loud enough, then God Almighty Himself would have no choice but to listen. To fix her.

Because He would not dare take her from me. Better not or—

Well, I never managed my way past the *or*. Anyway, it was on one of those days when I was stomping around, making calls, demanding results, badgering everyone Sister didn't have the strength to push . . . and Sister asked me to clean the top of the refrigerator. I stared at her like she'd lost her mind. She might be dying, for Pete's sake, and she cared about whether anyone could see the film of dust on top of the refrigerator? I told her I'd take care of it later, after the next call, and she insisted that it needed to be done right then. When I refused and started dialing, she made her way to the kitchen and, while I was deep in another harangue, dragged a chair over, planted one foot on the seat and began to mount it.

The snap of bone, I swear to you, was as loud as a gunshot.

I never let my mad go like that again. Not when Jelly was screwing around, not when Big Lil smirked at me, not at my most aggravating customer. I had precious little to cling to after I lost Sister, and not the slightest scrap I was prepared to sacrifice.

An irony, given that I'd lost everything I'd been clutching to me since.

"Why were you angry?"

"She gave up. I was still fighting." And flat refusing to listen to the one thing she begged of me at the end. My regrets still ate at me every single day. After all she'd done for me . . .

The stars above me got wavery, but I had not earned the right to cry.

Suddenly, I couldn't breathe. I leaped to my feet and put some distance between me and Val. I stared up at the sky, praying that somehow she'd hear me. "I am so, so sorry, Sister," I murmured. "I just couldn't give up like that."

Behind me, I heard Val start to gain his feet, but I didn't want to talk anymore, not to him or anyone unless it was Sister. If only I could have the chance to meet her just once more, face to face. I'd told her this a thousand times in my mind. Lit candles in churches. Meditated under trees.

But I'd never known if she heard me.

I took off running and left Val behind.

Frances Marie Sparks Brown (October 17, 1849-January 1, 1934)

Frances Marie Sparks, a native of North Carolina and daughter of Daniel and Kezziah Sparks, married Thomas Brown in 1865. They lived in Grayson County, Texas, before moving to a 410-acre farm near here about 1876. During the 1880s and 1890s, Frances served as a midwife and lay doctor for families in the area. Known as "Aunt Fanny," she often rode 6-8 miles by horseback at night to deliver a baby. Despite her husband's death in 1912 Frances skillfully managed her farm and reared 12 children while continuing to nurse many of her neighbors back to health.

CINNAMON TOAST DREAMS

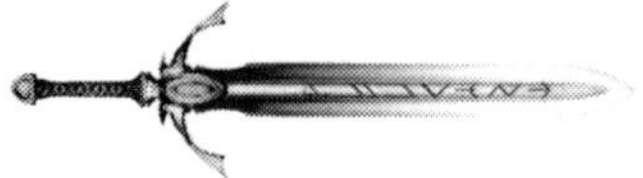

Morning found me in the store long before Lorena. I'd made one more attempt to go to sleep then given up so that Alex would stand a chance of getting a good night's rest. I tiptoed around the trailer gathering clothes, then took a sponge bath in the bathroom of the café.

I only turned on one light over the sink in the kitchen for fear of waking somebody up. By the glow cast into the dining area, I spent some time rearranging the salt and pepper shakers, the assortment of Tabasco sauce, ketchup and sweeteners at each table, trying for something that would put some pizzazz in the joint.

Then I crawled into a booth and catnapped a little until dawn's first faint light woke me up. Ragged and weary, I brewed a pot of coffee and started dragging out the ingredients for pancakes, hoping I remembered everything I'd seen Lorena set out the day before. She hadn't taught me how to do pancakes yet—yesterday had been a lesson on potato salad.

I poured myself a cup of coffee and drank it while dancing the steps of Lorena's minuet, trying to cement in my mind the order of the lunch prep. I thought about going ahead and peeling potatoes, but they'd have turned brown long before time to boil them, I feared. Okra, though—I thought I could maybe chop it and put it in the fridge in baggies until—

No. I'd be lucky to remember the order of things. I was far from ready to wing it. And anyway, I'd have needed to turn on more lights or risk losing a finger. The mental rehearsal would have to do me.

Chop potatoes. Check.

Ditto onions and dill pickles. Check.

Boil potatoes for—

Oh, lordy, I'd have to ask her how long. I did recall that I had to turn the burner down right after the water came to a boil, and—

"What on earth are you doing, child?"

I bobbled my coffee cup and barely avoided spilling it all over me. I whirled to find a bemused Lorena inside the back door.

"I, uh, couldn't sleep. Thought I'd get a head start. Want some coffee?"

She gazed at me so long that I got antsy.

"I set out all the ingredients for pancakes. At least, I think I did. Maybe today you could teach me about making them."

She wasn't going to get distracted. "Why couldn't you sleep? You certainly worked hard enough yesterday."

If I started talking about Sister, I would cry. I had never seen anything that crying improved. "I just had things on my mind. No big deal."

If only she wouldn't study me like that. I busied myself pouring her a cup of coffee. "Only cream, right?" At her nod, I added cream, then stirred. When I walked over to hand the cup to her, the sympathy in her eyes nearly undid me.

"You're lonely, aren't you, child?"

If she kept going in this vein, I would be blubbering. "How could I be? I've got a car chockfull of company." I managed a weak chuckle. "Shoot, I've hardly had a minute to myself since the day I left Austin."

Those too-seeing eyes never left me, until I was ready to beg for mercy. Finally she turned away and tied on her apron. "For pancakes, you begin with the dry ingredients. Come over here and watch."

I breathed a huge sigh of relief and approached her side. "How much flour do you need?"

"I couldn't tell you; I don't measure when I cook. I just eyeball it, then judge by the consistency when the batter is mixed."

I resisted a groan. That left way too many points in the process for me to screw up. "I'll get some paper and a pencil. Maybe you could let me measure what you assemble."

She placed one hand over mine. "No, dear. You're a smart little thing. You'll catch on. Just trust yourself."

So much of my life had been winging it, and I was weary of the constant need to dance around, trying to find someplace to light.

But Lorena was demonstrating confidence in me, and I hated to disappoint her. And anyway, she'd called me a smart *little* thing. Shoot, the novelty of that had to be worth something. No one had called me little in a very long time. "All right," I said dubiously. "I'll try."

And so the day began.

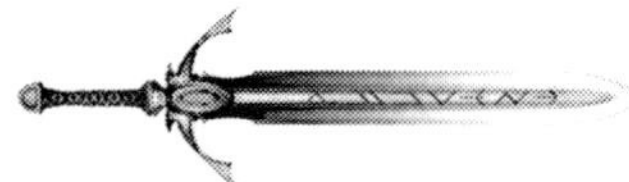

That evening, after closing, I should have been exhausted, and I was, but I was also jazzed. I'd messed up half the batch of pancakes I'd made, but the other half were dadgum near perfect. I'd also started making plans to rearrange some of the stock on the store shelves to increase sales, though I hadn't discussed that with Lorena yet.

I had the itch to brag, to celebrate, but there was nobody to do it with. Lorena knew, of course, and she'd puffed up my chest with her compliments. Val was nowhere in sight, and when I'd asked Alex if she wanted to hang, she'd said she would, but I could tell she really wanted to be with Jeremy.

So it was just me, and I needed to move around. I decided to explore this odd little burg I'd landed in. I snagged Isis from the RV and took her along. She and Alex were so tight these days that I wasn't sure whose cat she was now, but I wasn't ready to give her up.

I went in the opposite direction from where we'd driven, well, okay, been towed, into town. The evening was still quite warm, but trees lined the road, and the shade was more than welcome. It was a novel experience for me, just to walk with no particular destination. There was little traffic, but I got a particular thrill when two different pickups and a car passed me and inside each one was someone I'd met at the café. They nodded at me or waved, and a little further down the road, a lady whose house I passed called out to me from the porch. I couldn't remember her name, but she sat in her rocking chair and told me how glad she was that I was helping out Lorena.

Visiting, I was visiting. Just like we were neighbors. I couldn't get over the feeling.

Maybe a mile down the road from the café, I spotted a little cemetery and wondered if that might be where Lorena's people were buried. It was a sweet place, small and tree-shaded, neat as a pin. I was not comfortable with death and had never voluntarily entered a cemetery, but this place was different. Peaceful and serene. You could almost feel the love, the respect for tradition.

I wondered if Sister would have liked to be buried in a place like this.

Which was just stupid to think about. If she'd wanted a headstone, she wouldn't have insisted on being cremated. I did as she'd asked, but I hated those ashes, couldn't wait to be rid of them. I couldn't bear the thought that the woman who was everything to me had been put through fire after everything else she'd suffered. Trying to figure out what to do with them had made me about half-crazy. I couldn't stand to keep them and think of her that way, but I didn't want to part with her, either.

Big Lil, of all people, had solved my problem. She'd taken charge when Jelly had told her how paralyzed I was by the decision and had made arrangements for me to spread them over the ocean off South Padre Island. Had actually chartered a boat and ushered me out there and, when I faltered, had helped me survive sticking my fingers in there and holding what was left of Sister in my hand.

The letting go was awful.

She's free now, Big Lil had told me. *In the end, that's all any of us want.* I latched onto her reasoning with everything in me because I thought I'd lose my mind if I didn't.

Whatever complaints I might have about Big Lil, however little we had in common or how eager she was to see me go from her son's life, I will always owe her for that one act of kindness. It isn't always the best thing to go easy on folks. Big Lil made me face a hard thing, and I learned I could survive it.

As I looked around this place, I wished Sister's body could have rested somewhere like this, nestled in the bosom of family. Some place I could have visited and cared for. Put out poinsettias at Christmas and a flag on Memorial Day and July 4th. Special flowers on her birthday in January. I guess Mama had been cremated, too, because we never visited a grave, but then, we were always on the move. I was too little back then to know what all was going on, and I never asked Sister when I got older, so once she was gone, it was like I never even had a family. My pitiful store of memories was all I possessed.

Folks in Jewel took good care of their loved ones, I could see. Many of the graves had flowers planted, not just plastic ones stuck in a vase. Some of the graves were really old and gone wild, but very few of them.

I decided I would ask Lorena about her maiden name so on my next visit, I could locate her people. Maybe pull a weed or two, if she hadn't beaten me to it.

In the meantime, I found some Cashwells and stopped for a minute to pay my respects.

Then, ready for sleep at last, I retrieved Isis from her prowling and headed home. Or back, more accurately.

I could call it home for a little while, though.

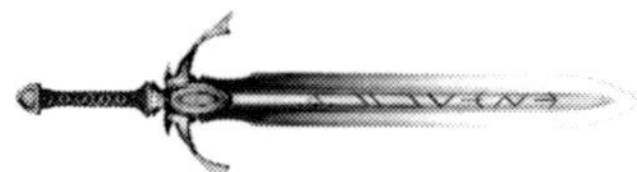

The next morning was a banner day for me. Lorena actually sat out front and visited with customers for a few minutes at lunchtime.

I only managed to scorch one batch of okra. The potato salad was pretty dadgum good, if you ask me.

Lorena had an interesting system set up. The price was the same every day, five dollars, so folks paid at the beginning, inserting their money in a metal box decorated with cowboy-on-bucking-bronco cutouts right next to where the plates were stacked at the beginning of the buffet.

People could have cheated, maybe, but I could tell by watching that they didn't want to. Lorena had the respect of one and all. I watched her and marveled. She knew everyone's children and grandchildren and parents, always took the time to chat with each one while still keeping the food coming.

Every dish on the buffet line was cooked fresh, and the smell was out of this world. Somehow there was always okra, golden and crisp, and rolls hot from the oven. Most of the vegetables were grown in

Tommy's and Charlie's gardens. Once they'd all been grown in Lorena's, but she admitted that the demands of the lunch trade had gotten beyond her. During the winter, she told me, she counted a lot on produce she and her children and grandchildren preserved during summer weekend marathons. That's where all those rows and rows of jars of corn, green beans and tomatoes in the storeroom had come from.

She set a hard pace for herself, that woman. I understood completely why the store closed at six. Even a force of nature, as Lorena clearly was, could only put in so many hours on her feet.

I came up with an idea that I thought was brilliant. I told her I wanted her to sleep in one morning, and she seemed excited about it. After heaven knows how many years of having breakfast and lunch ready for everyone else, I wanted her to sleep and sleep, maybe even let me bring her breakfast in bed. She deserved much more than that, but it would be a start. She was the most admirable woman—make that person—I had ever met.

I could not begin to imagine what Glory had been thinking. I wanted to give the rat bastard Ray a piece of my mind, except men like him kinda scared me. Not because he was mean or anything, don't get me wrong. It's just that I had spent very little time in my life around men like him, real fathers. Men in charge, so sure of themselves, so certain of their place in the world. My world had been mostly comprised of women.

Still, I had a powerful urge to get right in his face and make him explain what on earth he was thinking to get involved with someone like Glory, however intriguing she might have been, when he was married to a woman as close to a saint as I ever hoped to encounter. So far, though, I hadn't worked up the nerve.

"Eudora."

I snapped out of my daydreaming at the sound of Lorena's voice and realized that I was about to burn the okra again. I grabbed for the basket in which it was frying and yanked it toward me too quickly. Grease spattered on the front of the apron she had forced me to wear. It popped on the skin of my arm and on hers—

Hands as quick as her wits, Lorena snatched the basket at the same moment she pushed me aside to protect me.

"Come here." I scrambled to see if she was hurt.

"Hush, child. I'm fine. Let me look at your arm."

It stung only a little. I shrugged it off. "I am so sorry. I didn't mean to—" My voice trailed off as she competently emptied the basket in the trash and calmly started another batch, which pained me greatly, knowing just how much work preparing each one was.

"I'm sorry. I'm an idiot. I don't know why I thought I could do this."

"Don't be ridiculous," she snapped. "You will do fine, just fine. Have some faith in yourself, Eudora."

What I heard in her voice was a confidence I wished I could share, and also a little disappointment, like maybe she'd been looking forward to the treat of sleeping in. I looked at her and realized it must be hell to be the strongest person around, the Rock of Gibraltar for not only a family but a whole town.

I studied her hands, knuckles swollen with arthritis. I felt how much my own feet ached and thought about year after year of standing all day, only to have the man you loved rip away every last bit of comfort you had. A hard life is bearable when there's love in it. Love softens the edges, takes you away for a bit.

"All right, I'll do it. Soon, but not just yet." There was no choice. I'd promised. I'd failed at too much, and I might screw this up, too, but I'd go down swinging.

Lorena ducked her head and busied herself with the next batch of okra. I looked over her head and noticed that Ray was focused on her with his forehead all wrinkled up. Then he darted a glance at me and surprised the living daylights out of me by giving me a nod, his expression conveying approval and maybe even some respect.

Never in a million years would I understand why he hadn't taken steps to clear the air before they lost more precious time.

I would screw up my courage and ask him soon.

But for the moment, I had okra to fry.

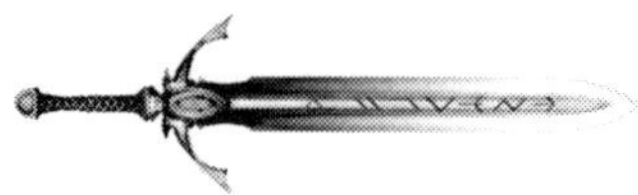

The next day, I graduated to pie crust. In all my life, I never expected to love cooking, but under Lorena's patient hands, I was actually becoming pretty decent at it. Imagine that.

It wasn't as though I'd never cooked, I don't mean that. When Sister was working to support us, I would come home from school and have something on the table when she arrived. It was a limited menu, though, learned from the Junior Cookbook handed out in the six weeks spent in my first fifth-grade class. I had three that year.

Best I recalled, Mama wasn't big on cooking. We could seldom afford to eat out, but there were a lot of sandwiches and boxed five-for-a-dollar macaroni and cheeses. Iceberg lettuce with mayonnaise—only for us, it was store-brand Miracle Whip—on it. Every once in a while she'd splurge and mix ketchup and a little hot dog relish in it to make French dressing.

The next night, supper might be leftover French dressing scooped up with saltine crackers, and Mama would call it party dip.

So when I learned to make exotic fare like Vienna sausage wrapped in a canned biscuit, I thought I was pretty hot stuff. To say nothing of the one year I got to be in Camp Fire Girls for an entire semester and learned how to make a complete meal in tinfoil. Sliced potatoes, carrots and onion over a hamburger patty, salted and peppered, then tucked tight in foil and cooked in the oven as a substitute for coals . . . I thought I was Betty Crocker her own self.

I couldn't resist sometimes, though, a little experimenting. The time I added Velveeta was not my most sterling success.

But Sister didn't complain. And she'd always thank me, however awful the results might be. I understood, however, that we didn't have enough money to be wasting food, so my era of experimentation died young. Best to stick with the tried and true, even if we ate a lot of the same thing over and over.

On Sundays when Sister didn't have to work, we had a ritual. Most mornings, Sister was up before me. I usually had to get myself off to school and take care of myself afterward until she got home. I knew not to answer the door, and we seldom had the money for a phone, so she didn't have to tell me not to let callers know that I was home alone.

But Sundays, Sister slept in whenever possible. And when I heard her stir, I had my specialty ready for the oven.

Cinnamon toast, with sugar as thick on top as I could mound, lots of bright yellow oleomargarine smeared beneath, completely covering the bread. It was so sweet your teeth would ache as you bit into it, hissing and doing that pant where you're trying to rescue your scorched tongue. There is nothing that burns quite like hot sugar.

But boy, it was good.

I'd bring it to Sister in bed, along with coffee I'd learned to brew just the way she liked it. She'd let me have some, too, though mine was mostly milk. I'd perch cross-legged on the bed beside her, and we'd talk and talk, all the words we'd had to store up during the week because she was so tired by the time she made it home, and she still had to check my homework. Then it was time for bed because I had to be rested for school the next day.

But on Sundays over cinnamon toast was Dream Time, saved for talk of all we would do one day, where we would go and what we would see. That's where I learned about New Mexico and Pueblo Indians and told her I wanted to see Scotland. Where we planned out the house we would own and the car that would be new, the rich food we'd eat and the clothes we'd drop to the floor for the maids to pick up.

I understood why the work week was different, but sometimes, in the middle of the night, I'd just go sit on the floor beside her bed and stare at her, trying to see into her mind and hear all that had happened to her that day.

Sister never talked about her problems, not until I was grown, and even then not much, but I could see them on her face. I never forgot what she'd given up not to leave me, and I tried to make it up to her every which way I could.

In the end, of course, she left, anyway. And I deserved my fate for the peace I had robbed her of in those last weeks.

I will make it up to you when I find you, Sister, I swear it.

Please let me find you.

"Eudora!"

I snapped to and realized that Lorena was shaking her head at me. "You are such a dreamer, child. What's going on in that head of yours?"

Dreamer? Me? I hadn't dared to dream since the last time I'd shared cinnamon toast with Sister, a stupid impulse I was positive would bring her back from the grave she was rapidly approaching.

My toast burned her tongue. I don't know how to quit remembering that.

"What is it, Eudora?" Lorena asked softly. "What's wrong?"

I swallowed hard and reminded myself not to discuss the past with her. There was nothing to be gained by it.

Her work worn hands rested on mine. "The piecrust will get tough if it's rolled out too much." Her voice was unbearably gentle. I wanted to lap her up like cream, to bathe in how she had warmed up to me. Been so kind. "Jeremy is so lucky," I blurted. "If I had a grandmother, I'd want her to be just like you."

She was startled. "Well." She cleared her throat. "Well, now." She patted my hands, and I wanted to turn them over and weave our fingers together and hold on.

Something sad slipped over her face, just for a second. "Let's cut this one up, dust the strips with sugar and cinnamon and bake on a cookie sheet for a treat, shall we? Then we'll start on the next one, and you'll get it just right, I'm certain."

I hesitated before the lifeline I wanted so badly to grab. Cinnamon and sugar and a second chance . . . how could that not be a sign?

But I didn't quite see how it was going to get me to Sister.

Still, for the moment, it was enough. I smiled at her and headed for the cookie sheet.

And resolved not to wish for more.

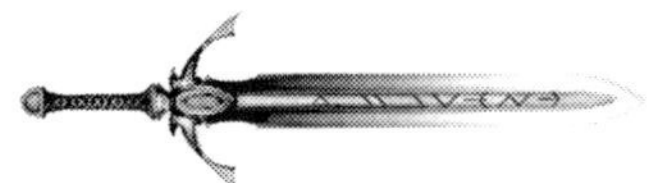

Mah dawgs is tired.

There was a neighbor man once, an old fellow who would say that when he shuffled down the block after getting off the bus. I wasn't clear where he worked—our stay in that neighborhood was even shorter than usual, and it was before Mama died, so I was real young—but that expression tickled me so much that it was still the first thing that popped to mind when my feet hurt.

As they did at that moment. Worse than ever before, even at Fat Elvis. The very idea of crossing the distance between the store and the RV was enough to make me weep.

"Hey, Red, whatcha up to?" Val sauntered near, his hair slicked back from the shower, his clothes obviously fresh. He had taken to spending the entire day with Ray and Jeremy and Tommy, working in the garage, yet to look at him now, he might have been lolling on a beach.

"Trying to get the strength to lay down and die," I answered.

"Whoa, you're not sick, are you?" Then he shook his head. "What am I thinking? You've been on your feet all day. Poor baby."

"You don't know the half of it."

"I was hoping . . . " His gaze swerved away, which surprised me, as Val was seldom hesitant.

"What?"

He shrugged. "I thought maybe you'd be a little itchy for some entertainment by now."

"What kind?" One could say I had my share of entertainment, between feuding but lusty seniors, lovelorn pregnant rebels and sword-wielding gun dealers. Still . . .

"Wondered if you might want to shoot some pool. Looking at you, though, I probably know the answer."

"Is there a way to shoot pool lying down?"

"Well, now, let me think . . . " He scratched his chin. Then grinned. "Nope. But would you want to come with me and just have a drink?" There was an eagerness to him that was at odds with his usual blasé air.

"I wish I could, but—" I lifted my hands. I thought if I didn't sit down in the next five minutes, I would weep.

"No big deal."

But I had the sense that it really was. "Maybe if I could just rest a little."

Val brightened in a boyish expression I had not seen from him before. I got a sudden vision of a younger, idealistic Val.

Except he'd never had that chance, had he?

I touched his forearm. "Let me just—" But I had been standing still too long, and when I stepped forward, a little moan escaped me.

"Hey, you're in real pain, aren't you?"

"I'm fine. Really." I tried to draw myself straight. Concentrated on negotiating the next few yards with some semblance of grace.

But the next thing I knew, I was being swept off my feet.

Literally.

"Val, I'm huge. You can't carry me."

"You're not wrong. You are an armload of woman, that's for sure, Red." He was carrying me, though, and he could move surprisingly well for not being that much taller.

"Put me down, Val." This was embarrassing, even to one who'd long ago accepted that she would never be petite.

"We're almost there."

I kept waiting for him to stagger. "Your back will never be the same."

He chuckled. "Hey, I probably won't sue you for the cost of the surgery. Maybe."

I scrambled to get down. "Stop it. Go away."

He maintained his grip. Guffawed. His fingers were like iron. He leaned in, opened the door and called out, "Alex? You here?"

Only silence greeted us. He stepped inside and towed me along.

I used my free hand and shoved against his shoulder. Hard. "Get out of here. Let me go."

Mirth was still alive in his features. "Red, you're taking this too personally." He got me to the tiny sofa. "Sit down."

When he released me, I flopped on the sofa and crossed my arms. "I'm here now. Thank you." I glared for emphasis. "Get lost."

"Nope. I'm on a mission of mercy, and you're not going to talk me out of it."

Talk him out of it? I was going to shove him down the steps if he didn't scram.

He dropped to his haunches before me, taking off one of my shoes and lifting that foot into his lap. His hands were warm and his fingers strong as he began to massage.

The urge I had to kick him subsided as my eyes rolled back in my head and my bones turned to jelly.

I was going down fast. Too fast. "No." I sat up quickly.

"What the hell, Red? I'm trying to help you."

"Keep your hands to yourself. I know all about you smooth operators."

Once again, however, Val was not what I expected. He settled himself on the floor, Indian style, and cocked his head.

With a grin as wide as Texas on that face. "Do tell," he said. "I can't recall a woman ever refusing a massage from me before." He leaned forward, his voice lowering as if sharing a confidence. "You really should have waited just a little longer, Red. You didn't get a representative sample of the goods." His eyebrows waggled.

He was enjoying himself so much that I was finding it difficult to hold onto my outrage. Val was nothing if not a charming devil. "So you say." I shrugged elaborately, getting into the spirit of things. "Men tend to exaggerate their prowess often, in my experience." Which was, of course, more limited than I would ever confess to a rake like Valentine Bonham.

The fire of competition sparked in his eyes. "Oh, Red." His voice was syrupy with fake pity. "Red, Red, Red." He uncoiled with a lithe grace that—okay, sue me—had my attention.

Through, Eudora. Through. With. Men. Remember?

"Stay right there." One long finger pointed straight at me.

"You've challenged my manhood, my honor and—" It was clear that he was getting a real kick out of this. "My skill at making a woman feel—" A look that could only be called smoldering, even though I knew it was fake "—verrry relaxed. So we will have ourselves a little wager."

I hauled myself straighter.

"Unh-unh-unh," he chided. "Put your feet back up and chill. It's a harmless bet. If I make you feel . . . recharged—" That eyebrow waggle again, so dang cocky. "Then you come play pool with me."

"And if you don't?" I asked.

"But I will, so it's moot. And you win, either way."

"How do you figure that?"

"Even if I fail, you can't possibly feel worse than you do now, and I promise you will feel much better."

"You're very sure of yourself."

"Hey, what can I say? I'm gifted." His expression was unrepentantly bursting with ego and good cheer. "Lie back, *mademoiselle*, and prepare to be astonished." He swept me a bow that would have done a courtier proud. Then he started rummaging through the cabinets, whistling.

The aggravating thing was, he was probably right. I didn't see how I could lose. I lay back on the too-short sofa as if I was Cleopatra awaiting her servants.

Except for one niggling thought. When, exactly, had the asp shown up in the story?

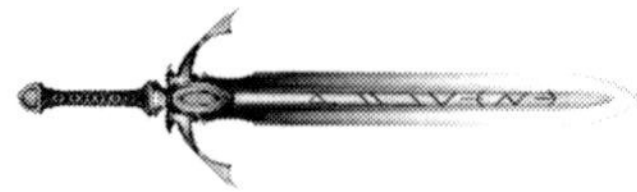

So there I was, hovering just inside the door of the Rough and Ready, but all I was ready for was to rabbit.

All because Val challenged me to spend an evening having fun. Won a wager by reducing me to the approximate texture of overcooked pasta after he finished with my feet. Of course, then I napped for an hour. He must really have wanted some company to have waited for me.

"You played pool before?" he asked, leaning close.

"No. Yeah." I frowned. "Well, sort of."

"Care to translate?"

But I was busy scanning the room and bracing myself.

"Red?"

"Wha—" My eyes focused on him at last. "Oh. Um, the guy I, um, left had a pool table. He showed me a little." Mostly about what two people could do on green felt besides shoot pool.

"Come on." He grasped my arm and towed me behind him.

"Hey, Val. Wanna play some cards?" Carl Vincent, whom I'd met at the café.

"You go ahead." I slipped from Val's hold and slid a glance toward the door.

"Fun, Red. It won't hurt you, I swear it." He shook his head at Carl. "Not tonight, friend."

Carl visibly wilted. "I—you said I could have another chance to win back my money. Darlene is pretty hacked off about me losing the trailer payment."

My jaw dropped. "You let him gamble away his house payment?"

"Like I could stop him," Val muttered.

"You go give him another chance, Valentine."

"I brought you here so you could relax, Red. Have some fun."

"How could I possibly enjoy myself, knowing that Carl can't make his mortgage? Do you know how far along his wife is?" I bunched my fists on my hips.

"All right, all right. But what are you going to do in the meantime?"

What if his commitment to going straight was wavering? "Why, I'm going to play, too, of course."

A cheer went up from the assembled group. Delbert Wallace leaped to his feet and pulled out a chair. "Here, Eudora." Color was rising up his neck, and it was kind of sweet. "You can sit by me."

I was a lousy gambler, but I felt responsible for Val's soul. "Thank you, Delbert."

Before I got the chance to settle, Val tugged me instead into the chair next to him. "The lady isn't familiar with poker. She can help me play."

"I want to play my own hand."

Val sighed. "Of course you do." He rolled his neck. "Okay, Carl, deal." He glared at Carl. "And pay attention to what you're doing this time."

How sweet. He was worried about Carl. I knew he was going straight. "That's nice of you," I leaned over and whispered.

His stare could have melted lead. "Shut up, Red."

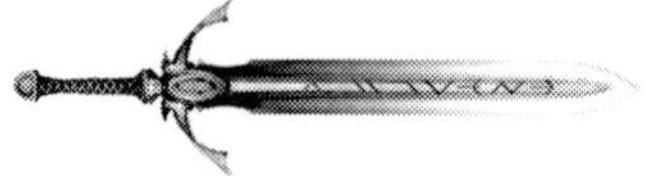

"Red," Val whispered in my ear a while later, "Stop trying to throw the game to Carl. You're not that good."

Well, of course I wasn't, but I couldn't seem to quit winning myself, and with every hand, Carl's spirits sank lower. "I have to do something," I hissed.

Val had an absolutely dead-solid poker face, but he let a blazing threat shine through his eyes, just for a second, as he looked at me. "I've got it covered," he said through clenched teeth. "Back off. You're screwing me up. Just play your hand."

"Hey, you two," complained an unpleasant guy named Brad. "There's a game going on here. Get a room if you can't leave each other alone." He snickered, and another player, whose name I hadn't caught, followed suit.

I did not like those two. They reminded me too much of the fanny-pinching lousy tippers I once served. "Maybe you two should get your own room. You seem mighty cozy."

Val's groan was quickly lost in the screech of Brad's chair on the grungy floor. Brad leaned over the table, palms down, glaring at me. "Watch your mouth, bitch. You're a stranger here. We have ways of dealing with folks who don't belong."

Instantly, I was reminded of the graffiti on Glory's wall. I stared at him, mentally trying to superimpose him over the figures leaping into the pickup that morning. His hair was the right color, a dark brown. I couldn't be sure, but I'd still met his type far too often. "Yeah? You don't happen to have spray paint cans in that penis substitute pickup of yours, do you? Keep it handy for scribbling filth on walls?"

"Red," Val warned. "Jesus."

"And what if I do?" Brad was halfway across the table now. "What are you going to do about it? Run tell the crazy bitch?"

Glory was no crazier than half the people I'd met over a convenience store counter. Beats me, though, why I felt the need to defend her. I didn't like one bit what she had done to Lorena, but this smacked of persecution. I couldn't hold still for that. "It was you, wasn't it, spraying graffiti on her building? There are laws against that.

Maybe I'll call the cops."

His face filled with ugly color, and he lunged across the table. "You have no idea who you're screwing with."

"Shit, Red!" Val dragged me out of my chair, shoving me behind him. "Back off, Brad."

"Hey!" I tried to elbow past Val. "I'm not afraid of him."

Val wheeled on me, his own face hard with fury. "This is not the time to be an idiot. Go out to the car."

I glared back, and he swiveled me around. "Now, goddammit. Before you get us both killed."

I'd let Jelly walk all over me. I'd swallowed a lot of guff from customers for the sake of my job. I was sick and tired of being a doormat.

But I didn't want Val hurt on my account, and it was clear that he was in this battle and had no plans to leave.

I cast a glance over his shoulder at Brad, who was literally trembling with fury in Carl's hold. Around us were restless mutters, and I had seen a club erupt into violence before. Male pride and alcohol are a bad mix.

But I did hate giving in to this creep.

"For you." I spat the words at Val. Looked back at Brad and let my expression tell him what I was trying to have the sense not to say. He was a redneck of a type I truly wished I never had to meet again, an insecure short man who made himself feel bigger by knocking everyone else down. He would have made fun of me in junior high, and he would have been the first to grope at me when I got breasts. And he would have bragged to all and sundry that he'd done a whole lot more.

In that instant, the ugly side of my mad was pushing very hard to break past my good sense.

"Please, Red. I don't want you hurt." Val's tone, in the midst of all the violence simmering in this room, was gentle and earnest.

It broke the back of my fury. So I backed down.

Again.

The taste of it was bitter, though, and if I spared Bigot Brad one more glance, I would not be able to do as Val was asking.

So, with a throat jammed full of humiliation, I turned away and began my walk toward the door.

"I'm not the only one ready to run Glory out of town, you skinny bi—" Brad's yell was cut off abruptly.

And, I hoped, painfully. But given that I was not the one dealing out the pain, that was cold comfort. As I crossed the filthy floor of the Rough and Ready, that was the closest I'd felt in a long time to the taunting I used to get as the new, gawky misfit, the butt of the joke in more schools than I liked to remember.

When Val caught up to me just outside, I shrugged off his hold. "Carl hasn't won his trailer payment yet," I said.

"What?"

"You have to go back in there. I'm not even going to think about how you can be so sure you can make him win."

"I'm not letting you out of my sight. Carl will be fine."

Tears of shame blinded me. "If I have to walk away from that . . . *creep*—" I was nearly growling. "Then you have to go back and make sure Carl winds up with his mortgage money. Or I will."

"Exactly how do you propose to do that?"

"Give him my winnings."

"You are insane. Anyway, he won't accept charity." But I guess he could see that I was dead serious. He uttered a few choice words and raked his fingers through his hair. He exhaled sharply through his nose, but his shoulders lowered a fraction, telling me I'd won. "Completely freaking insane. Maybe you should just add Carl to your menagerie." He threw up his hands before settling them on his hips. "All right. On one condition. I give you the keys to Jeremy's truck, and you get your fanny out of here now and go straight back to the RV. No trips to Glory's, no lurking in the parking lot. Do not pass Go, do not collect two hundred dollars." He leaned in so close my eyes nearly crossed. "Are we clear?"

Once again he was reading my mind, and I didn't like it one bit. That little victory wasn't much to brag about, but it was all I was going to get, I could tell. "Yes." He handed me the keys and started to turn, but I touched his forearm. "Thank you."

He snorted and shook his head.

"He just—" I began.

"I understand." His look was a mix of exasperation and wry amusement. "At least, as much as a head case like you can be understood." But his tone was fond.

"Good thing there's nothing going on between us, huh? You'd have your hands full."

"There is a God." His smile was wide and oddly sweet. "Go on home, Red." He headed back inside, and I was left to watch the space made by his absence.

Which was a whole lot bigger than I'd like.

Queen's Peak Indian Lookout

Discovered by white men in 1848. Permanent white settlement began in this region in 1858. Its early history is a long story of Indian raids. In memory of pioneer women, who, in the midst of such dangers, daily risked their lives for others, this monument is erected.

COUNTRY FOOD AND SWORDPLAY

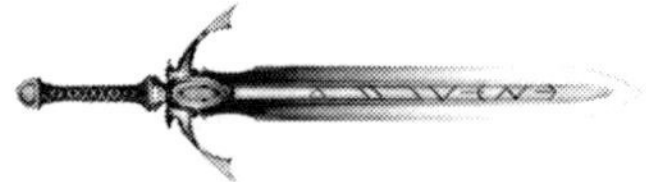

The morning after. How come you just about never hear that phrase used in glowing terms?

It's too bad no one's invented something like shock therapy to make a person remember—in advance—that whatever notion you have when you light out to have fun of an evening, morning will come. And with it, that cranky old scoundrel named Payback.

It was my own blasted fault, though, that I hadn't managed to say no to Val when he tried to lure me to the Rough and Ready. So while I wanted to whimper my way through the morning, I sucked it up and just stayed quiet.

But I was still worried about the threat to Glory. After work, I would have to do something about it. I was not buying that notion that she was a murderer. Crabby and eccentric, yes, but no killer, even if she did like to brandish that shotgun around.

Also, I was through dithering over the notion of swordplay. Somehow or another, I made up my mind, I would convince her to teach me a little before I left. Dark Agnes would have cut Bigot Brad's heart out. I might be no Dark Agnes, but I needed every bit of warrior instinct I could cultivate.

At the café, despite my lack of enthusiasm for being awake, the day went well. No scorched okra, no kitchen burns. *The Goddess of Fried Okra*, old Mr. Conkwright called me. I came around the counter to hug his neck for that. Take that, you homecoming queens. Take that, Jelly's bimbo. I even thought Big Lil might approve. I was no Kilgore Rangerette or Miss Texas, but she did respect competence in a woman.

Not that fried okra would ever pass those collagen lips.

Lorena gave me her own vote of confidence as she left the kitchen for a while during the height of the lunch rush and went to sit with a friend. "I know in my heart that you can handle this, Eudora."

Her faith in me was wonderful. . . if only I shared it. I did exert myself, though, and I was sincerely glad to be able to provide the break for her. That I juggled everything with only minor delays seemed little short of a miracle, but it felt good.

Ray came in for lunch and paused on his way to a booth to stand in the kitchen door. "No part today," he said. "Maybe tomorrow."

I nodded a quick thanks and kept chopping.

Once he was seated, Ray hardly took his eyes off her.

And when he wasn't looking, she was.

This battle of wills between them just had to be fixed. If only I knew how.

Even though I completely understood how much betrayal hurt, my situation with Jelly was different. There was nothing between us, really. Not like these two, with years of history and children and grandchildren. Struggling together and fighting the odds in world where people hardly stay married five years anymore.

There was something very private about the two of them, however, and it held me back from barging into the middle.

But, oh, it hurt me to watch them. To see the sorrow that was a shadow over both. The way she looked at him when she thought nobody saw, like her heart was breaking. How he watched her like she might vanish.

I was glad when lunch was over and he left. That afternoon I passed my hours in the store dusting shelves and was grateful for a decent stream of customers to keep me busy enough not to fall asleep face-first on the counter. Very pregnant Millie came in for milk for her two little ones.

"How are you doing, Eudora?" she asked. Lorena's influence seemed to trump any plans I had for my name. Most everybody had taken to calling me that.

"Fine, just fine. How about you?"

She pressed one hand to her enormous belly and rubbed circular strokes over it. "I am ready for this baby to show up," she said. "I'm hot, I'm fat, I can't sleep for an hour without needing to pee—" Then she laughed.

Laughed.

"It's Mother Nature's training for having a newborn."

One of her two boys skidded to her side then. "Mama, can we have a Popsicle?"

She stroked one hand over his hair. "You'll use a napkin? Not wind up with it all over the car and your face?"

Earnestly, he shook his white-blond hair, and his little brother followed suit. "We promise."

"All right, go ahead." As they charged for the freezer case, she grinned at me. "They'll be a disaster within five minutes. Bet on it."

Her cheer amazed me, and I told her so.

"When you have little kids, you either learn to chill out about what's not important or go crazy. I had all these notions with my first about exactly how things would be." She shook her head. "The big lesson in having children is just how little in life you can really control."

"Did your mother teach you that?"

"I'm not sure my mother has ever accepted that there are things she can't control. If you haven't noticed, there are few times when she chooses to bend on an issue."

She's your mother and practically a saint, I started to say to her, all worked up in Lorena's defense.

But then I saw the fondness of Millie's smile, and it confused me. To me, Lorena was everything perfect and right. Lorena's strength, her firm convictions, they made me feel safe. I didn't want to examine her for flaws.

Okay, so she was the woman who hadn't spoken to her husband in six months—but that was his fault. And if she seemed determined to make me into more than I thought I could be, well, no one in my life had ever believed in me that way. I wanted to be wrong.

So when the little boys raced back, already tearing the paper from their frozen treats, I managed not to really answer Millie. Not that I thought she was being a traitor to her mother, exactly. More that she didn't understand the luxury she had.

Lorena would love her children to her dying breath, would fight for them. She would never leave them lost and floundering.

I grabbed a bunch of napkins, helped her get the kids in the car without too many drips, and returned to clean up the mess, all the while aware of a little kernel of resentment for all that had graced Millie's life, and how lucky she was to be able to make fun of it.

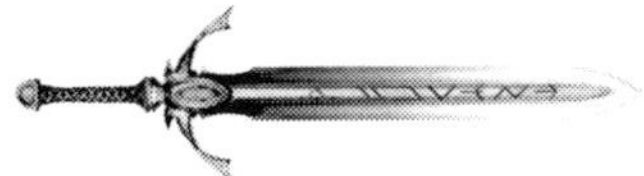

The old bicycle Jeremy's sister Sally loaned me was creaking as I strained to make it up the hill after work. Glory's was just over the top of this rise, I thought.

Yes, she'd thrown me out. No, I wasn't in the slow class on what *Get out!* meant.

But I couldn't shake the feeling that Glory was in danger, even if she'd brought it on herself. I also wanted to know—though I had no idea how I would ever ask—what she had been thinking when she got between Ray and Lorena.

Their situation was not my business, I knew that, but sometimes people can't see what they're doing to themselves. Jewel was not my home, and these people were not my family, but for the first time since Becky Marie, I had gotten involved. I cared. I still was set on finding Sister, but there was nothing I could do about my journey until my car was fixed. I intended to hit the gas the second I had wheels again, but the more time I spent with Lorena, the more I wanted to find a way to make things right there first.

Suddenly, there was Guns 'n' Glory ahead. It was hard to believe that only days had passed since I'd first laid eyes on the portable building with its windows wired like an eighth-grader's teeth. So much had happened since.

I lifted my feet off the pedals. Dragged them in the dirt. Thought about rolling right back down that hill.

Nope. No guts, no glory, excuse the pun. I dismounted from the bike and began to walk it toward the fence, only too aware of the ever-present shotgun. The two dogs with whom I had an uneasy truce. "Glory?" I called out. "Geri? Freki?" Big dogs with big teeth.

"Glory!" I shouted louder, though I didn't kid myself that my voice would carry all the way to the dome. I cupped my hands around my mouth. "Here, Freki. Come take a bite."

At last, a furious barking, growing louder by the second. I

retreated from the fence as they came tearing around the corner, mad-dog slobbering again. "Nice dogs. Remember me, guys? I left the cat at home this time. Good doggies." I mentally kicked my tail for not bringing treats. "Where's Glory? Where's your mommy?"

"I've been called a bitch before, but it wasn't literal, big girl." And there she was, shotgun in hand. "What are you doing here?" She didn't look happy to see me.

I wasn't sure how thrilled I was, for that matter. I had no way to know if she'd even answer my questions about her and Ray. Best not to come right out with them, though, before I scoped things out. "I want you to teach me." I jutted my chin. It wasn't the main reason I'd made the trek, but the more I thought about it, the more I wanted to learn.

"What?" Her brow was beetled, yet I realized anew that Glory was indeed not so ancient as I'd thought. Even attractive, damn Ray's hide.

Eye on the prize, Pea. "Swordplay."

"You're kidding."

"No."

"For the competition in June?"

Everything in me slammed on the brakes. Where would I be in June? "No, I just—I want to learn."

"Why?"

"Because I need to be strong. I guess I want—"

"Guessing won't get it. You got to know, big girl. Know inside yourself that you're strong. It's the only weapon that matters, and no one can teach that to you." She looked me over. "Besides, you got no meat on you. Couldn't even pick up my sword and swing it, bet you money."

I stared at her, stung by the easy dismissal. I thought she would be happy I was here, that I was taking her swords seriously.

She stared back, and I lost heart. "Forget it." I turned and stalked toward Sally's old bike, ready to ride away, to leave this mean old woman behind.

Then I remembered my other purpose for coming. Even if she was mean, she deserved warning. I whirled back to face her. "I think you're in danger, Glory. I don't know if it's those guys who wrote that stuff on your wall."

"I can handle the little pissants."

"But why would they—"

"Big girl," she exhaled in a gust. "You ask too many questions."

"You need to take this seriously. I heard these guys at the Rough and Ready talking about driving you out."

Her eyes went to slits. "It wouldn't be the first time."

"You need to get help. This is harassment, at the very least."

"Just stay out of it." Her voice was gravel-rough. "It's none of your business."

"I'm trying to help you." But she didn't want it; that much was evident.

"Best to steer clear of what you don't understand. You head on back to town now, hear?" She turned and started walking away. Now obviously wasn't the time to be asking about Ray.

"What about my lessons?" If I got her to let me keep coming back, I'd find the right moment. But beyond that, I just really, really wanted to see if I could handle a sword. I could almost feel the weight of it in my hand.

Her head was shaking slowly, as if she couldn't believe my gall, but I could have sworn I saw her lips twitch a little.

A deep sigh. "If you don't beat all . . . " At last, her head lifted. "The store closes at six. You be here at seven tomorrow night."

How she knew I was working for Lorena when folks said she never came to town, I couldn't guess, but Glory was an infinite mystery to me, and maybe that's just how things would be.

In the meantime, while I was waiting for my car to be repaired, at least I'd be learning something besides home cooking.

Country food and swordplay. Life preservers, each in its own way.

I stood there, grinning to myself, until she was already almost out of sight. "Thank you," I yelled at her retreating back, bisected by that silver braid.

She waved at me over her shoulder and kept going.

I hopped back on the bike and, for good measure, rang the bell on the handlebars in salute.

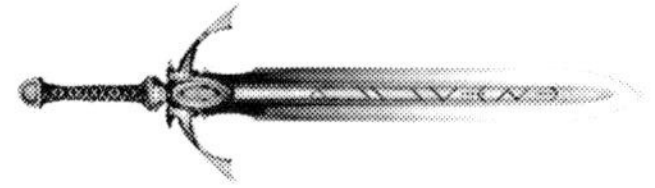

This was nothing like his usual gig, and Val couldn't figure out why he was still hanging around.

The food, maybe. He'd never had better, and that was saying something. He was no stranger to the high life, however temporary his visits to it. Lorena's cooking, however, would linger in memory. And he had to admit that he got a kick, weird as it sounded, out of hanging out in the garage with the kid and his grandpa Ray.

For all Val's extensive, on-the-job training in the way humans ticked, family was the one language he didn't speak. Oh, he'd watched them from afar, listened to his women talk about their own, yes, but that was as near the inner circle as he came.

Until Jewel. Now he was surrounded by one family, and their workings were . . . weird. But nice. Even the not-speaking grandparents.

Actually, they might be the most fascinating of the lot. Listening to the old man communicate with his grandson as much with a touch to the shoulder as a word or watching how, with a minimum of conversation, looks conveyed whole sentences.

Ray was gruff, but his hands were gentle on the boy, and love was in every sound, as present in a grunt or a nod of the head as in entire speeches given by others. He demanded excellence and hard work, but the kid would never appreciate, as Val did, the bounty he gave back by sheer example.

Boneheaded teenager Jeremy had no idea of the riches handed to him on a daily basis. Best Val could tell from observing Ray and his two sons, the line bred true, decent people producing more decent people, content to make it from one day to the next with no expectation of more.

It gave Val the shudders. He had to get out of here before he forgot what the world was really about. He felt the expanding roll of cash in his pocket and smiled. Then frowned. Simply winning at cards without any sleight of hand shouldn't have felt this good.

He was getting soft. Too long without a good con . . . he was starting to itch. Sure, he'd sworn to go off the grift, but what did people do with their time when they lived on the straight and narrow? Where was the challenge? The fun?

He couldn't keep showing up at the Rough and Ready every night to relieve the shitkickers of their currency. Oh, sure, he had run a small con, if you wanted to call it that, by throwing a few games, but that was small-time stuff. A good poker face and a long-range perspective.

He'd always been good at the former.

The latter terrified him. Smacked of planning. Commitment. Thinking of the future, even if it was only a few days.

He liked the high of life on the fly. Adrenaline racing because every turn was a hairpin, every edge razor-thin. Each step a flirtation with disaster. Seducing a good-looking woman in her marital bed. A husband arriving home early.

Oh, yeah. That worked out well last time. Look where it had landed him. Nowheresville.

Another night or two at the Rough and Ready, and he'd have a new grubstake, then he'd part ways with Red and Alex and get back in the game. East Texas had faded in memory, and he could only wonder how he'd lost his mind enough to think he'd ever give up life on the edge.

He was only alive when he was dancing with disaster, daring fate and human nature.

And, nearly always, snagging the win. It was the juice that kept him going, the reason to get up every day. He was different from these people, that's all. Maybe they had something going here, something warm and . . . comfortable.

But Valentine Bonham didn't do comfortable. Some people—most people—needed safety, but not him.

The road was calling him. A few more days, at most, to rest up and take it easy, enjoy being someone he wasn't. To play grease monkey and hang with Ray, to watch for Red's next mishap and ogle those endless legs, and to teach Alex what he could to protect her.

Then life, his life, would begin again.

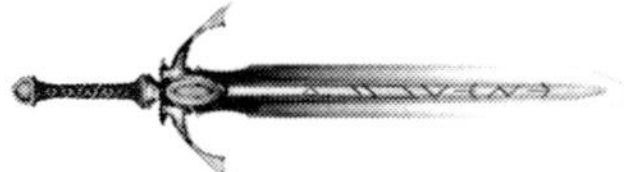

Sally had swapped me the use of her bicycle for a paint job like mine on her toenails. Each time I'd seen her, she'd cast greedy glances at those golden stars on a turquoise background, however ratty they'd become.

So I'd decided we'd have a pedicure party in the RV. Alex had deigned to participate, though it meant skipping an evening with Jeremy. Jeremy's mom begged off, but Millie said she hadn't seen her feet in forever, and she'd like to pretty up before the baby came.

The best part, though, was that Lorena planned to attend, mostly just to watch, she said, but I was of a mind to convince her to dabble just a bit.

What I wouldn't have given for a proper wax bath. I was

determined to improvise one and, to that end, I asked Val to help me with supplies, since the café and store took up most of my hours.

I had candle wax melting in an old crock pot I found in the Employees Only storeroom, iced tea and sodas chilling and bottles of nail polish lined up in a neat row on the microscopic counter. Val had done his best, though he never stopped grumbling. Not all the bottles were new, but I was not about to ask who he charmed them out of. Pickings were pretty slim in Jewel, though he did manage a bottle of startling green in a shade not present in nature. Otherwise, I was limited to your basic red and pink and coral.

I had an ace up my sleeve, however. Sequins I'd unearthed from my trunk, courtesy of a holiday scrunchie intended for my hair. A little bit of time spent picking at threads and, voila! Instant sparkle.

"Am I going to be an elephant like Millie?" Alex asked as she emerged from our tiny bathroom, face blotchy with nerves.

"Of course not," I answered, though what I knew of pregnancy would fit on the head of the last sequin I transferred to a saucer. It was what she needed to hear. Though she was getting noticeably bigger by the day.

"How do you know?" Alex was nothing if not skeptical when it came to me, but I saw the plea in her.

So I did my best. "Millie's husband Leo is enormous, plus she's had two other children."

"So?" She pretended not to care, but she took another nibble at her already ragged nails.

I wanted to grab her hands and say *Stop that!*, but I resisted. "Pret—um, Nicky is thinner and not so tall. You're delicate. Also, it seems to me that it's sort of like blowing up a balloon. The second time, it would expand easier than the first."

She nibbled again, staring in the vicinity of the faded red apples on our curtains. "Whatever." With a lift of the shoulder, she slid past me and walked all four paces to the door.

What she still didn't get, though, is that she could aggravate me but she couldn't fool me. Whether or not I deserved the title as Goddess of Fried Okra, hard knocks had made me the Empress of Nonchalance. The Grand Master of *Ignore Them Before They Ignore You.* No one changed schools as often as I did without learning that defense eventually. I cared too much, of course, but I knew how to cover it up.

"Stars or cherries?" I asked her.

She turned in mid-gnaw. "What?"

"Come here. Sit down. You can be my first customer."

"I don't have any money."

"I'm not asking for any. Tonight is a party," I said to her as I eased her onto the bench and tested the wax again before slipping her right foot into it.

"Ouch!"

I'd already tested the temperature, so I knew she was just being cranky. "Give it a second. It'll feel like heaven in no time."

She was all tensed and furious, her fingers curled around the edge of the cushion in preparation for launching herself off, when a knock sounded at the door.

"It's open," I called out and turned, still gripping Alex's leg.

"Quartermaster Bonham checking in, General."

But I didn't need to hear the voice to know it was Val. Alex's expression was plenty. He had an effect on her unlike anyone else, even Jeremy. With Jeremy, she alternated between lovesick and flirty.

With Val, she simply . . . glowed. "Hey," she greeted him. "Hitler here is boiling my foot in hot wax."

"Tough break, kid." He winked at me. "But better you than me."

She smiled at him eagerly. "You could stay, you know."

His eyebrows winged skyward. "Let Red write bad words on my toenails? I don't think so."

Alex's giggle delighted Val as much as it did me. He lingered, though I wasn't sure why.

"So," he said to me, "The colors work out okay?"

Given that Val was a) a guy, b) had spent hours that afternoon on what he clearly deemed a fool's errand, and c) refused to let me pay him for the supplies, he was a total hero. "They're great. Thank you."

He was jingling change in his pocket, odd for a man who was normally so self-possessed.

"You okay?"

He shrugged. "Absolutely." A pause, then he looked at me. "Can I, uh, see you outside for a second?"

I glanced at Alex's foot. "Could it wait a few minutes? I can't leave just now."

"I don't need you," Alex pointed out, but I could only imagine the mess she'd make of Lorena's trailer if I didn't oversee the removal of the paraffin.

"I guess—" Before Val could finish, we heard Sally's excited voice and Millie's softer one just outside the door.

Val shook his head. "Never mind. No big."

"You're welcome to stay."

Horror bloomed in his features. "A trailer full of women doing weird things to their feet. A really attractive offer, Red, but I'm afraid I'll have to pass."

"What did you need to discuss?"

"Later."

Sally opened the door, and he was gone like greased lightning.

"Eudora, I've decided I want cherries on mine, and Millie is trying to decide between hearts and lightning bolts—"

Sally's chatter dislodged my wondering about Val, and when I saw Lorena bringing up the rear, delight erased whatever traces were left.

Confederate Texas Poet
Mollie E. Moore
(1844-1909)

During the Civil War, wrote poems Texans memorized, cut out of newspapers, sent their boys on the battlefront: About the deaths of heroes, Texans' units, Confederate victories and such topics. She also did social work and nursing at Camp Ford, Tyler.

She was a lively, spirited girl who went horseback riding with a pistol strapped to her side.

After war, became nationally known poet, novelist, columnist. Married a newspaper editor. Led New Orleans society 20 years.

Near this marker site, at old Mooresville (now Proctor) often visited her brother's family.

DARK AGNES IN TRAINING

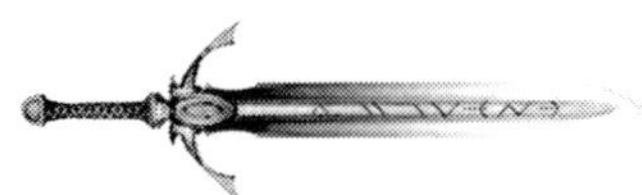

"So explain to me what this has to do with sword fighting," I gasped at the end of my one thousandth pushup. Okay, only thirty, but it felt like way more.

"You need biceps, and your deltoids are pathetic," Glory said. "Face it, Eudora. You are a wimp."

That got me hopping. I rose to my feet and glared down at her. "I have had a long day, slave-driver. Anyway, I don't have all that much time left in Jewel, and we need to get to the main program. I know how to do pushups."

"Couldn't prove it by me. Drop and give me twenty more."

"You should have been a drill instructor," I muttered.

"I was."

My head jerked up at that. "For real? You were in the army?"

Her upper lip curled. "No, Eudora. The real military. The Marines."

Whoa. I worked with a former Marine once. He was one bad dude. Dark Agnes would have been a Marine, I was positive. "How long were you in? Did you ever see action?"

"Twenty, girl. Or I'll add to it."

I propped my fists at my waist and opened my mouth to argue.

"Twenty-five."

"It's just a stupid contest, fans play-fighting." Not that I was competing, anyway.

She arched one brow. "I assure you it is not. Not while I'm in charge."

Oh, boy. The Wicked Witch of the West would be running the show.

"Thirty. Or do you not want to learn about swords?"

"Glory, I won't be here—"

"Goodbye, Eudora." She executed a very formal about-face and walked toward her dome.

My mad was fixing to run away with me. The urge to stomp my foot was just about unbearable.

But oh, how I hated to be a quitter. "Wait." She kept going. "Glory, wait, I'm sorry." No pause, and I remembered our face-off once before. "Please." If there is one thing that will stick in your craw more than saying please to a bully, I do not know what it would be.

"You don't understand," I continued. "I don't have much time. I have a journey to complete." She paused without turning around, and I swallowed hard. "I'll do the pushups back in Jewel, I promise. I just don't want to waste precious time here when I could be learning from you."

"What kind of journey?" she asked, facing me at last.

I hesitated. This woman had no respect for me already. My quest was private, and I didn't really want to share it with her.

"Fine." She began to pivot.

"To find my sister," I blurted.

"What happened to her?"

I stared at the ground, trying to find a good answer, one that would make sense to someone like Glory. Except there was no one like Glory.

Just spit it out, hon. Who's she to call you crazy?

Big Lil had a point. I lifted my head and just said it. "She died, but I know she's out there somewhere. She believed in reincarnation, and it makes some sense, don't you think?" I wasn't really waiting for her to answer but just raced on. "I mean, how else do you explain that sense of familiarity you get with some people or some places except that you've been there before, just in a different body? And anyway, I don't care if you believe me because I am going to find her, I just want to be strong when I do, someone to reckon with like Dark Agnes or even . . . you."

When I finally ran out of steam, she didn't move, just watched me for what seemed like forever. I was the mouse caught in the cobra's gaze, and I couldn't look away even though I was pretty sure I wouldn't like what she had to say.

But what did I have to lose, anyway? She'd already fired me from the lessons.

What Glory did, though, was the very last thing I would have expected.

She smiled. Glory, smiling. "I do believe I like you, Eudora."

What?? "But—" *Aren't you going to make fun of me? Make me feel stupid?*

"We'll settle on ten more pushups now, but you have to swear to do at least fifty tomorrow and add ten each day, if not more."

"But—"

"Now, Eudora. Or there will be no swords in your future." But the way she said it was oddly gentle.

My head was spinning, but I dropped to the ground and gave her ten.

"Take a rest. There's water inside. You have five minutes."

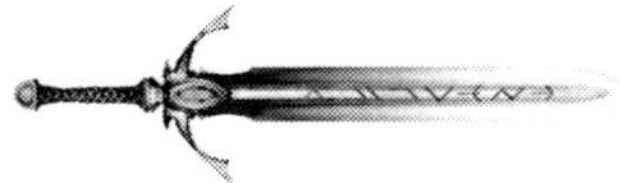

Somehow I survived that first lesson, including the session after the break where she taught me some footwork I was to practice. It was a further consolation that Glory also relented and sent *Sword Woman* home with me to finish.

It was more than a little disturbing to discover that at the end of one of the tales of Dark Agnes, she screamed and launched herself into a man's arms. Still, I chose to focus on the words of her companion: *And now you have naught to fear—and naught to be ashamed of. You have done as well against this horror as any woman or any man could do. And if, in the end, it comes to this, there is no shame for you to act as a woman, Dark Agnes, for you are quite a woman, indeed.*

Quite a woman. I tried to keep that in mind the next morning when I was so sore I thought I would have to crawl to the café. As the day wore on, the urge to whimper faded, less due, however, to my inner strength than to consuming enough ibuprofen to fell a horse.

Still, I showed up for my second lesson—high marks for me, I chose to think—and I got to actually hold a sword in my hand, even if it was wooden.

Lord have mercy, though. I cannot begin to understand how knights managed in full suits of armor. After an hour, I was about to fall flat on my face. *Uncle*, I wanted to say to Glory. *I give.*

But she was standing in front of me with a smirk on her face, just waiting for me to cave in.

I needed a breather bad, plus that smirk stirred up my mad like a stick poked in a hornet's nest. I lost whatever caution I'd had. "How could you have an affair with Ray?"

A mix of emotions raced over her features. "My relationship to Ray is none of your business."

"Lorena is." I closed the distance between us. "You hurt her. She's practically a saint. How could you?"

"This lesson is over." She wheeled and left me behind.

"Oh, no, you don't." Long legs are good for some things. I passed her and planted myself square in her path.

She glared at me and started to shove past.

I lifted my sword to bar her passage. "You answer me."

"Don't mess with me, big girl."

But I couldn't let this go. "She's a wonderful woman. I thought you were something special, too."

That threw her off, but only for a second. "You were wrong. Just ask anyone." She stepped around me, her practice sword loose in her grip because she knew I presented no challenge.

But I was sick to death of being a wimp. From somewhere I found the strength to swing in a downward arc and smack her weapon from her hand.

She whirled on me with a glint in her eyes. "You are going to push me too far."

"Yeah?" I waggled my fingers. "Come on, then." I was surely insane. The lessons had clearly demonstrated that she was in vastly superior condition, while most of the muscles in my body were jello. If jello could scream and weep, that is.

You would not believe how much of your body sword fighting makes a person use.

Lightning fast, Glory swept her sword from the ground and assumed a strike position.

Thanks be, I remembered the counter and lifted mine to block. Her blade hit with a crack that echoed down my spine all the way to my soles. I forgot the fancy footwork I'd practiced in my sleep last night and stumbled before the onslaught.

But then I managed to swing into a guard position before the next blow. Another couple of thrusts and counters, and I was starting to feel pretty good about my chances.

Then she hooked one foot around my ankle, and I fell flat on my butt.

Glory loomed over me, sword at my throat. *Crazy bitch*, I heard Bigot Brad say in my head. *She's dangerous.*

"Life is complicated, Eudora. Few things are as they seem." Her eyes were laser-hot, pinning me even when her blade was removed. "Take Kali, for example. She is *shakti*, the female energy, incarnate. She has the power to give birth and bring death. To recycle life into new life. She shows us good and bad, but in reality, she's neither. She's the universal mother who accompanies us into the darkness, who teaches us to transform our lives by embracing our own shadows, rather than fearing what haunts us and running from it. Death and life. Violence and creation. The balance of the universe. You look at one face and only think you understand." She stepped away, turned.

"Not a bad start," she cast over her shoulder. "You just might have promise. See you tomorrow."

Whistling to her dogs, she was gone.

I lay there with my head whirling. Lorena and Glory and Ray. Life recycled to new life. Embrace our shadows, don't run from what haunts us.

Night fell before I managed to move.

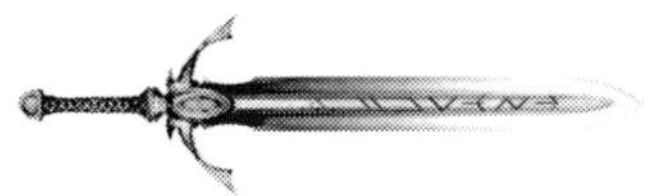

A woman of Lorena's age shouldn't have had to work so hard; her pace was about to kill me, I swear. So I cornered her in the storeroom the next day while she was taking inventory after lunch. "Let me do that." I held out my hand for the clipboard she was using. "You go rest."

One eyebrow arched, just one. But it was potent.

"I'm bored," I said, to spare her pride.

"Then go practice your swords."

My eyes popped. "How do you know about that?"

Her gaze left no room to hide. "I've lived here all my life. I know most everything that goes on." She pivoted and began on a new set of shelves.

I was not about to let her off that easy. I plastered myself into the tiny space between her and the stock. "People really don't like Glory. Why is that? I mean, aside from her sweet personality."

A corner of her mouth quirked. "She is a force to be reckoned with."

"So are you, but everyone loves you."

"Not really," she responded dryly. "If everyone loves you, Eudora, you're giving up too much of yourself."

Like I knew anything about being adored by many. "Maybe. I tend to think that having a lot of people care about you means you're doing something right."

Her eyes went soft. "Life has not been good to you, has it, child?"

Her kindness undid me. I wanted to lay my head on her shoulder, to crawl up in her lap. To have her tuck me in tight and sing me to sleep. I yearned to hold her gnarled hand. Sit somewhere quiet and just listen to her breathe.

I would have to get away from her scent of old-fashioned dusting powder and endless cups of hot tea before I did something stupid. Like think I should hang around. "I sure hope the part comes today."

On her face was disappointment. "You still plan to go."

"Of course. I haven't found her yet. My sister."

She looked very sad at that. She hadn't mocked me, though I could tell that the idea of reincarnation was far-fetched to her. A tiny, desperate voice inside me wanted to give in. To say I'd stay.

But I couldn't. Glory's talk about Kali and death and rebirth had to be another sign. It just had to. "I should talk to Tommy. See if he knows anything." I sidled past her and headed for the door.

Just outside, I paused. "Sleep in tomorrow," I offered, though it left me breathless. "Let me try it all on my own."

A long wait, then the tiniest of nods from her. "Thank you."

"You're welcome." With a gulp, I departed.

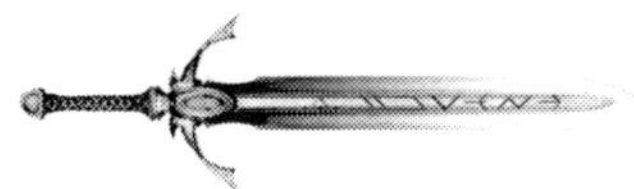

That night, showered after my workout with Glory, I was restless. Nervous about the next day.

The screen door opened suddenly, and I turned, surprised that Alex would be back this early.

But it wasn't Alex. "Hey, Red."

Abruptly I recalled that Val had wanted to talk to me the other night. "I'm sorry. I forgot you needed to see me."

I had on only one tiny lamp in an effort to reduce the number of bugs bashing their brains out trying to get through the window screens, so his face was mostly shadows shifting at odd angles as he moved around.

But something about his expression was . . . off.

"You okay?"

A quick jerk. "Oh." A frown. "Yeah."

"What did you want?"

"It wasn't important." He was silent for endless seconds, then held out a hand. "Come with me."

"Where?"

"Dancing."

I goggled. "Dancing?"

He pulled me to my feet. "Let's have some fun. Get the juices running." There was something a little wild and desperate in his eyes.

"What's wrong?"

He retreated a half-step. "Nothing. Sheesh. It's not against the law to want to liven things up, is it? I mean, you could grow roots here. Sink into quicksand and never—"

"Antsy to leave?"

"Maybe." A pause. "Yeah."

"Why?"

"Why not? It's the back of beyond, remember?"

It was. Still . . . "They're good people. You like Ray and Tommy.

Jeremy."

His expression softened. "That kid has no idea how lucky he is. The old man is cranky as hell, but he's teaching Jeremy what a man is, how he acts, without saying ten words a day. Just by who he is."

"So stick around."

"Not my style, Red."

"Val." I touched his arm gently. "You don't change a life overnight."

"Or maybe you never can."

"I won't believe that." The jitters that had plagued me all evening increased. "I need to be going, too. I have a sister to find. What am I doing here, cooking and—" I started to pace.

"Becoming a part of this place," he answered. "There's no reason for you to keep looking for her, you know."

"What?" I couldn't breathe.

"Red, you've jumped on this idea like it's salvation. You don't honestly believe in reincarnation, do you?"

My throat was too dry to answer. My fingers were clinging to a ledge that kept crumbling.

"You act as though finding her is going to make you someone better," he continued, his expression fierce. "You're already good enough. Why you can't see it is beyond me. You're the strongest person, I swear to God, I ever met. You take your heart and just lay it out there for everybody—hell, you even believe in a sonofabitch like me, knowing I'll break it."

I found my voice then. "You're not as bad as you pretend."

He snorted. "Don't kid yourself. I'm good at leaving, Red. You . . . you could learn how to stay."

I never thought I'd pity Val. He's so much more sure of himself and always has an answer, at least that's what I thought. Now I wondered if he wasn't mostly just lonely.

Like me. Only worse, because he didn't believe it could be any other way. "Where would you go?"

He shrugged. "Wherever the wind blows."

I hesitated. Swallowed hard before I offered. "Would you want to come with me? To New Mexico?"

"Damn it, Red, have you not heard a word I've said? One day you'd look up and I'd be gone. I'd feel like shit, maybe, for a day or two, but I'd do it. And you'd be all broken up and blaming yourself when any fool could tell you that all you did wrong was to take me too seriously. Anyway, if you had one lick of sense, you'd be scared, being out on the road so close to broke."

I had to turn away from his concern. Of course I was scared. I wasn't sure I remembered being any other way.

"You have to stop taking stupid risks like getting into a fight with Nicky. Or picking up someone like me."

"I thought you were hurt."

"My point exactly. You're naïve, too trusting. You take on blame and responsibility too easily."

"While you don't accept either?"

"There's no point in it. People get what they want from you and move on. It's only smart to do the same. But do you get that? No. So I have to worry about you. I don't do worry."

He stalked away, muttering. Wheeled and jabbed a finger at me. "I knew better, damn it. I don't spend time with women who don't know the score. A little fooling around, some let-the-good-times-roll, everyone's happy and then—" He snapped his fingers. "Time to go. Simple and easy."

That he couldn't see the toll that life had exacted of him was perhaps the saddest thing I'd seen in a very long time. "You always leave first, don't you? What you really want is the home you never had. There's one right here in this podunk town. All you have to do is be brave enough to grab it."

"That's it." He threw up his hands and headed for the door. Then whirled on me once more. "I have had just about enough of you and your idealistic bullshit."

The madder he got, the more cheerful I felt. The more I was positive I was right. I smiled.

"Stop that."

"Stop what?"

"That. That look."

"I am sure I don't know what you mean." I was all Big Lil, coy and breathy. A little eyelash fluttering.

Out of his throat came a low growl. "Red, you make me—" Abruptly, he started chuckling. Shaking his head. "You are certifiably insane."

"I'm right, though."

"Yeah, yeah, yeah. Whatever. You ready to dance?" All Mr. Sunshine now.

Well, why not? Night had always been my time up until my car broke down outside of Jewel. I'd had a long day, but I decided I wouldn't mind a little chance to howl at the moon myself.

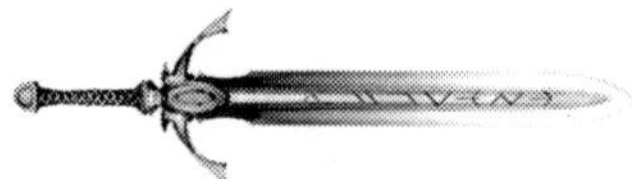

We pulled into the parking lot, and I couldn't help tensing.

"I'll check inside first," Val offered. "See who's there."

No way. I yanked my shoulders back and held my head high. "I'm not afraid of them."

"Of course you're not," he sighed. Then grinned. "I thought I might warn them who's coming. Give 'em a chance to escape out the back."

I smiled back and relaxed. "I bet they're quaking in their boots, but hey, check it out, I'm getting muscles." I did a curl and brandished my tiny bicep.

He dutifully gave it a squeeze. "Oooh, I feel so safe now. All that from cooking?"

"Nope."

"What, then?"

"Swords."

He did a near-vaudeville double-take. "You're kidding." He peered closer. "You're not kidding. So you're the new Dark Agnes, huh?"

I thought of how often I'd landed in the dirt. "A long way from that." But I couldn't help smiling again. "I made Glory fight me. I got tired of drills."

"No shit? How'd you do? Kick her ass?"

"Nope, but I got in a few good licks."

He waggled his eyebrows. "Girls fighting. I love that."

"Men are so easy."

"Hey—" He splayed his hands. "Charge admission, and you could get your car repairs covered quick. Even faster if some clothes come off or there's mud wrestling involved."

I laughed, but I was pleased to have surprised him. Impressed him a little, even.

He gripped the door handle. "You ready, Agnes?"

In the spirit of things, I shook a finger at him. "Don't make fun, or I'll use you for practice."

"And don't think that doesn't scare me." He emerged from the car and came around to my side.

I couldn't help melting a little. I'd never had a man open the door for me before. "A gentleman."

"Oh, Red, the things I could show you about how a woman should be treated."

Our eyes locked. Temptation did a quick jitterbug in my chest.

Thank goodness Val broke the tension with his killer smile and an outstretched hand. "Come on, Agnes. Let's dance."

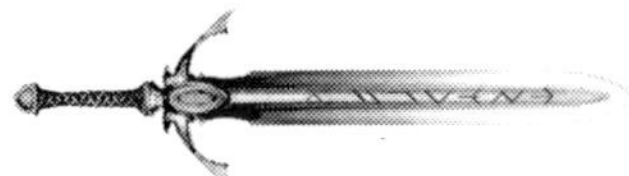

I don't believe I drank all that much. Yes, the day had been long and I was extremely weary, but there was more than either in the way one beer and one shot of whiskey went to my head.

Or maybe it was Val who went to my head.

Uh-uh. Nope. Through With Men, so liquor, definitely.

The evening was a blur of dancing, at first to hell-raising country that got the blood pumping as I circled the floor with a bunch of the guys I'd met at the café.

Somewhere along the way the tunes slid to slow and smoky. Val cut in, locking his arms around my waist and holding me close. The jukebox kept playing, and being in his arms felt natural, the scent of him, the warmth everywhere his flesh touched mine.

It was the smallest of shifts to bare my throat to his lips, to feel his breath whisper over my skin, to let his fingertips tease secret shivers from hiding.

"Come with me." It was a dream, that voice, a lure to nerve tendrils rising beneath my skin. He drew me into a night serenaded by the purr of cicadas, the whisper of gentle breezes. The trip back to the empty RV passed in a blur, and my senses soon reveled in a sumptuous feast: the glide of bodies over cool cotton sheets . . . the sigh in my bones when he eased my hair from its braid. The tingle as he teased the strands across a breast . . . the warm, wet suckling of a nipple. The wiry rasp of my tender arch caressing the hard curve of his calf.

Longing . . . I became pure longing . . . head arched, back bowed, goosebumps rising. I craved, I was reckless. I was hungry.

I yearned, and I embraced that yearning. And yielded completely, the surrender peeling me open . . . exposing the tiny, frightened creature so long curled inside. In exuberance, in the staggering, sinful beauty of our joining, I wallowed in the blessed absence of lonely. I gave and I got . . . and I lost myself in wonder, forgetting to shield the fragile heart of me now cradled in a warm palm, wrapped in silken comfort. Fed and rocked to sleep.

I'm sorry, Red. The faintest of whispers as unconsciousness claimed me.

"Not me," I murmured, closing my fingers, one after one after one, to capture the dream, the gift . . . the so-sweet surcease of belonging.

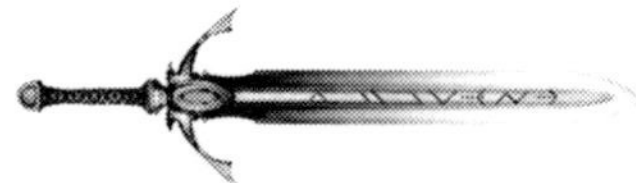

Val watched her longer than he should have. Brushed a kiss at the corner of her mouth, twined his fingers once more in her curls. Traced a path down her smiling cheek as she slept.

He closed the door behind him with a soft click.

Confederate Lady Paul Revere

Sophia Porter (1813-1899) settled 1839 at Glen Eden, site now under Lake Texoma. North of here, husband Holland Coffee, early trader, built a fine home, welcomed (1845-1869) U.S. Army officers, including Robert E. Lee and Ulysses S. Grant. During the Civil War, wined and dined passing Federal scouts, found they were seeking Col. Jas. Bourland, Confederate defender of the Texas frontier. While guests were busy, she slipped out, swam her horse across icy Red River, warned Col. Bourland, helped prevent invasion of North Texas.

IF WE REST WE RUST

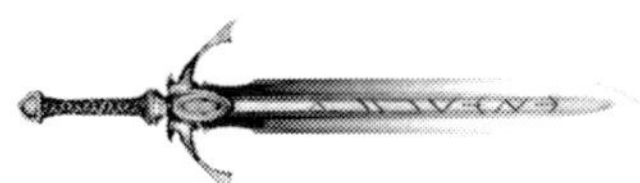

"Wake up," shouted the helmeted woman. Her horns dipped as she swung her sword over her head to strike.

I fumbled for my own weapon. My only hope was to leap away from the gleaming blade. Before I could manage anything, she struck my shoulder—

"Pea, you've got to get up. You're late."

"Hunh? I can't. I have to—She's going to—"

"You promised Lorena. Your alarm keeps going off."

Lorena. I opened my eyes, then yelped when the light hit them. "Off! Turn it off!"

"Not until you get out of bed. You told Lorena you'd take today by yourself."

"Oh, golly." I sprang straight off the mattress and nearly knocked Alex down. "Sorry." I grasped her shoulders to steady her. "What time is it?"

"Five-thirty."

"Oh, man. Oh, no. I have to—" One foot caught in the covers, and I stumbled.

Alex steadied me. "Take a second to wake up. I'll start the shower."

"I don't have time. Too much to do." Frantically, I tried to get myself together, search for my shoes, for clean clothes. Last night's excesses hammered inside my skull. I couldn't help letting out a little moan.

"What's wrong?" Alex returned with a mug in her hands, and the scent of it hit me.

"Coffee. You made coffee?" I hadn't even known we had a pot in the trailer. Then I realized that she was fully dressed. "What's up?"

"I'll help you. Go on and shower."

"But—"

"I paid attention. I can get some things started." Her eyes looked uncertain. "Unless you don't trust me."

"No, but—"

"But what?" *Pride's a teenager's worst enemy, and that girl's supply of it is running low*, Glory had told me. "You don't want to disappoint Lorena."

"I don't." Of all the days to oversleep . . . "Alex, I'm so sorry. I promise I'll hurry. I don't know how to thank you enough for waking me up."

"No big." A shy, pleased look skated over her features. "I should go." She headed for the door, and I stared after her, amazed at the difference from the Goth rebel I had found at a truck stop.

"What?" She halted at the doorway.

Better not to say what I was thinking, so I lifted my coffee cup in salute. "You're a lifesaver."

She smiled at me, really smiled, and I realized how little attention I'd been paying her lately. "No problem."

Then she was out the door. A glance at the clock made me shriek and race for the shower.

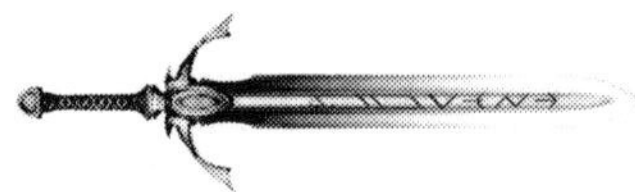

I heard voices as I approached the café at a dead run. For a second, I wondered if it was Val with Alex. Memory fluttered. We'd danced, we'd . . . I frowned as I struggled to remember. *I'm sorry, Red.*

What—

Ray loomed in the doorway. "You told Lorena you were ready."

I halted at his guard-dog tone. "I am."

He nodded up at the clock above the serving window. "Got about three minutes 'til Delbert and Bo walk in." He glanced past me. "Coffee done, Alexandra?"

"Yes, sir."

Sir? My head whipped around to see if she'd been replaced by some alien.

The sound of Delbert Wallace, my poker buddy, and his friend Bo arguing could be heard just outside. I snagged an apron and yanked it on, tying it as I walked to the grill that was already warming.

Ray took his time scrutinizing me. I was all too aware that just by staying there, he could make it clear to the whole town that I'd broken faith with Lorena.

And he'd be justified in doing so.

At last, he spoke. "You gonna mess up like this again? 'Cause she deserves better, you know. A damn sight better."

I flinched at the truth of it. "She does. She's the best woman I ever knew."

"She is that, all right."

I frowned. Odd words from a man who refused to speak to her.

Still he lingered, and I tried not to panic over the seconds ticking away. "I promise this won't happen again."

"Better not." He stalked out.

I kept my head down as I began to cook because I knew, whether any of these people ever would, that I had failed someone who meant a lot to me.

The front door opened, and then, blessedly, we were too busy to think.

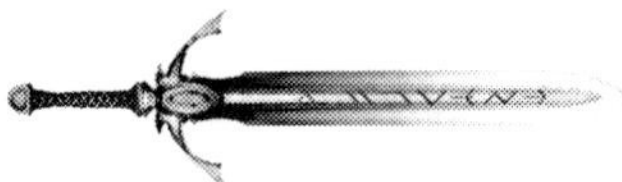

At last, the booths and tables were empty, and Alex and I had survived both breakfast and the lunch rush. Not without mistakes, that was certain, but we'd managed without major incident.

"Give me five," Alex exulted. "Did we kick butt or what?"

When she leaped to slap my palm, I couldn't help but grin at the glowing young woman who had somehow replaced the scowling teen. "We did, indeed." I was seized by the urge to close my fingers around hers. Hang onto this moment.

"I have to find Val and tell him," she said. "Wonder why he didn't come for lunch?"

"I don't know." But inside, I shivered. *I'm sorry, Red.* I could ignore no longer the pocket of dread inside me, as more scraps of last night drifted upward.

I'd broken my vow with Val.

And he was gone, somehow I knew it.

Just as, I realized now, I'd known, beneath the fury of my fight to save Sister's life, that she was dying. That I was helpless to change anything. I hated being helpless, then and now. Alex would be hurt by Val's abandonment, and I didn't want to spoil her triumph of the morning, so I kept my dread to myself. As for me, well . . . I wasn't going to spend another second thinking about Val . . . or last night. "You were great, really. I had no idea you'd paid so much attention when Lorena was teaching me."

Her face was pink with pleasure, but she shrugged like the old, don't-give-a-shit Alex. "Doesn't take a genius to wipe off tables or fill glasses."

"Don't do that." At my bark, her shoulders stiffened, and I had a sudden déjà vu moment, only the barker was Sister and the stiff shoulders belonged to me. The topic of our disagreement was long forgotten.

The shame of it was not. *I am so sorry, Sister, for all I put you through.* "Alex . . . "

But the shining moment of triumph had gone *poof* like it never existed. A deep sigh escaped me, and the short night and hours of work smothered me. I just wanted some sleep.

Actually, what I really wanted was to be back on the road with the same hope I'd had when I started. Still, I tried again. "It means a lot that you pitched in. I thought I could do it all, but I guess I got in too big a hurry to do something nice for Lorena before we go."

If anything, Alex grew more tense. "Why do we still need to leave?"

"My sister," I reminded her. "You know I have to look for her." Though I couldn't help casting a glance at Alex's belly. Where was Sister, really, inside Alex or in New Mexico? Or somewhere else altogether?

I was exhausted by the constant wondering.

"That's just crazy." She crossed her arms over her middle.

My mad scraped up some energy. "Oh, yeah? Well, who are you to say what's sensible, you who's still flirting with that poor kid? You have to tell him."

"He knows. He wants to be her daddy."

Her. She used to say it was a boy, but whatever she believed, my heart just flat shuddered. I knew how much she wanted to keep this child, but she could ruin three lives if she trapped Jeremy into marriage.

I opened my mouth to argue, but she spoke first. "Don't you say we're too young. His parents got married right out of high school, and Lorena and Ray were the same ages as us when they had Tommy. Lorena would back me. She likes me." Her expression dared me to contradict, but I couldn't because it was true. Lorena did care about her, and not only for Jeremy's sake.

Then suddenly, she grabbed her belly.

I leaped from my chair. "What's wrong?"

"Nothing." Her smile was a thousand suns. "The baby kicked."

"But you're okay, right?"

"Of course. Want to feel?"

"Um . . . " I stayed right where I was.

Her face fell. "Never mind. You don't have to."

"I want to, Alex." She couldn't imagine how much, but I was scared. "It's just . . . " That little life was precious, and it had to survive. I was so off balance anymore, and maybe here was Sister observing me up close and what if I communicated my turmoil and she decided I was still too much trouble and she chose not to be born in that body . . .

"Forget it." Alex started for the door.

"No!" I reached for her, but at the last second I snatched back my hand. "I—It's a miracle, isn't it?" Maybe I could give her words and that would be enough.

She turned to me, her eyes ripe with some ancient knowledge, and with it she nailed me. "You're afraid." The notion seemed to tickle her. "That's it, isn't it? You're chicken."

She was daring me, and normally, I'd rise to the challenge.

But what was normal anymore?

She didn't wait for an answer. "Would Dark Agnes be afraid of a tiny little baby?"

This baby? Yes. If she had a lick of sense. "How do you know about her?"

She snorted. "I was there at Glory's, wasn't I?"

"But you were mostly sleeping."

"Glory doesn't exactly whisper when she talks." She cocked her head. "You're going there at night, aren't you? She's teaching you about swords."

"Of course not."

"There's no need to lie about it. Jeremy and I followed you."

"You did not."

A tiny shrug. "He wanted to show me this creek he likes to wade in."

"Yeah, sure. His favorite place to make out, right?"

"So what? He loves me."

"You barely know each other, and anyway, he's so goggle-eyed over you, he can't see straight. He has no idea what being a father means." Poor guy was outgunned. Alex might have been younger than him, but she was wily. Dangerous in her abandon, her sense of nothing to lose.

Oh, lordy. From the frying pan into the fire, except at least this fire wouldn't mean to burn her. Jeremy was a good kid, but that's all he was, a kid. "Alex . . . " I was about to remind her of her poor judgment in the past. That the bruises Pretty Boy put on her not long ago had barely left her skin.

She charged ahead. "He says he knows what he's getting into, so you just go on and leave, if you insist on this insanity. I'm staying here. I'll talk to Val. He'll make you understand. He's the only one who ever can."

Reality landed smack on top of me. I couldn't dodge the news any longer. "Val's gone, Alex."

"What?" Her eyes got huge. "No." She took a step back. "You're lying. He wouldn't. I'm going to check." Alex stomped out of the café, and I stayed right where I was, my palms itching to be pressed to her belly.

Sister, please just—

I was about to say *Give me a sign. Show me some answers.*

But I'd always put a lot on Sister's shoulders. *Too much*, I thought now. And I kept doing it.

I blinked as it occurred to me, for the first moment since I'd left on this trip, to wonder if Sister would want me to find her as much as I needed to do it.

Which was the scariest idea yet.

Just then, a customer walked into the store.

I all but hugged him for the distraction.

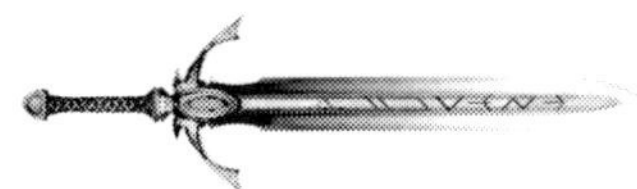

The hours since the lunch rush had been endless, and I'd been dusting and re-shelving cans to pass the time while contemplating new arrangements, but this was Lorena's place. I was only a stranger, drifting through. I started counting out the till, and the bell on the back door dinged.

I could feel Lorena's presence behind me, but I held up a finger and knew she would understand. Finally, I finished the stack of twenties and wrote down the amount.

I faced her. "I overslept this morning. I'm sorry I let you down."

"Did anyone miss getting breakfast?" Her head tilted as she regarded me.

"No, but—"

"Then you must not have been too late."

"No, but that was due to Alex, not me. I slept right through the alarm."

She smiled. "So did I. It was lovely. Thank you. I can't remember the last time I slept in." She stroked my arm. "Having you here is a blessing, Eudora. And not only because you work hard and could quite easily run this place without me."

She couldn't be allowed to think that. "If Alex hadn't pitched in, it would have been a disaster. I didn't live up to my promise."

"Would you like another chance?"

"You'd give me one?"

Her mouth curved. "I believe in you, Eudora. I wish you did."

There was a lump in my throat the size of Isis. What this woman meant to me was growing every day.

But I'd just landed here by accident. Lorena, Ray, Glory . . . none of them had anything to do with Sister and the powerful need in me to set things straight with her. To thank her for all she'd done. Apologize for making her last weeks filled with strife and not peace.

"You are awful nice to say that." I wanted to repay her somehow.

"I'll be glad to handle the cooking until my car's ready."

Her smile went hollow. "The part's here. Tommy's already working on your repairs."

I could only blink. For days now, I'd been focused on waiting for that one event.

"Easy for you to just load up and be gone now, isn't it?" She moved from the door. "Leave all of us behind."

Her sudden distance hurt me. "I won't dump Alex on you," I said stiffly.

"Even if she wants to stay?"

"I brought her here. She's my responsibility, at least until—" Until her parents rejected her, as she was sure they would? Or until the baby was born and I knew if she was Sister?

"Until what, Eudora? Do you honestly believe you're going to find her?"

If Lorena had stabbed me straight in the heart, her challenge couldn't have hurt worse. I'd thought she, of all people, was sympathetic. If I believed she was right, I didn't know what I would do. "You don't understand. She's my sister, my only family. I miss her like my right arm. There's so much I did wrong, and I see now that I didn't appreciate her enough—"

"Eudora." Lorena's hand grazed my shoulder. "It's a lovely thought, your notion, but life seldom gives us do-overs. We have to make the best of the time we're given."

Sister was all I had. Fear made me desperate to quiet Lorena. "Is that what you're doing with Ray? Making the best of your time with him?"

She reared back like I'd slapped her. "My marriage is none of your business."

"Maybe not, but what kind of example is that for your children? Your grandchildren? What do they learn about marriage?"

"It's not your concern."

"Yeah, because I'm not family, right? I don't really belong, so there's no reason to stay."

"Don't twist my words."

I shoved the cash register drawer shut, handed her the bank bag. Grappled for control before I destroyed everything between us. "I'd appreciate my wages, please. I need to pay Tommy, so I can go as quick as he's done."

"I don't pay in cash." Her voice turned glacial. "I must have the check for proper records, and my checkbook is at the house. You'll have to wait for morning. He's not positive he'll be through today, anyway, though he hopes so."

Great. I was counting on cash, off the books. Instead, she meant to do it all proper and take out taxes. I would be that much poorer, but I was not going to beg. "Fine. I'd better go. I need to pack and clean the trailer."

"What about Alex?" she asked. "What will you do with her after this?"

"I have no idea." I stalked toward the door, then turned. "She thinks you'll welcome her here, that she and Jeremy will marry and live in some vine-covered cottage." And if she did, what happened to Sister?

I could go on to New Mexico, I supposed, then check back here once Alex's baby is born if I didn't find her. Or I could—

What? Suddenly, I could barely put one foot in front of the other. I had the awfullest urge to cry.

"Eudora—" Lorena called to me.

I knew I should wait, find out what she meant to say next.

But I couldn't. Right then, I just needed to be alone.

Fort Parker

Built 1834 for protection from Indians. Named for leaders who brought first Predestinarian Baptist church body to Texas; elder Daniel Parker; his father, elder John; brothers Jas. W., Benjamin, Silas, John. Also here were Kellogg, Frost, Nixon, Duty and Plummer families. On May 18, 1836, raiding Comanches killed Benjamin, John and Silas Parker; Samuel and Robert Frost and others; captured Elizabeth Kellogg, Rachel Plummer and son James, and Silas' children, John and Cynthia Ann. In captivity, Cynthia Ann married Chief Peta Nacona; her son, Quanah, was last Comanche chief. With her baby, Prairie Flower, in 1860 she was captured by Texas Rangers. She, the baby and Quanah are buried at Fort Sill.

THE NERVES THEY DONE GOT ME

Dawn was tiptoeing into the darkness, and I was wide awake. I'd packed up last night so I'd be ready to go as soon as Lorena wrote my check and Tommy was finished.

That had taken a whole thirty minutes, including breaks to stomp around the trailer. I was so mad at Lorena I could have spit. I thought she was on my side. Thought she understood me. Sympathized.

I never expected her to make fun of me.

Alex hadn't shown, like she was psychic or something. She must have taken Isis because I'd scoured every inch of the RV and couldn't find her. I probably should have been glad to have the cat off my hands, but I wasn't. She, at least, would not have been arguing with me about my journey.

So that was one more thing I had to do in the morning. Find my cat and reclaim her, never mind that she slept with Alex way more than with me. Traitor. I was surrounded by them. Beginning with one Valentine Bonham, not that I cared one whit about a con man who was probably right now fleecing some unsuspecting woman who couldn't get past his arresting face and smooth moves.

Yes, I know Val warned me, and yes, I said I was Through With Men and he couldn't hurt me.

But without him, the whole town seemed just a little emptier. I kept remembering the teasing, the arguing. Those last gentle touches I wish I'd been more awake to savor. It was lowering to admit that for a teeny minute there, I'd actually been tempted to borrow Jeremy's truck and see if I could intercept Val.

He's a mere male, I could almost hear Dark Agnes saying, and I'm positive that she would have whacked off his head, not chased after him. That Big Lil would have looked down her nose at me for even considering it.

But I didn't follow, okay? I should have thanked Val, I guess, for the wakeup call. Sad what a little flirting and close dancing could do, making a person all mushy in the head. Okay, and the great sex. My vow sure hadn't stood up too well, had it?

I wondered if Val was snickering at pathetic me when he left.

You got it all wrong, hon. You scared the bejesus out of him.

My eyes popped. Could Big Lil be right?

Of course I am, are you kidding?

I sat up, cheered by the thought, and it occurred to me that, long before Glory or Dark Agnes, Big Lil might have been my introduction to warrior goddesses, big hair and all. Her sharp tongue was her sword, her unbending will her armor. The mental image of Big Lil in nose-cone breastplate, wrist gauntlets and stilettos made me chuckle, but there was no one here to share it with. Even if I would have.

I realized I was done with sleep. Might as well wait outside the café for Lorena, then get my check and go on.

Even if the road ahead seemed really empty.

I dressed quickly and left the RV, but my mind drifted back to Big Lil's imagined get-up. Suddenly, I recalled the bracelet that was Mama's. It wasn't much, a band of tarnished silver with machine-stamped hieroglyphics, its dots of cheap turquoise long ago gone dark green, but I could picture it on my arm, the ornament of a warrior, a swordswoman. Someone with veins of strength amid all my fool's gold.

I was gripped by the need for my own totem, something to remind me that the O'Brien women had heft of their own. Mama might have shown poor judgment in men, but she had the guts to tackle life with two girls and no money. Sister was too young to be a mother, but she stuck by me when others would have flown. I might have been no Athena, sprung from the forehead of Zeus, but I did not come from a line of sissies.

It was in the trunk of my car, that bracelet. I hadn't unloaded much beyond the basics as an act of faith that my car would recover, that I'd soon be on my way. Now I would be.

I decided I'd pay my faithful steed a visit before getting my check from Lorena. It wasn't quite five a.m., but the garage was never locked, anyhow. I'd asked about that once, but Lorena had just stared at me like I was an alien. Folks in Jewel were not thieves, I was informed. Houses didn't have to be locked. Cars, either.

In case I needed a refresher: I was not in the city.

The sky was lightening from night's monochrome to pale rose rimmed in gold. As I passed the house where the not-speaking couple lived, my throat got a little tight at the thought of leaving what had become so familiar.

I'd be fine. I would. No reason to quail just because The Nerves made me think I could feel strands of my hair coming loose at the root, all set to fall in drifts as I walked. The Nerves—I snickered as I remembered Laura Lee, a high-strung lady in a pompadour wig who worked with Sister years ago. *The Nerves they done got me, child. Made all my hair fall out. It's that daughter of mine, bound to send me to an early grave, I swan to goodness.*

I wondered whatever happened to Laura Lee. To her wild child. I was still grinning when I pushed open the office door of the garage—

And spotted Ray, slumped at the ancient gray metal desk, head in hands.

I froze, started to back out.

"What are you doing here?" he barked.

"I—I was just going to look in my car for—" Then I registered that his face had aged just since the day before, and he was wearing a threadbare, wrinkled shirt. He hadn't shaved. "Never mind me. Are you okay?"

Palms flat on the desk, he shoved to his feet. Gave me his back as he busied himself pulling a parts catalog off the shelf behind him. With a jerk of his head, he indicated the door that led to the bays. "Go on. Grab whatever it is and get out."

His manner was so forbidding that I hurried to do as ordered, but then a chill ran through me. "Is Lorena all right?"

"How would I know? Think the dadblasted woman ever gives me the time of day?" But his usual gruffness wavered.

If he was here at this hour, was she at the café early? "Is she cooking already?"

"No." His head whipped in my direction, his expression fierce now. "She's gone."

"Gone?"

"Drove off in the middle of the night."

"Why? Where's she going?" And how had I slept through it?

He slammed the parts catalog shut. "She just packed up and left."

"Left?" I blinked. "You mean like . . . *left?*" I stalked over to him. "What did you do?"

"Nothing. Not that it's any of your business."

"She wouldn't just go without a word to me."

"You think she owes you an explanation when she didn't even give one to me?"

"But last night we agreed—" *Take it back*, I wanted to demand. I was the one who was supposed to go. I grabbed his arm. "You played some part in this."

He might be an old man, but he was strong. He flicked me off like a gnat. "I didn't do a damn thing. Matter of fact, she was upset when she got home. You know anything about that?"

"How do you know she was upset, if you two don't talk?"

"Man don't live with a woman this long and not hear what she don't say." There was a quiver in his voice that yanked me out of my panic enough to focus on him again. To remember how often he stole glances at her in the café, how his eyes followed her as she moved around.

"You still love her." I shook my head. "I do not get you people. You have everything, a family, a home—" I swept my arm in a wide arc. "And you're wasting it on some stupid feud over a driver's license and—" Recalling the *and* part, the cheating part, made my mad sputter out, replaced by contempt. "Of course she left you. You hurt her. Had an affair with the woman everyone hates. How could you?"

"Lorena don't hate her own sister. The two can't get along, but she don't hate her."

"What?" Surely I had lost my hearing. "Her sister? Who's—" *Oh. My. God.* I swallowed hard. "Glory? Glory is—" My eyeballs were about to pop out of my head. "Lorena and Glory are . . . *sisters?*" If ever two women were polar opposites, it was those two. Aunt Bea and the Valkyrie. Earth Mother meets Sword Woman.

My head was reeling, but eventually one important fact leaked through. "You . . . had an affair with your wife's . . . sister." I stared at him like he had two heads. As though he were the devil himself. "No wonder she left you. The only question is why she waited so long."

"Left you, too."

No. She knew I needed to go. "She wouldn't." Would she? "I can't stay here. She understands that. She'll be back. She has to."

Easy for you to just load up and be gone now, isn't it? Leave all of us behind.

Had she escaped first, to keep me there?

Oh, no. No, no, no, no.

My legs didn't want to hold me. "She's forcing my hand." I had to tip my hat, though—it was a gambit worthy of Big Lil. "Well, it won't work, I'm telling you." I stabbed my finger at him.

Then I remembered that without my paycheck, I was going nowhere. "You write me a check for my wages, so I can pay Tommy."

"You didn't work for me. I don't owe you anything."

"She's your wife. It's your income, too."

"Unh-uh. Garage is mine, café's hers."

I threw up my hands. "Texas is a community property state. Even I know that. She can repay you when she gets back."

"Why would I want to? Woman deserted me."

I whirled and started to pace. The unfairness of it made me itch to throw a hissy, but I couldn't force him to pay me, and Tommy had a houseful of kids to support, so I couldn't expect him to let me have my car for free.

How could she do this? I thought she cared about me. I looked at Ray's slumped shoulders, and mine wanted to follow suit.

So you just fold, do you? Some warrior you are. I could practically see Dark Agnes's lip curl with contempt.

"No. I do not fold."

Ray frowned. "What?"

See what Lorena had driven me to? I was answering Dark Agnes out loud. "All right, all right. Look, I'll handle things for a few days—" Somehow. Even though my chest was tight and my heart was racing. "But I can't just hang around forever, so you'd better start figuring out where she is. When you find her, you tell her that I will do my dead-level best, but people are not going to like this one bit, and she may not have a business to come back to if she stays away long."

I was nearly breathless by the end, and it was all I could do not to take off running. I made it to the door before I remembered the bracelet I came for. I reversed my path and bumped into Ray, who was following me.

We jumped apart, but he grasped my shoulders. "Calm down," he ordered. "You're running around like a chicken with its head cut off."

I bristled. First, because I had never liked that saying, however often I'd heard it. It was just not an image a person wanted to focus on.

And second, because it was insulting. I was not panicking. I just needed to get away for a few minutes to clear my brain and—

"Breathe," he said. His voice was surprisingly gentle, and in that instant, he was once again the Texaco Man, sure and steady. "Lorena has faith in you for a reason, Eudora." The use of my strong name helped.

Even if it did remind me of both Glory and Lorena. How odd that both of them would call me Eudora.

Or not, now that I knew they were related. I shivered just a little as I gathered myself.

Ray patted me awkwardly. "You want some coffee or something?"

"You have some?" I sniffed the air and didn't find it amid the scents of grease and gasoline.

"Nope. I was thinking we could head on over to the café and you could make it."

She had been cooking for him at home, I was now certain. He was of that generation of men who were helpless in the kitchen, and he wanted me to take care of him, too.

Well, he had another think coming. "No, but I'll show you how to make your own." I cocked my head and awaited his reaction.

"Younger generation going to hell in a handbasket," he muttered.

But I would have sworn he winked.

Ray being playful. The world had definitely tilted off its axis. Something in me eased a little, but I still felt the need for a little bolstering. "One second," I told Ray and went to retrieve my bracelet.

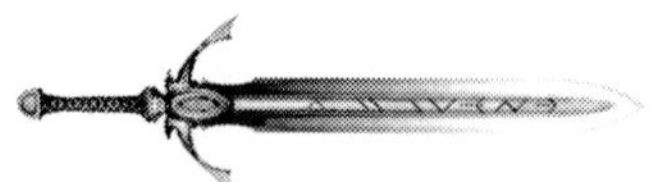

"Here we are." Inside the café, I nodded at the coffee maker with its two pots, one for decaf and one for regular. "You grab one carafe, and we'll do this together."

"Don't see the use in decaf," he grumbled. "Pot sits full half the day."

He was right about that. I wondered if Lorena understood just how much attention he paid to her and her surroundings. "It's Lorena's place," I said primly. "We do things her way."

"Like I don't know that. Woman's been calling the shots for fifty-three years."

"Somehow I doubt it was in her plan for you to have an affair."

"You're not going to stay. What's it to you?"

"I care about Lorena."

"You think I don't?" That look was back again, that shadow of misery.

"Then why on earth would you hurt her that way? With her own sister, of all people?" I was still trying to wrap my mind around the fact that they were related. "What could be more painful?"

He didn't answer; instead, he reached for the carafe dangling from my fingers and proceeded to fill both, then measure out grounds and insert filters as though he'd been doing it all his life.

I was goggling at what I was witnessing, but I didn't want to get off track. "What if she never comes back? What if you lose her?" My chest was tight and my head was about to explode. Didn't he get the risk he was taking?

Still no response.

I couldn't breathe. I really couldn't breathe. My knees gave way, and I started to slump—

Only to be caught in strong arms and lowered to a nearby chair. "Put your head down," Ray said. When I didn't respond, he did it for me, shoving my head between my knees.

Like a jack in the box, I popped right back up. "You have to find her."

Just then, the front door opened, and the first customers walked in. Delbert and Bo, always the early birds.

I cast a panicked look at Ray.

"In or out, girl?" he challenged.

I took a deep breath. Grabbed hold of the band on my wrist. "In." I headed for the refrigerator.

"I'll start the bacon," he said. "You make the pancake batter."

"You don't know how to cook."

One eyebrow lifted, and I recalled how smoothly he made the coffee. "You do know." So why—"Well, I'll be." I shook my head in admiration. "Does she realize?"

Only a grunt in answer.

"You two are unbelievable."

A shrug, and he reached past me for the bacon. Handed me eggs and milk.

The Texaco Man on the Food Channel. Wouldn't that be a kick?

I got busy mixing, already planning who to grill first regarding Lorena's whereabouts. I would be asking the woman some hard questions when I tracked her down.

Which you could bet the farm I would be doing.

Meanwhile, the rat bastard and I had some cooking to do.

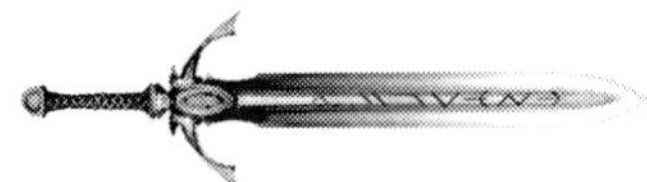

I was crazy busy after that, running the store and cooking at the café, but Alex pitched in to help. We found we worked well together—as long as I kept my mouth shut about leaving Jewel.

After the first morning, Ray didn't show up to eat for two days, and he worried me. On the third, he returned to the café, but he was wound so tight he barely ate half of what was on his plate. Jeremy told Alex that Ray had explained Lorena's absence as a little vacation, but the kids knew something was off. She'd never gone on one without Ray, plus Ray's behavior had them all concerned. Charlie took to dropping in for lunch to sit with his dad and Tommy, and Millie came over each morning to ask me if she could help. My sense was that she just wanted to be in the place her mother had always been, her presence taken for granted by all of them.

I always thanked her and gave her some task she could do while sitting, but having her there made me nervous. Her belly was so huge that I was scared to pieces that she would split wide open like an overripe melon. Birth her child right there in the café where I was barely holding my own.

At night, I began to mop twice, just to be sure the floor would be clean enough if we had to deliver that baby on the spot.

We? Who was I kidding? I knew less than nothing about babies. Not even my convenience store first aid training had taught me diddly about that. Her ever-closer due date cheered me, though. I couldn't picture Lorena missing out on the birth of her daughter's child.

Meanwhile, Ray avoided talking to me, I guess because he thought I'd badger him about his progress in searching for her. I wouldn't have, though. I'd already been asking around, for all the good it had done me.

So, time to take the next step. I would go out to see Glory. I hadn't wanted to talk to her ever again once I knew that she was a woman who would cheat with her own sister's husband. I would never understand how she could do that. Whatever fondness I'd had for her had vanished.

But I realized that there might be something crucial I might get from her: insights into her sister's mind. She and Lorena might have nothing to do with each other, but they were still sisters. Love or hate, sisters know each other like nobody else.

So imagine my surprise when I got back to the RV that night after closing and found a package on the steps. A sword, a real one. Even had a dandy scabbard I could wear strapped on my back. A message from Glory, I guess, that it was time to get back to work on my lessons.

I drew the sword from the leather scabbard and held it in my hand, weighing the feel of it, as perfect as if it had been made just for me. I slashed it through the air. Admired the balance, the gleam of its sharp edge.

Mine. My very own warrior woman sword. Anticipation shivered over me.

Hurriedly, I changed my clothes and hopped on the bike. Discovered that wearing a thirty-inch sword across your back while cycling was a wee bit awkward, and I was already tired from working all day. For a second, I considered how wise it was to be doing this tonight.

But truth was, nothing could have stopped me.

Geri and Freki were my escorts as I negotiated the road up to the dome. I reminded myself to stay calm and cool and unemotional.

Glory was already outside, warming up. Once I would have been admiring her grace, the economy of her motions. Not today. My good intentions evaporated at the sight of her. I stalked toward her, my mad flaring high that she had lied to me about something so important. "Why didn't you tell me Lorena's your sister?"

Slowly she revolved, not speaking until she finished her move with a flourish. "Why would I?"

"Because—"

Glory attacked, and whatever I was going to say was lost as I scrambled to draw my new sword from the scabbard.

Then I was busy fighting for my life. I managed one block and a feint before my weapon went flying through the air. Glory's sword whistled as the point came way too close to my breastbone.

My heart was about to pound right out of my chest, but I would be dadgummed if I'd let her know it. "You might not want to mess with me. Lorena's gone, just vanished. Poof, like I don't have anything else to do with my life but cook."

"Pick it up," Glory ordered.

"Did you hear me? Lorena's left. She's your sister. Aren't you worried?"

"In case you hadn't noticed, we don't talk."

"But why not?" An incredulous stare from her. "Well, of course, that. But did you before?"

"Not really."

"Why not?"

"Never got along."

"Is that your fault or hers?"

"Just how it is. Always has been. No skin off my nose."

"Are you kidding me?" I advanced on her. "I would sell my soul to spend five more seconds with my sister, and you don't speak to yours. You—you cheat on her. With her own husband!" I threw up my hands. "I swear do not get you people. Your televisions don't carry soap operas so you just create your own, is that it?"

She stood straight and still and utterly untouchable. "Are you ready for your lesson or not?"

"First you're going to help me figure out where she is."

"How on earth would I know?"

"You should. Think back. You grew up together. You have to know how her mind works."

"Nope." She crossed her arms. "She and I have nothing in common. Now, are you here to train or chitchat?"

I resisted the urge to scream. "No. I'm done."

"Good thing I didn't waste any more time on you. You could never have cut it anyway. Too soft."

That did it. "As opposed to you, who's so busy being a hardass that you have no man of your own and have to get involved with your sister's?"

She pointed her sword at mine. "You gonna hang around and jabber, then grab the sword and get to work."

"I've been working all day. I'm tired. I need a drink of water." I headed for the dome.

She stepped in front of me. "Use the hose."

"I want ice water like usual."

"Hose." She was clearly not moving.

I swerved around her. The woman was tap-dancing on my last nerve. "You want me to leave some money on the counter, that it?" I sneered.

She bumped me. Set me back on my heels.

I cocked my arm to pop her one.

"Stop it, you two."

I blinked at the new voice, and Glory knocked me flat on my bottom. Then swore.

I raised my head, and there, to my utter astonishment, stood Lorena. My throat worked, but no sound was forthcoming. I glanced from her to Glory, who was frowning to beat the band.

"You said you wanted to hide out," she accused.

"You're handling Eudora all wrong."

"My turf, my choice. Get back inside."

"Don't you order me around."

They were like two squabbling kids. I rose and stepped between them, still gaping. "Lorena, what are you doing here? After—after she—" I pointed at Glory.

"You, of all people should know the answer to that."

"Me?"

Lorena glanced at Glory. "When you spoke of your sister and how much you long to see her, I couldn't forget it. I headed toward Abilene, but with every mile, I kept thinking about how I have a sister I never speak to."

"She says you two don't like each other. Why not?"

"It's not that we . . . It's complicated."

"Because of Ray, I get that, but what about before?"

She hesitated. They exchanged glances. At last, she spoke. "She and Ray used to date, did you know that?"

Good grief. Soap opera, indeed. "No." I turned to Glory. "Did you love him?"

An irritable shrug. "I wanted out of Jewel more. I left."

"And I never wanted to be anywhere else," Lorena said. "I started flirting with him to get your goat, you know."

Glory scowled.

"So you were always rivals?" I asked. Though they weren't paying me all that much attention.

"We had little in common," Lorena finally answered. "She traveled all over, while I stayed and built a life here. We lost touch. Then she came back to town a few years ago, and I hoped things would be better between us, but . . . things happened."

I looked from one to the other, sensing I was missing something, but neither would look at me, so I took a stab. "Did you know she'd married Ray before you returned?"

One nod.

"Were you upset?"

"Maybe. He was a good kisser." Glory smirked.

"Still is," Lorena countered.

Eww, too much information. Nonetheless, I pressed on. "So you, what—still wanted him? Decided to get even?"

Glory wouldn't look at us. "I'm not discussing this with either of you."

The moment was sticky with misery. It would probably have been smarter to change the topic, but not talking had helped no one thus far. Dicey as the subject was, here was an opportunity that might not come again.

Oh, lordy. Oh, man.

I took a deep breath. "Well, that's just stupid." Glory's glare nearly stopped me dead, but I barged on. "You're sisters, see, and that means something. Yes, sisters hurt each other. Sometimes they say things they wish they could take back, but blood counts. Family counts. You cannot waste it. Do you know what I'd give for the chance you have? Do you?" I could have wrung their necks. "Maybe you were hurt that she married him, but maybe she was hurt that you didn't keep in touch. You picked a real bad way to get back at her, having an affair with her husband, but maybe—"

I stopped because I'd never seen Glory so vulnerable, her

expression so lost as she watched Lorena, and it got to me. "You have to work this out," I said. "You have to."

But Lorena wasn't listening to me, either, totally focused on Glory. At first she seemed confused and then, astonishingly, a curve began to form on her lips. "You didn't do it, did you? You and Ray didn't actually have an affair."

Her voice was so quiet, I wasn't sure I heard right.

"Did you?" she prodded.

Glory kept staring at her, then one single tear fell down her weathered cheek. Finally, she shook her head.

Holy cow. "But—What—" I was clearly talking to myself. The two of them had eyes only for each other. Lorena took one step toward Glory, then another. Glory didn't move, but all the fight had gone out of her.

"Why?" Lorena asked. "Why make me believe you did?"

"He thought it would get you mad enough to talk to him. The distance was killing him."

"He was the one who refused to speak to me first. He could have broken the silence at any time."

"He's a man. Ergo, an idiot." They shared a smile. "Anyway, I owed him."

The air around them was so full and charged, it was practically a tornado. I had the inescapable sense that something more was going on here than I understood.

Glory cleared her throat. "He's a good man. You belong together."

They stood so close yet so far apart, across a chasm of years. Of misunderstandings. Slowly, Lorena's arms encircled Glory's shoulders, and I realized that while Lorena seemed small and Glory huge, they were actually close to the same size.

Glory's shoulders started to shake, and it was Lorena who comforted her, Lorena who, despite Glory's bluster, was the strong one. Two sisters together at last, holding each other the way I wanted so badly to hold and be held again by my own.

They forgot I was there. I should have gone then and left them alone, but for a minute, I just wanted to stay. The love was spilling over, and I yearned to lap it up a little while. I heard them murmuring to each other, and it was beautiful and it hurt.

I picked up my sword, stuck it in its scabbard and looped the strap over my shoulder. Started down the hill toward the bike.

"Don't tell him where I am yet, Eudora."

I halted, think of how Ray looked the morning Lorena left. How decent he'd been to me, pitching in that way. I turned. "Why make him wait? Why not straighten things out?"

"No." Her head shook vigorously. "I'm not ready. I was only watching out for him, trying to keep him from getting himself killed. Instead of apologizing, first he froze me out, then he made things worse by deliberately creating an impression he knew would hurt me. If we're going to have a future, he has to make the first move."

"Do you know what the so-called rat bastard did the morning you left? He helped me cook."

Lorena's eyebrows rose. "He didn't."

"I was freaked because first Val took a powder, then I find out you did, too. He—" I was interrupted by Glory's snort. "What?"

"Coulda seen that coming a mile away."

"I disagree," said Lorena. "I believe Valentine was rather smitten with you."

"Well, you were wrong."

"I'm so sorry, dear."

Lorena's sympathy would tease out tears I refused to shed. "Doesn't matter. I knew better."

"Durga," Glory muttered.

"What?" Both Lorena and I stared at her.

"You could both take a lesson from her. She's a Hindu goddess born from the combined breaths of all the gods, who were losing a battle with an army of demons. She emerged a full-grown warrior who won the battle. Her name means beyond reach. She's a virgin in the full sense of the word, not just sexual but beholden to no man. Her power is not dependent on any male, no father, no husband. That's where she gets her strength."

"Is that supposed to be some sort of lesson?" I asked. "Men can only make you weak? Well, I got the memo about that already." I couldn't stand thinking about my mistakes another second. "I'm out of here." I started walking away.

"Eudora." Lorena's voice was gentle. "Come back."

I wanted to. So much.

But I couldn't. I shook my head and kept going. "Take some time. Just—"

"What?"

"Nothing." *Just please hurry so I can find Sister and get my own chance.*

But I didn't say it.

"Come back tomorrow. Promise me."

Why? So I could watch them together and wish? Eat my heart out? "I don't think so. Let me know when you're ready."

"Don't chicken out on your lessons," Glory taunted. "Unless you're too soft, after all."

"What's the point?" I whirled. "Why should I?"

"Because you're not through learning who you can become," she said.

"I agree," said Lorena.

They were standing beside each other, two faces of a goddess. Earth Mother and Sword Woman.

I'd learned that many goddesses came in threes. Three Fates. Three Muses. Kali, the Celtic Morrigan, the Greek Moerae, the Norse triple Norns. A triad was powerful, and I was suddenly and insanely jealous that I couldn't be part of such a set.

These two didn't need a third, however. They were already complete. Halves of a pair when I had lost my own. They belonged, and I did not.

But if I could find Sister, I would, too. "I have a journey to complete," I reminded Glory. "As soon as Lorena's ready to come back."

"And what do you hope to accomplish on some wild goose chase after a ghost?" Glory challenged. "Stop kidding yourself."

Lorena doubted. Val, too, and so did Alex. Now Glory.

"Sister's not a ghost." But she seemed so far away from me, I wanted to clap my hands over my ears. Chant really loud. "And who are you to talk, with your obsession with myths, your stupid sword games? I'm no warrior goddess and neither are you."

"Don't do this." Defeat was in Lorena's voice. "Forget it. I'll go back." Her posture echoed her tone.

I couldn't help but think of all she'd done for me, how she'd taken a chance on me, how much I'd learned from her about being strong and wise and kind, and I was about to repay her by taking a powder just like Val. By not staying the course a little longer.

But Glory's words echoed and made me shiver in fear. *Wild goose chase.* Doubt crept in on stealthy predator feet.

"No." Sure of so little, I was nonetheless positive that I couldn't make Lorena leave yet. "Don't. I'll keep quiet. It's the least I can do for you. Just . . . will you let me know when you're ready?" There was a boulder-sized lump in my throat. "Maybe Glory's right, but I have to try. Otherwise . . . " I could not bear to think about otherwise.

Then I took off running, even though they were calling to me. The sound of their voices died off as I grabbed the bike and pedaled down the hill to the road.

WASP Training Base

Women's Airforce Service Pilots (WASP) trained here in military aircraft during World War II from Feb. 21, 1943, through final graduation Day, Dec.7, 1944.

Avenger Field first served as a training base for British Royal Air Force Cadets in 1942, then for U.S. Army Air Forces Cadets Aug. 1942-April 1943.

The WASP program was started under Gen. H.H. ("Hap") Arnold to train women to fly every kind of mission short of combat, releasing male pilots for overseas duty . . . .

Of 25,000 girls who applied for WASP flight training, 1,830 were accepted; 1,074 won their silver wings. The WASPs flew 60 million miles on operational duty; 37 lost their lives serving their country. WASPs had civil service—not military—status, but were granted eligibility to apply for reserve commissions in the Air Corps after the WASP program ended when the Allies were winning the war in Europe and the U.S.A. pilot shortage was past.

Avenger Field was closed after a short post-WASP span of service as a missile base.

PEARLS LIKE A HAIR SHIRT

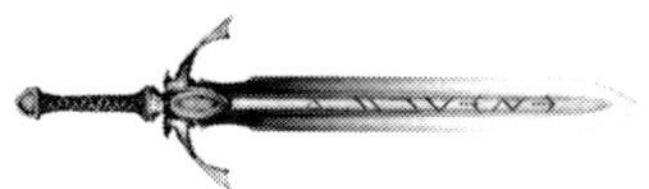

I pumped like crazy in the opposite direction of Jewel. I didn't want to talk to anyone I knew. Didn't want to see a single soul.

I saw the lights of the Rough and Ready ahead and considered stopping for a drink. Anything to make this ache the size of a mountain go away. The only times I'd been in there were with Val, though, and he was the last thing I wanted to be thinking about. Not that he was anything to me, except a good example. He got out while the getting was good.

Give me a few days, and I'd be the same.

I was pedaling so hard I didn't hear the shout at first, coming from a pickup in the parking lot.

"Well, lookee here, boys," said a voice I'd just as soon never have heard again. "It's the nosy bitch. Your poker stud split, sugar. Wanna come have a drink with us?"

The menace in Bigot Brad's voice chilled me. I remained silent and kept riding as fast as I could. There were four of them and one of me.

"Stuck up, too, I guess. Thinks she's too good to drink with us."

I glanced over my shoulder and saw them getting into his pickup, and I knew I wouldn't get around them easily. The pickup engine cranked up. I rose and started pumping hard.

It wasn't nearly fast enough. The truck soon passed, then swerved in front of me. I skidded on the gravel, and the bike slid from beneath me. Rocks cut into my bare legs, and the spokes of the wheel caught my foot. As I fell, all I could hear was laughter.

"Well, well, well." A door slammed and footsteps approached.

Frantically, I was trying to get my foot free. At last I did, and I scrambled to rise. I wanted with everything in me to run, but I stood my ground, though my insides were shaking.

"So how you and Glory doing, huh? You two gotten real cozy?" Brad swaggered toward me as his friends piled out of the other side.

"Get back." *Come on, Dark Agnes. Big Lil. Someone.*

Help me.

"Make me," he taunted, and his buddies sniggered.

But the voices were silent. There was no help for me.

Sister, I need you, I pleaded.

"Not so brave without ol' Val, are you? You know, boys, she's got one hell of a rack on her." His leer sickened me.

I thought of Dark Agnes and the black-haired brute. She was all alone in the world, and she managed. I remembered Sister taking on the system single-handed to defend me, to keep me safe.

There was no one but me now. I had my sword, but I wondered if I had what it took.

Don't wait on your enemy. Take the fight to them, Glory had taught me.

I dug deep for the courage and drew my weapon.

"What the hell?" Bigot Brad and his boys started pointing and laughing.

I swung it in a single deadly arc Dark Agnes would have been proud of.

And sent Brad scrambling backward. "You crazy—Get around behind her," he roared to his friends.

Fear ripped through me. He wouldn't hesitate to hurt me if he could. I feinted, then slashed at them, but they circled me like a pack of wolves. I jabbed and sliced. Focused hard on every last move I'd seen Glory demonstrate. I might be doomed, but I'd go down swinging.

Suddenly, a light swept over us, freezing them for a second.

Tires squealed to a stop. "Move, Eudora!" came a shout.

Glory?? I didn't dare take my eyes off them to look.

"I said move!" she yelled.

But where to? It was definitely her, though. Thank heaven.

A shotgun blast brought a tree limb crashing right behind my attackers.

"Hey!" cried one of them. "She's got a gun!"

"No shit," yelled Bigot Brad. "Distract her. I'll get mine."

"Glory, watch out!" My words died off as her jeep leaped forward, cutting Brad off from his vehicle.

"You crazy—"

"Get going," she ordered. "Now."

"I'm calling the cops," postured one of them. "They'll put your ass in jail, you whacked out, murdering—"

"You're on probation, Ronnie Earle. You'll be right there with me." A rack of the shotgun sounded like thunder. "Throw your weapon out, Brad."

He glared at her, his fingers flexing on the pistol. At last he cast it to the ground. "You'll pay for this."

Glory lifted the shotgun slowly and pointed it straight at him. "You sure jabber a lot." Her smile was chilling. "Bring it on, boy."

I wouldn't have gone near Glory again, if I were them. Bigot Brad, though, was not someone whose test paper I'd want to copy from.

"Don't think we're done." In his face was pure menace, but in seconds, they were gone.

The only sound I could hear was Glory's engine running. She bent to pick up his weapon and stuck it in her glove box. "Best load up your bike and let me drive you home, Eudora."

My knees were locked in place, otherwise, I would surely have collapsed to the caliche.

"You can drop that blade now." She pried it gently from my hand. My arms fell to my side, and I started shaking.

"How bad you hurt?"

I looked at her, still mute.

"It's okay." Her voice was gruff yet oddly gentle. "Just lean on me a spell."

She couldn't possibly imagine how much I wanted to, but I stayed where I was. "What are you doing out here?"

"Looking for you," she said.

"Me? Why?"

"Lorena was worried, the way you took off."

"And you?"

She shrugged. "Maybe." She glanced over. "Your form was pathetic."

That startled a bark of laughter out of me. "It scared them, though—at least for a minute." If I ever stopped quaking, I thought I might be a little proud of myself.

"It's a start," she conceded. "We'll work harder tomorrow night."

Tomorrow night. That assumed I'd return to the dome. "What if I decide not to?"

Glory scowled. "Be crazy to quit when you got the guts to take those boys on."

I had guts, Glory said so. Wow.

I was still marveling over the miracle of a compliment from her when she spoke. "Sure you're all right?"

I nodded, though I'd probably be sore as all get-out. "I just got banged up when I fell off the bike. I only need a little cleaning up. I'm worried about you, though. Those guys already had it in for you and now . . . "

A bad-tempered shrug. "I can take care of myself. Come back with me. Lorena can fix you up."

She would, yes, but I needed to be alone right then. Too much had happened for one night. I didn't want to do any more talking, and though Glory could go hours without a word, Lorena wouldn't. She'd feel the need to do something about Brad, too.

"Glory, I told you what I heard them say about you."

"You coming or not, big girl?"

Topic closed, clearly. Fine and dandy. "No. I'm heading—" *Home,* I started to say. Except it wasn't. "How long you think she's going to hide out up there?" *How long before I can leave?* was the real question.

"Beats me." A frown. "Best be soon, though. Need my privacy." The protest seemed to be more for form, though, with no real heat in it. "You can ask her tomorrow. Come on, load up your bike and I'll drive you." She walked off, giving me no chance to refuse.

I was sick of being told what to do. "I'll get myself back." I sheathed my sword, then righted the bike. Mounted and tested it for a few feet. A squeak said something was rubbing, but maybe I could make it back to the RV. I had to try or go crazy with how everybody had plans for me, how everyone thought they could just order me around. *Don't tell Ray. Get in this pickup. Ask her tomorrow.*

Mere weeks ago, life had sucked, and I had been lonely.

But things had sure been a lot simpler.

Slowly I rode the bike back to town, despite the aches and pains that were screaming at me not to be so stubborn.

Glory followed me all the way.

Then hit the gas and took off before I could say thank you.

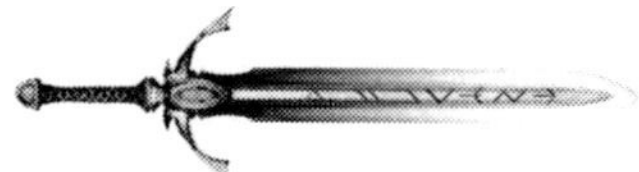

I did go back, though, dang my hide, the next night. Glory and I worked out first thing when I got there. Only when she had me dripping sweat and about to plop in the dirt did she signal an end to our session by walking off without a word. She didn't hang around while I stayed and visited with Lorena, but I thought I understood. Lorena was easy with me, and we laughed a lot. Glory wasn't much for laughing—I'd never seen her really smile except that one time when Alex had told her I needed a keeper—and at the moment, she had a lot on her mind keeping an eye out for trouble.

As for Lorena, I still believed she and Ray should be talking out their problems. I had no idea what it would take to break the stalemate, but however much I thought she should, I also treasured that time with her.

That night we even danced a little. Lorena told me that she'd danced so little in her life that she had to make up for lost time. Now that she wasn't on her feet all day, they got a little itchy to move, she swore.

So she started with the Lindy, a dance that was big in her salad days, as she called them. It's a very energetic step, so mostly I was the one to do all the hopping and juking around, but it still lit up her eyes and made her grin. I'd be any kind of fool I needed to be, to make that happen.

Then we sat down so I could do a foot massage for her. I settled on the floor in front of the overstuffed Longhorn chair that had become Lorena's throne. First I soaked her feet in warm water and washed them with a sweet lavender soap I found in the RV. She always sank a little deeper into her chair as if her bones were rearranging themselves.

"Tell me about your people, Lorena," I requested, mindful of the graves I had seen at that sweet cemetery.

"My great-grandmother loved to dance," she said. "She looked a lot like you, Eudora, china-blue eyes and red hair, a tiny thing, not quite five feet."

"That's a pretty big difference," I pointed out. "I could make two of her."

"Pshaw. You're a good size, honey. No one's going to overlook you."

"I should only wish," I muttered.

She bent forward to grip my chin. "Being remarkable is a good thing. Count your blessings. No man will be able to treat you like furniture."

"Stupid rat bastard," I hissed. But then I recalled how lost he'd looked that morning she left. How he wasn't eating.

I still couldn't get over how they were wasting love that others would kill for. I kept searching for a way to convince her to let me tell him where she was. To make her see the insanity of letting time slip away when she could be spending it with him.

But the woman brought new meaning to the word stubborn. Meanwhile, haranguing her would only mess up the time I had with her, and I was lapping that up like cream. "How about a cup of tea?" I asked, rising.

"Tea would be good."

I focused on the steps she'd taught me for brewing a proper cup. *Warm the pot first. Sprinkle in leaves. Pour water gently so as not to bruise them.*

I stared out the window over the sink and spotted Glory pacing in the growing darkness like she was on sentry duty. She was making herself an outcast in her own home—not that Bigot Brad and his threats weren't something to consider.

"Why do people hate Glory?" I asked Lorena. "There has to be more than just an affair with Ray to it. It's not just that they dislike her personality, either. The graffiti called her a murderer."

Lorena was silent, her head bowed so that I could see the fragile line of her nape. Her spine reminded me of a strand of pearls, which brought to mind the mystery of Glory's necklace, so out of tune with the rest of her getup.

Idly I wondered if Lorena's scalp ever hurt from how she scraped back her hair. After I rubbed her feet, I thought I'd offer to brush it. Surely that'd feel good, too.

"People around here do think she killed someone."

Whoa. "Did she?"

"Not . . . well, it's complicated."

"How?"

She glanced outside then back. "Glory had a childhood friend, Molly Cannon, who was the only person who was able to get past that hard shell after Glory came back to Jewel. Things happened while she was in the service that she won't talk about, but I can tell you that they only made her more troubled and fierce." Lorena stared off into the distance for a bit, then stirred herself to continue. "Molly had emphysema and toward the end, she was suffering tremendously. She begged Glory to help her end it."

I gasped.

Lorena's gaze whipped to me, but all I could do was wave her to go on.

Because I could not breathe. My skin was prickling.

"No one knows for sure," she went on, "but everyone believes Glory did it. She's never discussed it with anyone, but heaven knows how much she must have suffered over it. Now she wears Molly's pearls like a hair shirt."

Those pearls, so incongruous with the combat boots.

I could hardly focus. My mind was a cyclone hurling debris, gale force winds all riled up to maim and destroy, Lorena's words ripping right into me.

Because Sister had asked the same thing of me.

Begged me.

"I was one of those condemning her at the time," Lorena said sorrowfully, "But now I realize how much strength it took to perform what was an act of mercy."

Strength I didn't have. I'd said no—not only *no* but *hell, no.* Yelled at her for giving up. Went on a rampage of finding new treatments, each one more bizarre than the last. I ignored that she was a skeleton, getting worse every day, long past the strength to fight.

If you loved me enough, she'd accused. *It's because I love you*, I'd shrieked. And worse. *If you loved me, you wouldn't ask.*

Like Sister hadn't given up her whole life since sixteen—hard, miserable years of keeping me safe—out of love. And the one time . . . the only time she really needed me . . .

"Some folks around here talked about calling in the authorities. Ray stopped them."

Ray. And in doing so, fertilized the fields of gossip. Made an affair later seem fated and cast Glory even more the villain. *I owed him*, she'd said.

Oh, Glory. You stacked the deck against yourself. You knew they'd believe the worst of you. I saw a different Glory then and understood a little better her isolation. The crust she'd formed around herself to deal with being despised. Feared because she'd done something few people could face.

So had she decided that since she was already a pariah, being seen as an adulteress was no big deal? There was so much I wanted to ask her, the only person who would understand. If she had it to do over, would she? Were her regrets any more raw than mine?

But first I'd have to tell her what I'd done, and I was in no way ready for that, nor could I admit it to Lorena. If Lorena despised me for my choice, I would not be able to bear it.

"Is the tea ready yet?" Lorena asked, as if we'd only been talking about the weather.

Chilled to my marrow, I grabbed the pot in both hands. My palms were turning bright red, but my chest was redder, full of blood gushing out of old wounds I wished I couldn't feel. Barely, I got the pot to the trivet in time, then finally, with trembling fingers, I managed to give Lorena her cup of tea.

Once she sipped it with a pleased sigh and settled into the cushions for Act Two, I kept my face averted, focused on the oil I poured into my palm and began to minister to this woman I adored, praying my misery wouldn't communicate through my touch.

All the while, I wondered about the woman outside. Why had Fate put Glory in my path, after all—not to teach me strength but to shame me? To show me where I went wrong?

Oh, Sister, talk to me, please. I need a sign. Will you ever forgive me?

But Sister stayed silent, and my skin felt tight enough to burst, all the acid boiling and ready to escape if I couldn't find a way to shove it back, push it down, lock it away before it spilled over and hurt someone.

"What is it, Eudora?" The concern in Lorena's voice made me want to weep. To scream and scream until—

Desperate to escape my thoughts, I leaped right over the edge into crazy. Jerked to my feet, threw myself into a dance of the demented. Cast my head back, let my hair fly, begged the music to take me over, to free me. I spun off into the center of the room, whirling like a dervish, like some crazy mystic transported by the voices in his head. I thought about Agnes and Sonja cavorting with Conan on the outer skin of this shell. I needed the tornado inside me to latch onto their fierceness and suck it right down into me, so I'd be bold and fearless and nothing would bother me. I would hack my way through the jungle of doubt, unearth the temple where all the answers were buried. I'd stride across the clearing and God help anyone who tried to stop me—

"Eudora!" Lorena's voice, raised in alarm. She stopped me in mid-spin, her eyes huge and frightened.

Glory charged through the doorway, ready to take me apart.

"Eudora." Softer now, the way you'd speak to a deranged intruder, hoping to calm him before he shoots. "Honey," Lorena said, all gentleness. "Come sit down. Let me make you some tea."

I shuddered in her grasp. "That's my job," I said dully.

"Not right now. Sit here." She led me like a tall child and sat me in her chair. "Tell me what's wrong."

I sprang up like a jack in the box. "No!" I shook my head, looked around and came to myself at last. One long exhale, then, "I'm all right."

She and Glory traded glances. Glory shrugged and melted back into the outdoors.

Lorena studied me. "There's been a sorrow in you from the first day, child. Can you speak of it?"

Could I? I'd never told a soul. I could not imagine ever doing so. My sense of urgency clawed back. "How much longer are you planning to stay up here?"

Her eyes were too wise. "How long would it take me to convince you not to go?"

"Lorena, you know I . . . " I was so weary, so very much did not want to argue with her again over whether my journey was a fool's errand.

"I do." She patted my hand. "We won't tussle over that again. But that's not the only reason I'm here. I'm worried about Glory."

That brought my head up. "Why?"

"She's in pain. She's all alone, and that's my fault. I'm making progress with her, slow but coming along." A small smile curved her lips. "She wouldn't like knowing it."

"Amen to that."

"She needs to be brought into the fold, then people like Brad will leave her be."

Brought into the fold. I pictured Glory one of a flock of soft, woolly lambs, and that notion pushed at my crazy cloud. Put flight to some of my misery. Glory was more like the wolf in sheep's clothing, to my way of thinking. I found a smile. "You sure don't lack ambition."

"You can help me. You've already proven yourself to the townsfolk, and Glory trusts you. Between us, we could make people accept her."

Glory? Trust . . . *me?* I goggled at the notion. Lorena would think better of it if she knew all the ways I had failed Sister. She thought I was someone I was not, however much I wished she were right. I would have to tell her everything when the time came for me to leave—then she wouldn't be asking me to stay. She'd be happy to see the back of me.

But I could not tell her yet, I just couldn't.

Shaky as I felt, I was nowhere near ready for Lorena to hate me.

Indian Emily's Grave

Here lies Indian Emily, an Apache girl whose love for a young officer induced her to give warning of an Indian attack. Mistaken for an enemy, she was shot by a sentry, but saved the garrison from massacre.

KNIGHT IN JOHN DEERE GREEN

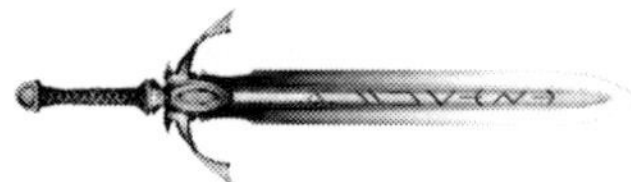

Before I left, I asked if I could bring Alex the next night. She and I had barely spoken outside work because I was gone so much, and I was worried about her. I couldn't continue my journey without knowing she was okay.

The idea wasn't without risk, though. Alex might tell Jeremy where his grandmother was, so the choice had to be Lorena's. I wasn't surprised that she said yes. Lorena, like her sister, had no shortage of grit.

Turned out that having Alex at the dome was a blessing. She couldn't stop giggling over the dancing, but when we finished, she cheered. She provided a much-needed spark of youth and a distraction for all of us. Even Glory came inside for the night, though she still stood by the door.

As I watched Alex learn the Lindy, I now understood Glory's on-the-outside-looking-in expression. Alex didn't worry about the future and seemed able to easily forget her past, while I was neck-deep in mortality, as were Lorena and Glory. We lacked the illusion that life grants pretty endings.

Alex, however, was a first-quarter moon growing ever brighter. I, for one, wanted to keep her that way, full of the clueless optimism you only possess at sixteen.

"Come here." She held out a hand and drew me into the dance. *Lose the gloom*, she mouthed to me, her back to Lorena, her forehead in a frown.

A wake-up call that Alex was young but not innocent. More a woman than I was, since she'd embraced a state I'd dodged for a long time.

For one glimmering instant, I pictured myself, belly rounded with child, then another breathless second when I thought I could feel the weight of that child in my arms. The sheer, outrageous joy of the notion knocked me right out of my misery.

So I joined in the dance, and when Lorena tired, Alex and I kept moving.

Afterward, I painted suns on Alex's big toenails to parallel Lorena's evening stars.

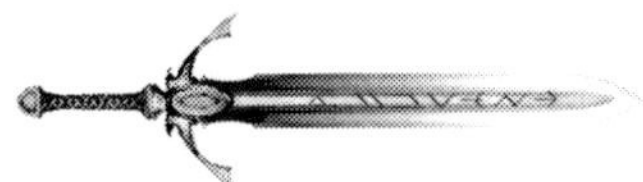

"One winter, my mother was housebound with three small children and snowdrifts to the tops of the trees," Lorena told us when we were settled in at her feet. I squirted oil into my palm and began to massage her left foot, kneading the sole and sliding my thumb over the arch. My touch was the only way Lorena would let me say what she meant to me. I'd tried, but words embarrassed her.

She sighed deeply, and for a moment, all we could hear was the cicadas outdoors. Glory had joined us, for a change, seated next to Lorena. Alex removed one of Glory's shoes, and Glory stiffened. At a sharp glance from Lorena, she frowned but complied.

Alex mimicked me, soaking Glory's feet first.

I nodded to urge Lorena on with the story. "Where was your father?"

"He was snowbound in town. It took him three days to get back to her, and even then, he had to borrow a horse to do it. We lived on a country road, and no one around those parts had ever heard of a snowplow." She chuckled. "Now that I'm grown, I can just imagine how Mother felt—did I mention we all had the measles?"

"Holy cow."

"Oh, I don't think she believed those cows were one bit holy. Spawns of Satan was more like it, since she had to shovel her way to the barn twice a day to milk them, then shovel her way back because the high winds kept blowing the snow into new drifts, obliterating her path. The well froze up, so she had to melt snow to have water, and the telephone lines were down, so she had no idea where Daddy was."

She paused to groan as I worked over the bony knobs of her toes. "Oh, child, you will make my eyes roll back into my head." She cast me a fond smile. "But don't you dare stop."

I smiled back. "I won't. So what were you all doing during this time?"

Her eyes shone bright with mischief. "Complaining nonstop about not being allowed to go out and play in the snow. Can you imagine it? Ungrateful wretches, children can be. Would have served us right if she'd thrown us out in the snow, fevers, sensitive eyes and all."

"You have to be patient with your kids." Alex was frowning. "You should try hard to understand them."

I started to defend Lorena, but Lorena beat me to answering. "That's true," she said calmly. "A good mother is strong for her family and puts her children's needs before her own. That's what my mother did then and so many other times, though she likely wanted to wring our necks."

"But she didn't," Alex insisted, and I wondered if this didn't have to do with her family, not Lorena's.

Lorena was unperturbed by the challenge. "No. You'll be driven to the edge of your strength sometimes, don't imagine you won't, but you can resist. A mother does what she has to in order to keep her family safe and whole."

Alex opened her mouth to respond, but just then the dogs started barking like crazy. Glory jumped up and charged outside barefoot, gripping the shotgun she had laid aside.

Then I heard the sound of an engine, and Bigot Brad immediately leaped to mind. I was only seconds behind Glory, shouting to Alex, "Stay with Lorena." I was wishing Glory would open up the safe and get me a gun instead of my sword, but whatever was required to defend Lorena and Alex and the baby, I was ready.

But as I raced outside, what I saw was not what I expected.

Ray, on his lawn tractor, steaming up the road, bellowing, "Lorena Beth Cashwell, I want to talk to you."

"You leave her alone." Glory tried to block him, but he simply steered the tractor around her. "Ray Cashwell, you stop now!" She lifted her weapon.

"No!" I screamed and took off running, shoving myself between her and Ray's unprotected back. "Glory, put it down." I forced my voice softer. "He loves her, can't you see that?"

"She's not ready." Her face was fierce. Desperate. "I won't have him dragging her off."

Then it dawned on me that Glory might be afraid if Lorena left, she would lose her again. "Glory, it'll be okay. She'll come back."

She shook her head. Shoved me aside and raced up the path.

I took off after her. "Ray!"

Then Lorena appeared in the doorway, and the look on her face froze Glory in her tracks and me, too.

Love, rich and glorious. The shine of tears in her eyes. "What are you doing here, old man?"

Ray shut off his engine and cleared his throat. "I'd think that was obvious, old woman. I'm here to take you home."

For a second, I could see everything in Lorena just melt, and I wanted to cry, watching it.

But then she drew herself up the way only Lorena could. Despite the hair that was tumbling over her shoulders, she was the woman with the scraped-back coronet. "How did you find me?"

I glanced at Alex in the doorway behind her, wondering if she'd betrayed us.

"I've known for a couple of days. Followed Eudora."

Ouch.

"Got tired of waiting for you to come to your senses."

"Well, you've wasted a trip, then." She turned to walk back inside.

"Lorena." He dismounted unsteadily from his tractor, took a step, then halted as she vanished through the doorway. I had never seen a sadder expression in my life.

Glory let her shotgun hang limply at her side. "Ray," she said softly. Reached out for him. "Give her some time."

He recoiled. "You don't touch me," he growled. Shook her off and started for the door—

BOOM! Behind us, the night suddenly shattered. The sky erupted into flames.

In the first shocked seconds, I froze. Ray whipped around to stare down the hill toward the road.

"The shop!" Glory shouted.

Bigot Brad, it had to be.

"I'll kill him!" She raced for her jeep.

Already back on his tractor, Ray charged down the road as fast as the tractor would move.

I ran, too, and jumped into the passenger side of Glory's jeep. Right behind me, Alex grabbed at my door handle. "Stay with Lorena," I ordered.

"No. I'm going with you."

I spotted Lorena heading toward us.

"Go back," Glory yelled at her. "Stay and call the sheriff."

Lorena only shook her head and kept coming. I didn't doubt one bit that she'd walk all the way if Glory refused to take her.

"Alex," I pleaded, very conscious of her condition. "You go inside and call."

But Alex yanked the door open.

"Alex—"

"You can catch up faster, big girl. We don't have time to argue."

"But—"

"Please." For Glory to want to call the authorities, much less to say please . . .

"All right." I raced inside, hearing her engine rev behind me. I made the call, but refused the dispatcher's request that I remain by the phone. As far out as we were, I had no idea how long it would take them to reach us, and anything could happen by then. I had to be with Lorena and Alex.

Charging down the hill through the skittering shadows cast by the trees, backlit by flames leaping higher and higher, I didn't know what to expect ahead. This was surely Bigot Brad's doing, but would he and his buddies be armed to the teeth? I gripped my sword harder as I ran, wishing yet again for a weapon with range, never mind that I had no training.

As I rounded the last clump of oaks, I saw the gun shop in flames. Ray hobbled around the building, chasing two figures who were easily outrunning him.

"Ray!" Lorena went after him. Glory and Alex were right behind her.

Abruptly, Ray staggered. Doubled over.

"Ray—" Lorena cried.

He turned and saw her. "Get back!" Abruptly, he swiveled toward the gun shop, listening intently. First tiny pops, then loud reports, more and more rapid.

"The ammo—" Glory voice was strangled. "Propane tank—explode—" was all I could make out over the crackling of the flames.

I raced to help Ray and Lorena, shouting to Alex to run for the road.

Then . . . one instant of utter stillness. As though the universe held its breath.

The hairs on my whole body rose.

Whoosh—The roar of the damned, the voice of hell. Heat and light and deafening thunder. Shouts and screams and all I could think was I had to save Lorena and Alex both, that Sister could die again and I'd never find her—

The ground shook and I yelled—

Lorena—

Alex—

Sister!

I was knocked flat, with no room for breath.

Nancy Parker Cabin

Home of "Grandma" (Mrs. John) Parker, local herb doctor. Here she brewed medicinal tea in a huge pot over an open fire; walked miles in Indian-infested country to visit the sick. Lived here over a decade. Sold cabin after eyesight failed, 1888.

SCAR TISSUE

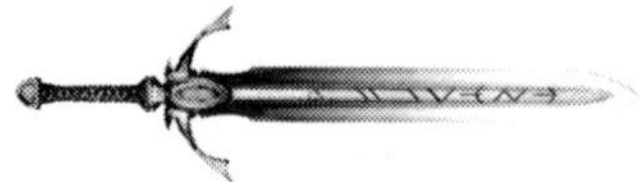

I'm frying okra, but it keeps burning, every single batch. I'm crawling through a smoke-filled kitchen, calling for Sister.

Then I'm in a green meadow, surrounded by people laughing and playing, but I don't know any of them.

At last I see Mama and Sister smiling, both beautiful and whole. There's a man beside Mama, very tall with auburn hair. Beneath the nearest tree is a baby whose mother has blond hair cascading past her shoulders. She turns, and it's Alex, and I cannot bear it. Around the tree trunk strolls a smiling Ray, his arm tucked into Lorena's. Glory steps into my field of vision, shaking her head at me. Alex joins in, then Lorena and Ray. Mama and Sister and the man who must be Casper, everyone pointing behind me, telling me I have to go back, that I can't stay, that I have to be alone again, and I start crying.

Please, I beg them. *Please let me stay. I don't want to be alone anymore. Please . . . please . . . please—*

"Big girl, that's enough. Wake up." Glory's voice wasn't sweet and cheerful, it was impatient and crusty and . . . real. Oh, lordy, real.

I opened my eyes to searing light. "Glory?" Whimpered and shut them fast. "Hurts. What—"

The roar of flames. The hot slap of hell. I struggled to sit up. "Lorena. Where is she? Where's Alex? Ray?" Oh, God. Oh, God. My dream. Were they all dead? But Glory was here and she was in it . . .

"Shh," she murmured and awkwardly patted my arm. "You lie back, Eudora. You rest now."

It was bad. It had to be bad or she'd tell me. "Are they all . . . gone?" Tears welled from my eyes.

"Good Lord, no." But her expression was solemn. "Lorena's bruised real bad, and her hair's all singed. Alex—" She looked away.

I gripped her hand. "Tell me."

"They're checking the baby. The blast knocked her about ten feet, and she showed some signs of early labor. They say sometimes stress can cause it, especially since she's underweight."

"I need to see her." I shoved aside my covers. I just couldn't stand the thought of how scared she must be.

"Hold your horses. You got shaken up pretty good. You calm down, and I'll go get the nurse."

I glanced around. "Where are we?"

"Emergency room in Abilene."

Then I noticed what I should have earlier, that one arm was bandaged. "Are you okay?"

"I'm fine." Her tone made it clear that hovering would not be appreciated.

"What about Ray?"

"Damn fool." She blinked hard. "Acting like some hero, trying to carry Lorena out of harm's way."

"Glory, tell me."

"He—after, he—" I'd never seen her so shaken. "He stopped breathing, turned a bad color. Thought my arms would fall off, doing CPR."

"Is he—" I bit my lip. "Is he dead?"

She scowled. "Of course not. I managed until Tommy got there, then I showed him how to help until the paramedics—" Her face crumpled then.

"You saved him, Glory. You saved Ray's life."

A terse shake of her head as her shoulders stiffened once more.

"Everyone will thank you. They'll understand that you're not a—" I pressed my lips together.

"A what? A murderer?" She stared at me defiantly. "Well, you're wrong, Eudora. I am exactly that. I killed my best friend."

"But . . . she asked you to. That's not murder, it's an act of mercy."

"Is it?" I'd never seen this fierce woman look so uncertain. "If it was so damn noble, then why does it eat at me still? How come I can't have some peace?" She paced to the end of my bed. "She begged me, goddammit." She jerked to a halt and wheeled around, her face a ruin, her shoulders bowed. "I didn't want to," she whispered. "I wanted her to live."

"I know." I clasped her forearm.

"Don't you patronize me." She wrenched away. "You can't possibly understand."

"Glory—" This was the moment. To help her, I had to give up my darkest secret. Tell her how it was to make the other choice. That she'd done the right thing.

If only I were strong enough. Brave enough. "Glory—"

"Leave me alone," she cried. "Just mind your own damn business." She yanked open the curtain that surrounded my bed.

"No!" I stood and took a step, but my head got dizzy, and I had to grasp the sheet. "Glory, wait. Please—I do know. I do."

She hesitated, and I knew I had to speak up now.

But I searched for the words and came up empty. When she shook her head in disgust and started to go, a sob broke out of me, snapping the stranglehold of my fear. "My—my sister, she was dying. She—she asked me—"

I was going to throw up. I clapped a hand over my mouth, but somehow the words clawed their way out. "She begged me, too, just like your friend. She wept from the pain, and she pleaded with me to help her. To end it. She—she'd skipped doses to save up enough, but she'd gotten too weak to reach the pills she'd stuck in the back of the drawer. All I had to do—all I—"

I broke then, just . . . broke.

Arms came around me, gentle ones. Glory, of all people. "It's okay," she soothed.

But it wasn't. It would never be. Rage uncoiled from deep in my gut, and I shook her off. "You don't get it. She gave up everything—*everything*—to take care of me," I yelled. I wanted my sword then, so bad. I could feel it in my fist, picture how I would slash at that damned striped curtain, knock everything off the table beside me. Charge through the world and dare them all to come close to me. "Get away from me!" I screamed. I heard a commotion outside, but I didn't care what anyone did to me.

Glory stood her ground. When a nurse peered through the curtain and a security guard stepped forward, she waved them off, and such was the force of her that they obeyed.

"Listen here," she began, but I kept shaking my head.

"Leave me be, Glory, just—"

"Hush up now." Her tone that could not be refused. She grabbed hold and started rocking me awkwardly even as I struggled. I was big, but I was no match for her then.

She kept on rocking until the screaming drained out of me. Then she spoke again. "I can't say what I did was right, Eudora." She pulled back, and her eyes gripped mine so I could see the truth in her. "I hurt real bad, too. Every damn day."

My throat was raw with tears I had no right to shed. "The only important thing she ever asked me to do, and I—" I couldn't look at Glory anymore or those people staring at me like I was nuts, but I had to tell her the worst so she'd see that I was beyond redemption and give up on me. Give me what I deserved.

"I got mad at her, Glory. Her hurting so bad and those pills so close, and I—I—" I hunched over, filled up with hate for myself. "I just want to tell her," I sobbed. "That I'm sorry. That I was scared to lose her, that's all, scared of being alone. That I'd do it right if I could."

"Right or wrong isn't that simple. I still don't know."

"But you didn't leave Molly sobbing from agony. You weren't a coward, you acted. You didn't—" I had to force out the words. "You didn't miss her dying." I buried my head in my hands. "She was alone at the end, Glory—alone when she made sure I never had to be. I know exactly what wrong is. I just don't know how to live with it."

A long pause. Then one hand came to rest on my head. "You go on, Eudora, one day at a time. All you can do."

"I'm too tired." And I was. So weary I thought even one step was beyond me.

In a surprisingly tender gesture, she brushed my sweat-soaked hair back from my face. "A hurt like that makes a scar on the inside of you that never goes away. Scar tissue's strong, though, tougher than the flesh around it. You use that scar, and you build on it." Then she smoothed her hand over me again and again, and each stroke seemed to ease out some of the misery. "And maybe how you live with it is you use that foundation to help someone else. You can't go back—what's done is done. You got to go on, that's all, but you can, big girl. You are stronger than you know."

I couldn't see it. I sure couldn't feel it. All I could do was shake my head hopelessly.

"Sit up now, hear? Wipe your eyes," she said gruffly. "Stop feeling sorry for yourself."

Oh, my mad stirred up then. Got on its hind legs and hissed at her.

"That's better." A satisfied nod. "Now get yourself squared away while I go see if I can spring you. Alex needs you, and so does Lorena. We don't have time for a pity party." She didn't give me a chance to say anything, just pushed through the curtain and disappeared past the throng of people who suddenly found other things to get busy doing.

I glared at where she'd disappeared, then I sank back on the bed, weary to my toenails. I stayed like that, real still, and tried to figure out how I felt. Bone-tired, yes, but . . . lighter somehow. I probed around the hurt real gingerly like your tongue tiptoes around a sore tooth, and I was surprised to find that the poison lake inside of me had receded a little.

I would always carry that scar, though, the one that bore Sister's name.

Which was only fair, I guess, since Sister was the best part of whatever strong there was in me.

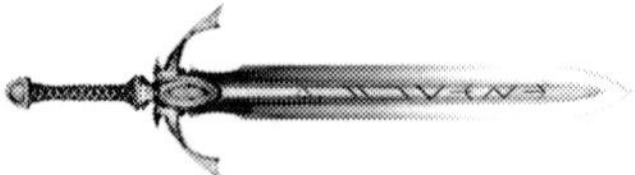

Alex was undergoing tests, so the nurses wouldn't let me see her yet, no matter how much of a hissy I was willing to pitch. Fortunately, Glory dragged me off before I got myself arrested. Security was already following me after my earlier outburst.

"I'll take you to Lorena, but you are not going in there acting like some madwoman," she growled. "She will only worry more about you, and neither she nor Ray needs that now. You settle down, or I swear I will restrain you myself."

Truth was, I could barely put one foot in front of the other, so I didn't actually mind her bossing me around. Especially when my brain cleared enough to see what I was missing, the devastation in her eyes. "Poor Glory," I murmured. "You love them both." She didn't flinch when I slid my hand around to clasp hers, a sure sign of just how upset she was.

We shambled down the hall, an odd couple, hard to tell exactly who was leaning on whom. When we got to Ray's room, I pressed my palm to the nearly-closed door and pushed gently, digging for the strength to be all cheerful and bright.

Until I saw them. And stopped in my tracks.

Lorena was perched on Ray's bed, her head on his shoulder, holding onto his arm as he slept. His cheek rested on her hair, the way they must have fit thousands of times before.

There it was, captured in one snapshot glimpse. Love, the forever kind, the sort that might stumble and get off track but somewhere down deep, where you can't screw it up forever, is solid rock. Lives and families can be built on that foundation for anyone lucky enough to get a ticket to enter that world.

The rest of us just stand outside and wish.

I was about to back from the room when Ray opened his eyes, his brows lifting, a question in his gaze.

It wasn't hard to figure what he was asking. Would I run now? Or would I stay and help her through all of this? He didn't know about my search for Sister, but it probably wouldn't matter to him anyway. Lorena meant everything to him.

Just as he knew she meant a whole lot to me.

But what about my journey? Sister's year would be up real soon, yet how could I leave these people when they had been so kind to me?

I couldn't. I nodded to Ray. He nodded back, then settled against Lorena and fell asleep.

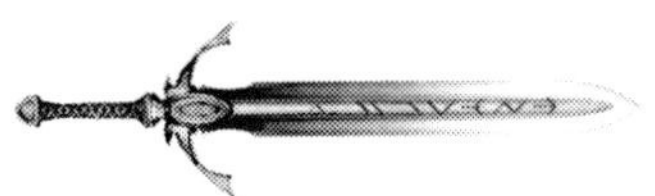

When I finally got to see Alex, Jeremy stood protectively by her side. I couldn't blame him; she looked tiny in that bed, wired up to all kinds of monitors and IVs. When she saw me, her eyes widened.

"Hey," I said.

"Are you okay?" she asked.

"Yeah. I, uh, I just wanted to check on you." I ate her up with my eyes, but I stayed by the door. Glory waited in the hall.

Alex studied me, then spoke to Jeremy. "Would you give us a minute?"

He didn't like leaving, I could tell. As he neared me, he leaned over. "Don't you upset her. The doctor said she has to stay calm and quiet or he'll throw all of us out." The goofy, calf-sick boy had vanished, and I glimpsed the man he would become.

"I won't." I squeezed his arm. "I promise."

Then we were alone.

"What are they saying?" I asked her. "The doctors."

"She's going to be all right. She has to." She put one hand over her belly. "They showed her to me on the ultrasound," she said, eyes welling. "I saw her fingers."

My own throat got tight. "I'd like to have seen it." I thought I really meant it this time.

"I can't go yet, not until she's born," she said. "But if you'll wait I'll go with you after. We will, that is."

I frowned. "You don't want to leave Jewel."

"But you need a keeper." Her lips curved a little. "Val agreed."

I rolled my eyes. "And you're designated?"

"He's not here to do it." She hesitated. "I miss him. Do you think he's okay?"

Oh, boy. How to answer that without shattering her illusions about him?

"He thought about stealing your wallet that first night, you know, but he didn't." She pressed her lips together. "I wanted to, too."

So much for thinking she was the one with illusions. "But you didn't either." And with that, I sent up a little prayer that Val had stayed on the straight and narrow, then consigned him to the Fates. All three of them. "You know I don't really need a keeper, right?"

"Maybe." She shrugged. "But if you're set on searching for your sister, you shouldn't have to go alone."

If she knew the designs I had on that precious life she carried, would she be so quick to offer? My throat ached because this half-grown girl was looking out for me like I was the one who needed taking care of.

For too long, I saw, I had been. She was pregnant, she was barely more than a child, and she was more grown up than me. I walked closer to the bed. "You don't want to go, Alex, and you shouldn't. You and your baby can be a part of all this. You can make a home here."

Hope stole from the shadows. "So could you. You're so important to them."

You could learn how to stay, Val had insisted.

I went very still, trying to wrap my mind around the notion. I knew how vital they'd all become to me, but that the reverse could be true floored me.

"You're not that tough, you know. You're lonely, just like me, like Val. That's why you're searching for your sister's soul, because you want a family."

From the mouths of babes. "I never had a home but her. I miss her so much."

"There's a home right here, for you as much as for me," Alex said.

In that moment, I acknowledged that this place and these people had begun to sink roots into my heart, to send tendrils winding through my veins that would not easily be plucked out.

New life, a new Eudora, could bloom from them.

In some ways, it already had.

"Well, I can't leave yet anyway. Lorena will need my help for awhile." I sat on the bed beside her. "Let's see how it goes."

"For how long?" Her eyes narrowed, and I guessed I'd earned that skepticism.

I was surprised to actually feel playful. "At least enough time for me to convince Jeremy that you're too young to get married."

She spluttered in outrage, and I chuckled. Hugged her then, and she clung to me. "I'm scared, Pea."

"Don't be. We're all here for you, Lorena and Glory and me. This baby is going to be fine. Anyhow, I dare any stupid contractions to beat Dark Agnes."

Alex giggled a little, then burst into tears.

My own eyes were none too dry. I hugged her once more, real quick. "So." I had to clear my throat. "The doctors want you to rest. I should go."

She grasped for my hand. "Stay." She ducked her head. "That is, if you don't mind."

I was, to put it mildly, flabbergasted. "I would like nothing better." I scooched onto the mattress beside her, and I felt her relax against me. We laid our heads back on the pillow, and it was like all the air just leaked out of me. I was so tired I couldn't move even a pinky toe.

Alex's fingers squeezed mine. "I'm glad you're here, Pea," she whispered. "Please stay."

She wasn't talking about this room, I was pretty sure. She meant Jewel. I kept my eyes closed so I wouldn't have to lie to her, and soon she drifted off. I lay there, comforted by the warmth of her next to me.

But even as exhausted and sore as I was, it was a long while before I slept.

Katherine Ann Porter
(May 15, 1890-September 18,1980)

Born Callie Russell Porter in Indian Creek. Katherine Anne Porter moved to Hays County with her family following her mother's death in 1892. She left Texas in 1915 and worked as an actress, teacher, reporter and publicist in such places as Chicago, Denver, Mexico, and New York. Her first book of short stories was published in 1930. Her acclaimed 1962 novel, Ship of Fools, was followed by the Pulitzer prizewinning The Collected Stories of Katherine Anne Porter in 1965. Upon her death in 1980, her ashes were buried next to her mother's grave in Indian Creek Cemetery.

BROUGHT INTO THE FOLD

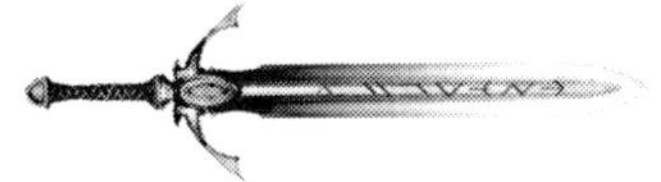

So I spent my days running the café and store.

With, if you can imagine, Glory's help. She was barred from cooking, though. Some causes are just lost from the beginning. She could wash dishes to beat the band, however, and bit by bit, the townsfolk were coming to accept her presence. Bigot Brad and his buddies might not have, but since they were now guests at the county jail for vandalism and assault, phooey on what they might think.

I myself didn't have a lot of time to ponder my interrupted journey, though I kept a map in the glove box of my newly smooth-running car, and some days I consulted it. Not often, though—Glory and I were also swapping off shifts helping Lorena tend to Ray and Alex in Lorena's house, where Alex and I had moved in for the time being. Millie helped out when she could.

Until, that is, her baby decided to arrive. Not—after all that mopping I'd done—on the café floor, oh no. She chose Lorena's kitchen to get things started. We stuck Millie in my bedroom, then

Lorena had me call Millie's husband and the midwife. In no time flat, the whole family had showed up.

Yep, I said midwife. A home birth, if you can believe that.

It took hours, I swear. And every time I edged toward a door to get the heck out, somebody nabbed me. Lorena, I am positive, sent Tommy with an invitation to watch, which I declined so fast the poor man hadn't finished asking yet.

Then it was Sally, wanting to talk about her new idea to go to beauty school, followed by a sister-in-law of somebody, wondering if I knew a man she'd met from Austin. Finally, I decided I might as well cook, since my escape routes were blocked and that baby appeared to be in no hurry.

A chocolate cake was cooling and the ingredients for the icing were laid out. Potato salad was done, and I was slicing ham along with tomatoes fresh from Tommy's garden. If that baby didn't show up soon, I was considering making pies next. Fried okra, of course, had to be saved for the last minute.

Suddenly, a cheer went up, and I heard laughing and crying. Through the kitchen door burst Alex, eyes shining.

"What are you doing out of bed?" I demanded.

That *whatever* look was spreading over her features, I could see it. Since she'd left the hospital and I'd become her warden, Hallmark moments had been scarce between Alex and me. I don't know what I was thinking, all those pictures in my head about soulful talks and shared laughter, accompanied by rainbows and violins.

"It's a girl, a sweet baby girl. Want to go see?" Apparently, her delight trumped her irritation with me.

"After you lie down."

Mutiny tightened her mouth. "I'm fine. Lorena said I could stay."

"Alex—"

"Pea, come on. Give it a rest. Come see her." Her eyes shone. "Lorena says she has Millie's mouth. I wonder how much my baby will look like me." Her expression turned dreamy.

As I watched her, it hit me, the damage I could do to her, staking a claim to her child. Hovering, hoping for signs of my sister. Even if Sister was in there, a new baby should mean a new chance. Alex had so little; didn't she deserve at least that? Didn't the baby?

But how could I let that hope go?

Yet even as I clutched at it, the enormity of what I'd been considering crashed in on me. I had no right.

Even if I had such a need.

If I relinquished that possibility, though, I didn't know how I could bear it. I sought my voices, all of them, any of them.

But only silence greeted me.

I didn't look at Alex anymore. I couldn't. By rote, I stirred the potato salad again. Stood there, staring into a desert where my hopes had once thrived.

"You should take a look, Pea," she said, blessedly unaware of the expectations I'd placed on her, all my fine plans in which her baby had starred.

"In a minute." Carefully, I kept my back to her, and soon she left.

I remained in the kitchen alone, while in the next room, everyone else was celebrating, laughing, crying. Sharing stories of other births, passing on their common history.

Together. All part of one.

Oh, they would have welcomed me, I'm sure, but I was never more aware that I was the only person here who had no one on this earth she was related to, no connection by blood. I was merely filling in the spaces of others: guest boarder, temporary cook, part-time nurse. Nothing had changed for me, really. I had tried to belong, as I had promised Alex, but I didn't, not the way they did.

Then through the open door I spotted Glory, lingering in the hall, her face aglow even as she hung around the edges. I knew the feeling. But even Glory was blood kin.

I tried to picture myself walking in there, but I couldn't. I untied my apron, checked the burners—

And walked out into a night that seemed endless.

A future I could no longer imagine.

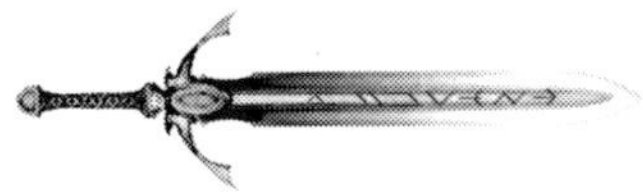

I sat in the front seat of my car, trying to read the map by flashlight. New Mexico seemed like Mars at that point, but I didn't really want to go back to Austin. Maybe I'd just close my eyes and stab a finger to pick a destination.

A sharp rap on my window like to gave me a heart attack.

"Open up, big girl." Glory's fists were on her hips.

"Go away."

"Don't make me yank you out of that car."

I snorted. "Like you could." Except that even several inches shorter, she might manage. I wouldn't bet the farm against her.

"What on earth are you doing, Eudora?"

I shoved the door open. "I wish to goodness everybody would stop asking me that."

"You should be inside with the rest of us. You're hurting Lorena's feelings."

Boy, she knew how to hit where it hurt. I switched topics. "Is Alex still up? She ought to get back in bed."

"Her doctor said limited activity after three weeks. And don't change the subject."

I stuck my chin in the air. "Limited, yes. That does not mean a party." I concentrated on folding up the map in my hand.

"Still having a tough time with her?" She didn't wait for an answer. "She fights you because she's afraid you won't stay, don't you know that?"

"What?"

"They all are." I noted that she didn't include herself. "Lorena's got enough on her mind."

"I'm doing everything I can to help her, but—"

"But what?" Glory's jaw clenched. "I swear you do try me, Eudora. What exactly is it you think you're going to find? And don't tell me your sister. You know better than that. It's time to get real, big girl."

Everyone had expressed doubt of one sort or another, mostly kind and gentle nudges or benign amusement.

Typical of Glory, she smacked me right in the face with hers.

The bubble-wrap of faith I'd tucked around me popped, snap by snap by snap, until there was no more borrowed conviction to cushion me. Sister had needed the comfort of believing in reincarnation, and my guilt and despair when she was gone had made me forget the Pea who wasn't half-crazy with grief, the one who'd once bitten her tongue half in two not to argue with Sister about her notion. Instead I had latched on for dear life to the idea that finding the eternal part of her would put me right back where we were before Sister went to the doctor and our world, the only world I knew how to live in, crumbled.

I'd operated in a fog for nearly a year now, I began to see, longer still if you counted the months of her dying. I'd tackled this journey looking for markers to light my path to her because I had no idea how to be on my own. How to settle myself . . . or to settle down.

I could hardly bear to think that wherever Sister was, the place I yearned for no longer existed.

That it never would.

The very thought knocked the stuffing out of me. "So I'm supposed to just, what, say *oh well, shit happens?*" My fingers were clenched into fists. "Presto, and I forget?"

"'Course not." She looked weary now, and old. "But if you don't find some way to put it behind you, you get bitter and hard."

"Like you have?" She flinched. Yes, it was a low blow, but I was fighting for my life. "Exactly how do I accomplish that miracle, huh, Glory? Tell me."

She straightened. "Get in the car," she snapped.

"What?"

"I have something to show you." She rounded the car. "Well, don't just stand there—hop in and drive."

I started to protest, but what good had arguing with Glory ever done, and besides I was as lost as I'd ever felt. I had no idea what my next step should be.

She directed me toward the gun shop, but instead of turning in, we went a little further down to the next caliche road. She got out and opened the gate. I drove past, then waited for her to close it again, as I'd learned one did in the country to prevent livestock from getting out on the road.

Through clumps of live oaks and mesquite and around a curve, at last we came upon a small frame house that appeared deserted. "Who lives here?"

Glory didn't answer, just looked through the windshield with the saddest expression I'd ever seen.

"Glory?"

She came to with a quick shake of her head, then opened her door and got out. "Come on," she said, visibly steeling herself.

The full moon illuminated the ground before us, but I grabbed my flashlight, just in case. I was not a fan of walking around outside in the dark, not in a place that was clearly working its way back to wild.

Glory made it to the steps leading to the covered front porch before she halted as if she'd hit an invisible barrier. I joined her but waited silently. Something momentous seemed to be happening, but I had no idea what.

After a bit, she spoke. "What's the longest you ever stayed in one place?"

Startled by the question, I frowned. "I don't know . . . six months, maybe, well, except for at the end." I had remained in the duplex where I last lived with Sister longer than anywhere else. I told myself it was to honor my promise never to budge once the choice was mine, but I recognized now that I had simply been too lost, too frightened. That I stayed because I was afraid to leave the last place she'd been.

"Running doesn't solve a thing, Eudora. Trust me, I've tried."

"I know that." And I did. "But you had someplace to run from, Glory. You had a place you belonged."

"And I had the sense to come back, even if I told myself I hated it." She faced me then. "So you gonna take off, just because everything's not all prettied up and happily ever after?"

"I'm not—" I stared at her. Because that was exactly what Mama always did, chased after the next better thing, the pot of gold that would vanish almost the instant she got there.

"Suck it up, big girl. Dark Agnes would kick your wimpy ass."

"I don't care."

"Yes, you do." A slow smile spread. She nodded toward the house. "You want somewhere to belong? You can have this."

My mouth dropped open. "This? You mean the house? Whose is it? Why—what—?"

"With one condition."

"Which is?"

"You get that bony behind of yours back to training, and you compete in June. After that, your life's your own, but until then, you don't even think about leaving."

June. So many months away. A whole winter, a Thanksgiving and a Christmas and—

"I have to sit down." I collapsed on the steps.

Gingerly she settled beside me, as though expecting an electric shock or something.

"Whose house is this, Glory?" But suddenly, I knew. It had that air of sadness I was all too familiar with, that feeling of unfinished business. "It's Molly's, isn't it?"

She gripped the edge of the step. "She left everything to me, told me to sell it and keep the money, but—"

I understood. "Ghosts aren't so easy to shed, are they?"

She sighed and shook her head. "And forgiving yourself is harder. I'm not promising miracles, Eudora."

We sat there in silence for a while.

"You want to see inside?" she asked.

"In a minute." I needed some time to let all this settle in. To figure out if I could handle what she was asking of me. "Am I your do-over, is that it?"

"What?" A line appeared between her brows. "Of course not." She was gathering up her prickly persona, but I could see all the way through it now, and I was pretty sure I was right.

So what would be my starting point in this new life? My do-over?

The answer, I discovered, had been right there in front of me all along.

Alex. To be there for her, to use the scar on my heart to be strong for her, be the family she needed. Maybe I'd found a sister, just not the one I'd envisioned.

Sister was gone. I would never get absolution from her.

God, it killed me to say that.

But somewhere inside, I thought I could face it now. That it didn't hurt as much as it once would have. I touched my bracelet. Under the harsh light of Glory's ruthless realism, I began to see all those markers I thought were Fate, all those turns in the road, differently. Maybe Sister hadn't been leading me to her, after all. Maybe I was finding my way to myself instead.

Whatever there was of Sister in this world lived inside me and nowhere else. All I'd learned from her about not giving up, no matter what life threw at you. About sticking like glue to those who were important to you. The only way I could make amends now was to live up to the powerful example she'd set.

"You would have liked Sister."

There was a long pause, and when Glory spoke, her voice was a little hoarse. "I expect I would." She patted my knee a couple of times, and then she stood. "You ready?"

She might have been talking about the house or forgiving myself or the sword competition. Maybe belonging in Jewel. I wasn't altogether sure.

But it didn't really matter. I rose and sucked in a big ole breath like you do right before you jump into the deep end of the pool. "Yeah. I guess I am."

And I followed her inside.

Sally Scull

Woman rancher, horse trader, champion "cusser." Ranched NW of here. In Civil War Texas, Sally Scull (or Skull) freight wagons took cotton to Mexico to swap for guns, ammunition, medicines, coffee, shoes, clothing and other goods vital to the Confederacy.

Dressed in trousers, Mrs. Scull bossed armed employees; was sure shot with the rifle carried on her saddle or the two pistols strapped to her waist.

Of good family, she had children cared for in New Orleans school. Often visited them. Loved dancing. Yet during the war, did extremely hazardous "man's work."

SWORD WOMAN

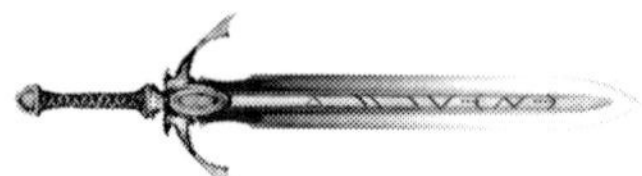

"You're up next," says the lady in the calico vest and skirt. It slays me how the people of Cross Plains, who appear more suited to rodeos and church picnics, get behind the Conan the Barbarian Festival when their forebears would have gladly run Robert E. Howard out of town on a rail. The more I read about the man, the more I realize he was one weird dude.

Yep, it's June, and I am in Cross Plains.

Yesterday, Alex, the baby and I accompanied Glory on the tour of Howard's home, a small, plain white frame house frozen in the 1930s. A sweet little woman in a polyester pantsuit showed us the room where he killed himself, proudly pointing out a typewriter just like the one he used, the one that wound up spattered with his blood.

I grabbed little Valentina (Alex, it turns out, has a sentimental streak) and left the room. Some things are not meant for tiny ears to hear. Who can be sure what babies comprehend?

So anyway, like I said, it's June, and I'm still living in Jewel, in

Molly's house, where Alex and the baby live with me and I am actually not too bad at babysitting. I am pretty much running the store and café with help from Alex and Millie and Glory, while Lorena and Ray have fired up the RV again.

I have my own cheering section here, though Valentina is farther away than I'd like, up in the stands with her mother. I do believe I could compete better with just one more sniff of the baby's neck, that talcum-powdered, milky smell that is all the innocence and hope in the world. "I'll be right back," I say to my escort.

"Not so fast, big girl." Glory grips my upper arm just above the cool engraved metal armbands she loaned me to go with my bracelet. "Don't chicken out now."

"I'm not. I just—" I search the crowd for familiar faces. I spot first Alex, then Jeremy, who is waiting anxiously for Alex to turn eighteen so he can tell me to butt out. I see Ray nod from beside him. Lorena, holding hands with Ray, smiles reassuringly.

I'm still not a part of a couple myself, but that's okay. I've got my hands full, being a sister, an aunt, a granddaughter. And who knows what to Glory.

"Eudora O'Brien—" My name is called over the loudspeaker, and my stomach is an icy ball of nerves.

"Remember, watch your opponent's eyes, and you'll know his next move," Glory counsels.

Yep, that's right, *his* next move. Conan is everywhere at this event, but not many women are into Red Sonja or Dark Agnes, though most of the men surely are. If I want to compete, I have to go against a Conan.

Good thing I found my mojo. My steel springs and whalebone. I've learned a lot from Sister and Mama and Big Lil, from Dark Agnes and Lorena and Glory, strong women all. I take a deep breath and get ready to walk out into the ring.

"Go get 'em, Red," a very familiar voice calls out from behind me. "Kick that Conan poser's butt."

No way. No freaking way.

I'm tempted to turn. To assure myself it's really Val, but even if it is, I am not the same person he left. I have a family now, even if it's nothing like the one I envisioned. I have experienced my own reincarnation as someone I would never have recognized but am coming to like quite a lot.

Though, to be fair, if Val has come back to Jewel, he's probably not the same person, either.

Just then the judge beckons me so instead of looking, I give a V for Victory sign over my shoulder, grip the pommel of my sword and start walking.

Maybe Fate's throwing me another curveball, but hey, everyone needs a little adventure.

Sometimes you just have to take the leap and see where the road leads.

Home of Whitney Montgomery, Poet (1877-1966)

Born in Navarro County in white-columned house across pasture south of this site. Began to write poetry when he was 15 years old. Author of more than 500 published poems which appeared in many major magazines; won numerous poetry prizes.

Moved to Dallas, 1927. Was editor and publisher of "Kaleidograph" magazine and press. Helped to organize and was vice president of the poetry society of Texas.

I Own a Home

I can not boast of a broad estate,
But I own a home with a rose at the gate.

I hold the title, and I keep the keys,
And in and out I can go as I please.

My home is not grand, but I live content,
For no man sends me a bill for rent.

And no man comes with a brush and a pail
To paint a sign on my door, "FOR SALE."

I can not boast of a broad estate,
But I own a home with a rose at the gate.

Reading Group Guide
The Goddess of Fried Okra

Find your personal signposts on Pea's road trip

1. Have you ever taken a road trip to find yourself? If not, do you wish you had . . . or think you might still do so?

2. Pea begins her journey lost in the landscape of grief, and for much of the book she is looking for Sister and hoping for signs to lead her there. How much of her search is motivated by a belief that she will actually find Sister reincarnated?

3. Pea says once Sister died, she lost all she ever knew of home, that all she knew of family came from Sister. What does it mean to have a family? Is family always comprised of those related by blood?

4. What significance does fried okra play in this book?

5. Is there a theme among the markers quoted in the book? Does your state have similar markers? What's the most interesting one you've ever seen? Which one did you like best in the book?

6. How do you feel about how Mama mothered Pea? Was Sister more of a mother than Mama was? Are there other mother figures in this book?

7. Female power is a theme in this book. Which characters demonstrate aspects of female power to Pea?

8. How does Pea learn who she is? What influences have shaped her as the book begins? Who are her guides as the book proceeds? Are there people in your life who've served as guides for you in your own journey toward understanding yourself?

9. Given Val's background, why do you think he's returned to Jewel? Do you believe he's gone straight or not? Is Ray as influential on Val as Lorena is on Pea? Do you think Pea and Val have a future together? If you do, what do you think that future consists of?

10. The importance of sisters is another theme in the book. How does having or not having a sister impact a woman's life? If you lose a sister, can you ever fill that place in your heart?

11. How important is the world of women in your life? Do you think that as you age, your women friends become more important or less so?

12. If someone very important to you begged you to assist them in dying or to allow them to die, would you? Could you? What do you think the ramifications to you emotionally would be, either way?

Acknowledgments

Sometimes life gives us gifts of pure grace; one such for me was meeting Pea. She began as an exercise in sheer fun—sitting on my deck in a wicker rocker, taking a few weeks off from my contracted writing to see if, after several years as a working writer, I still remembered how to play, how to write for the sheer fun of it, a joy too easily lost under the pressure of deadlines and expectations, both mine and others'.

I knew nothing about Pea, even her name at first—only that this woman was on the road searching for the reincarnated soul of the sister she desperately missed. It all seemed like a lark those first few days, drinking this killer Mexican iced coffee recipe while listening to birdsong under my live oaks and seeing where Pea would take me next.

When it was time to get back to my deadlines, Pea was never far from me, and over the next few years, I returned to her often, letting the flight of fancy take me away whenever possible. It led to such adventures as the Conan the Barbarian Festival in Cross Plains, Texas (yes, it's real, though the sword-fighting competition is only my idea of what should go on.) Then there were the back roads meanderings to check out various markers; in the course of doing so, my husband added to his collection of photos of oddball sights one misses when traveling by interstate highways. (And my thanks to Betty Dooley Awbrey and Claude Dooley, authors of a wonderful resource called *Why Stop?* which was invaluable in locating some of the markers.)

There are many I need to thank for believing in both me and this book: my family is already mentioned in the dedication, as is my dear friend Kathy Sobey. My longtime friend Barbara Pearce colluded with Kathy in beginning jars of quarters to save for frocks for the movie premiere (how lovely it is to have friends with faith.) Others, some of whom read Pea in various incarnations and all of whom encouraged me not to give up on her include Karen Solem, Chris Flynn, Marsha Zinberg, Beverley Sotolov, Karen Hicks, Bob and Margarite Holt, Nancy Munger, Mark Mitchell, Trista Black, Pam Parker, Charlotte Greene, Amber Pearce, Kerrie and Jim Steiert, Dinah Dinwiddie, Barbara Keiler, Patsy Meredith and Karyn Witmer-Gow. I will never be able to thank you all enough for helping me keep my faith alive.

To Deborah Smith and Debra Dixon of Belle Books, mongo

thanks for loving Pea as I do. Working with these bright, talented and dedicated women has been more fun than the law should allow, and I am filled with admiration for both who they are and what they've accomplished. Two savvier women one would be hard-pressed to find, and every author should experience the sheer delight of being immersed in such a charmed atmosphere.

About Jean Brashear

A 5th-generation Texan, award-winning author Jean Brashear enjoys cooking with the bounty of her former Marine husband's vegetable garden and likes making her own breads the old-fashioned way. (If you ask, she might share her recipe for biscuits so tender and flaky they will make you weep.) She and the man she's loved since they were teenagers live in Texas with their shaggy, stray, escaped-from-the-circus dog. Jean loves to hear from readers—her website is www.jeanbrashear.com

Photo by Ercel Brashear

Breinigsville, PA USA
24 March 2010
234845BV00003B/8/P